"So are you game?"

Matt looked at Savannah. "It's way past time to have a proper reunion of the original six-pack."

For some stupid reason, she glanced at Sam as if she needed his permission. Worse still, he sat there in silence, looking completely noncommittal.

"Talk her into it, McBriar."

Sam's smirk turned into a frown. "She can make up her own mind. If she doesn't want to do something, then I sure as hell can't make her do it."

In Savannah's opinion, he'd all but confirmed he would rather she not show up. That alone served as a good enough reason to attend the little soiree. She could tolerate Sam for a few hours. Besides, she truly wanted to connect with her old friends, even if she didn't count Sam among them.

"Are you sure you want to do this, Savannah?"

She turned to find Sam leaning against the railing, arms folded across his chest. "Of course. Why wouldn't I?"

"It means spending an entire night with me."

Dear Reader,

First love…

Two simple words that have the potential to evoke complicated emotions. If you've ever been in love, you're bound to have one because—let's face it—we all have to start somewhere.

Interestingly enough, I stumbled across a survey that claimed only twenty-five percent of women actually marry their first love. Maybe so, but I can almost guarantee the other seventy-five percent have never forgotten theirs. In my experience, when the subject has come up during a group discussion, I've noticed that some people have fond recollections, others express their foolishness and a few have even spoken of regrets. I venture a guess that every now and then many have asked themselves "What if?" What if things had been different? What if we had stayed together? What if I unexpectedly ran into him on the street? What would I say?

Those questions served as inspiration for *The One She Left Behind,* a story involving what once was and what possibly could be again if old recriminations can be put aside. A roller coaster ride into the past that changes two people's perspectives on life, love and forgiveness. One of my personal favorite plots—a reunion in every sense.

I truly hope you enjoy the first book in the Delta Secrets miniseries, where you'll meet a group of high school friends once known as the six-pack. In the meantime, I wish you fond memories, good friends and happy reading!

Kristi Gold

The One She Left Behind

Kristi Gold

TORONTO NEW YORK LONDON
AMSTERDAM PARIS SYDNEY HAMBURG
STOCKHOLM ATHENS TOKYO MILAN MADRID
PRAGUE WARSAW BUDAPEST AUCKLAND

Recycling programs
for this product may
not exist in your area.

ISBN-13: 978-0-373-71732-3

THE ONE SHE LEFT BEHIND

Copyright © 2011 by Kristi Goldberg

This edition published by arrangement with Harlequin Books S.A.

For questions and comments about the quality of this book please contact us at Customer_eCare@Harlequin.ca.

www.Harlequin.com

Printed in U.S.A.

ABOUT THE AUTHOR

Kristi Gold has always believed that love has remarkable healing powers and she feels very fortunate to be able to weave stories of love and commitment. As a bestselling author, a National Readers' Choice winner and a Romance Writers of America RITA® Award finalist, Kristi has learned that although accolades are wonderful, the most cherished rewards come from personal stories shared by readers and networking with other authors, both published and aspiring. You may contact Kristi through her website, www.kristigold.com, on Facebook or through snail mail at P.O. Box 24197, Waco, Texas 76702 (please include an SASE for response).

In loving memory of my husband, Steve—
Husband, father, healer.
My hero

CHAPTER ONE

AS THE CLASSIC COUNTRY ballad began to play, Savannah Greer's past came tumbling back on a white-water rush of memories. The song of love and leaving brought to mind another place and another time, a bridge long since crossed, but unfortunately not quite burned.

From her perch on a barstool at the diner's counter, she glanced over her shoulder, almost expecting to see the proverbial man from her past lounging in the back booth, weathered guitar in hand, his expression as bitter as the words he'd delivered more than a decade ago. But she only caught sight of a rotund farmer standing by the ancient jukebox, the culprit who'd unwittingly sent her imagination into overdrive with one careless selection.

Savannah turned back to the counter, took another sip of the frosted root beer and frowned. She'd never been particularly fond of the drink, or nostalgia, which left her questioning why she'd bothered to stop in at Stan's on the way to the farm. Truth was, she'd wanted to delay dealing with the grief over losing her beloved father, and being home would simply make it all too real. She also didn't look forward to seeing her mother again, yet prolonging the reunion would only fuel Ruth Greer's well-established disapproval of her daughter.

With that in mind, Savannah reached inside her

wallet, withdrew two dollar bills and handed them to the waitress—a fresh-faced young woman who had to be close to the same age she'd been when she'd shed this godforsaken Mississippi Delta town. The girl smiled, slid two quarters across the counter and said, "Y'all come back now."

"Have a nice evening," Savannah muttered, yet she wanted desperately to tell the teenager to get out of Placid while she still could, before the place sucked the life out of her.

She left the change on the counter and hurried toward the exit, craving freedom, only to face her past head-on when the door opened before she could escape.

He moved into the room like a shadow at sundown, all hard-shell insolence and towering height, his dark hair just long enough to be deemed disreputable in such a conservative community. He stared at her for a moment and when recognition dawned, a mocking smile lifted the corners of his mouth.

"Well, I'll be damned." Laughter rumbled low in his throat and crinkled the corners of his dark blue eyes, dredging up images of riotous storms and uncontrolled passion. He thumbed the brim of his baseball cap up from his brow and studied her from head to toe with all the cockiness of a seventeen-year-old jock. "Looks like Savvy's come back to town."

Savannah's feet refused to move from the worn tiled floor. She couldn't manage a step, not one step, for that meant she would again be moving toward him, not away.

You're not a child, Savannah. Leave.

Clutching her purse to her chest, she simply said,

"Goodbye, Sam," then brushed past him and rushed out into the humid June evening.

As she strode across the gravel parking lot toward her car, she heard the all-too-familiar voice call out, "Walking away again, Savannah?"

Ignoring the condemnation in his tone, Savannah quickened her pace. But against her better judgment, she paused to take another backward glance and discovered Sam leaning against the bed of a shiny black truck parked near the entrance, arms folded across his chest, looking as if he expected her to run back to him.

When her gaze again connected with his, Savannah's pulse beat a staccato rhythm in her ears as her nerves unraveled like an old woven rug.

What was wrong with her? She was behaving like some kid who'd gone to see the latest slasher movie, afraid to witness the terror on the screen, yet unable to resist some primitive calling to do that very thing. To face the fear. In this case, the man and the memories.

As she climbed into the safety of her sedan, Savannah attributed the unwelcome reaction to the remnants of an idealistic teenage perception of love. After all, she'd worked so hard to ignore those times when a warm breeze would blow across her face and remind her of him. She only needed to recall his parting words all those years ago to ground herself in reality.

Go on and leave, Savannah. I hope to God you never come back.

But she had come back—only to discover that if a person didn't kill all those feelings for an old love, they would remain dormant until one summer day years later, they broke through like spring grass, changing your perspective. Interrupting your comfortable life. Again breaking your heart.

Surrounded by tattered recollections of the town where she'd spent her formative years, among the place of shattered dreams, that realization pummeled Savannah like an iron fist. And so did awareness that her greatest fear had come to pass. Even after a dozen years, Samuel Jamison McBriar, her first love—her first lover—could still affect her.

As if time had done an about-face, Sam watched her drive away again, leaving him standing in front of the diner to deal with a truckload of recollections and more than a few regrets.

He had no one but himself to blame for the sudden shock of seeing Savannah Greer. He could've driven past the parking lot when he'd caught sight of the Illinois plates. He could've put off the encounter until he paid his respects at her father's funeral tomorrow. He could've waited one more day to satisfy his curiosity over how much she'd changed. The answer to that—not much. She was probably a few pounds heavier, not a bad thing considering she'd been rail-thin as a teenager. Definitely as pretty as he remembered. Her dark brown eyes looked the same and her hair was still golden blond, but not as long as before. He'd bet his last ten acres she still had a stubborn streak, one of the qualities that had attracted him when he'd been a sucker for girls who could hold their own in a battle of wills.

So, lost in his thoughts, Sam didn't notice a car had

pulled up in the adjacent space until he heard "Daddy!" followed by the sound of six-year-old feet pounding across the gravel. He barely had time to brace himself before his daughter threw her arms around his waist with enough force that he took a step backward to maintain his balance.

"Whoa there, Joe," he said as he lifted her into his arms and tugged at her dark brown ponytail.

She popped a kiss on his chin and grinned, displaying the blank space where her top two teeth had been the last time he'd seen her a month ago. "I'm not Joe, Daddy. I'm Jamie."

"I know that," he said as he set her back on her feet. "I'm the one who named you, kiddo. And it looks like you left a couple of your choppers at home."

She touched her bare gums. "The tooth fairy brought me five bucks, Daddy."

"Which she spent on candy even though I strictly forbade it."

Sam turned toward the sound of the voice belonging to the other blonde in his life. Correction. The second blonde who'd left him. But when it came to his ex-wife's parting, he'd played a major role. "Hey, Darlene. I thought you weren't going to be here for another hour."

She set a miniature purple suitcase down onto the ground at his boots. "From the minute she climbed out of bed this morning, Miss Jamie kept bugging me, so we started out early. Luckily I spotted your truck before we drove all the way out to the farm."

Jamie tugged on his hand to get his attention. "Can I get a chocolate shake, Daddy? I had my dinner."

Normally he'd give his permission without a thought, but he'd learned to defer to her mother to keep the peace. "It's okay with me, as long as your mom says it's okay."

Darlene waved in the direction of the diner. "Fine. Your sweet tooth is going to be your dad's problem for the next few days."

Sam caught Jamie's arm before she took off. "Sit by the window so I can see you, and don't talk to strangers." As if that were going to happen. Strangers were a rare occurrence in Placid, but he preferred to err on the side of caution. "I'll be in as soon as I say goodbye to your mom."

"Okay, Daddy," she called out, then headed at a dead run into Stan's, slamming the door behind her.

Once he made sure Jamie had followed orders and climbed into the designated booth, Sam turned back to Darlene. "I could've driven to Memphis and picked her up."

"I told you I planned to stop by Mom's and Dad's, remember?"

Right now Sam had trouble remembering anything except seeing Savannah again and the lingering bitterness mixed with the same stupid spark of lust.

"Are you okay, Sam?" Darlene asked when he failed to respond.

"Yeah. Why?"

"Because when we pulled up, you looked like you'd seen a ghost."

Not so far from the truth. A ghost from his past. She'd come and gone so quickly, he wasn't sure she hadn't been a figment of his imagination. "I just ran into Savannah Greer. She's in town for her father's funeral."

Darlene's expression went cold. "Well, that explains a lot."

He didn't have to ask what she'd meant by that. During their years together, she'd often accused him of carrying a torch for his former high school sweetheart. Not true. Savannah's disregard still burned like a brand, and ultimately the end of his and Darlene's marriage had come when they'd both discovered they made better friends than spouses.

Recognizing a subject change would prevent more speculation, Sam pointed at Darlene's swollen belly. "Are you sure that baby's not due until October?"

She laid her palm on her abdomen and scowled. "That's exactly what my husband said to me last night. Today he's not walking straight."

Sam laughed. "Tell Brent he has my sympathy, and warn him that your mood doesn't get any better until about thirty minutes after you deliver. But you do have some fine moments when your hormones kick in."

She reluctantly smiled. "I think he's already figured that out. And speaking of Brent, I need to go. I'll see you Friday."

"You bet." He hesitated a moment, feeling as if he needed to reaffirm that she'd made the right choice by leaving him behind. "I'm glad you and Brent are happy, Darlene. You deserve to be."

Finally, she smiled. "I am happy, Sam, and I hope you find someone who makes you happy, too. But that's not going to happen in this town. All the women are either underage, have a foot in the hereafter or they're married."

Didn't he know it. But he wasn't inclined to go too long without company and he did have a couple of local gals who readily accommodated him when he called. "I've got the farm to keep me busy. I'm doing okay."

She sent him a skeptical look. "Right, Sam. I don't know a man who doesn't want a woman's company every now and then, especially you. But then again, since Savannah's back in town, maybe you can remedy that."

She was determined to take hold of that old jealousy and shake it like a hound with a hambone. "That's ancient history, Darlene. I haven't seen her or talked to her in twelve years." Twelve long years. "I don't have a clue what she's up to now."

"My guess is she's probably married."

"She's not."

Darlene cracked a cynic's smile. "No clue what she's been doing, huh?"

The longer this conversation went on, the greater the risk for revealing that he'd kept up with Savannah through her parents. "I better get inside before Jamie orders two chocolate shakes and downs them both."

"True." Darlene climbed into her sedan and powered down the window. "Make sure she wears shoes most of the time."

"I'll try," he said as she backed out of the space and drove away. But he wouldn't force the issue. Nothing better than curling your bare toes in some good old black Delta dirt, exactly what he'd told Savannah during their first introduction. As if it had happened yesterday, he recalled exactly what she'd been wearing—a pair of leg-revealing white shorts, a fitted navy blue tank top and no shoes. He'd been a goner from the moment he'd laid eyes on her.

Strange that he remembered those details. Maybe not so strange at all. He remembered a lot of particulars about their time together, especially that day in this very diner when he'd intentionally stomped on her heart the moment she told him she was leaving.

Long ago he'd learned that everyone eventually leaves. Still, even after all this time, he couldn't stop the resentment that boiled just beneath the surface. And if he had any sense at all, he'd steer clear of her. Unfortunately, he'd never had much sense when it came to Savannah Greer. But he wasn't that kid anymore, and the man had no use for her.

As SAVANNAH STOOD BEFORE the white clapboard house that had been in her mother's family for three generations, she was immediately drawn in by the familiar song of the katydid, the pungent scent of freshly plowed earth and fragrant magnolia blossoms. But appreciation of the old home place hadn't come quickly or easily. They'd moved here from Knoxville the summer she'd turned fourteen, and she'd hated leaving the city and her friends. She'd basically thought her life was over. Had it not been for her father's encouragement, she might have seriously considered running away.

You'll learn to love it here, Savannah. I promise...

Like the remember-when song that had played in the

diner, her father's gentle voice filtered into her mind. The image of his kind green eyes had been forever etched in her memory like the butterflies he'd taught her to capture in her palms. She had always let them go after inspecting their wings. If only she could release the painful loss with such ease. If only she could get past the equally painful memories of her mother's constant scorn.

She reminded herself why she'd come back here— to say goodbye to her daddy. But now that she thought about it, in many ways her daddy had left her some time ago. The little girl still loved him, yet her adult heart couldn't forget how he'd never stood up to his wife, never sided with his child even when she had been wronged. He simply remained neutral in the ongoing battle between mother and daughter.

None of that mattered now. Her father was gone, and she wasn't little Savannah from Placid. She was grown-up Savannah from Chicago. And she could face whatever she must in order to put the past to rest.

Savannah drew in a fortifying breath and slowly opened the door. As she stepped into the foyer, the steady drone of conversation filtered into the entry hall. She set her bags at the bottom of the staircase and when she walked into the living room, all talk ceased. Thankfully, the first face she saw was a welcome one.

"Savannah, my goodness." Her mother's sister crossed the room and touched Savannah's cheek as if she were an ethereal presence. "Law, girl, you're still as pretty as ever."

Savannah drew her into a hearty hug. "It's so good to see you, Aunt May."

May dabbed at her misty eyes with an embroidered handkerchief. "Look, Ruth, your baby girl's come home."

Savannah turned her attention to the woman standing near the fireplace, her frame as rigid as the floor lamp in the corner. When she locked into her mother's stern gaze, she found no warmth in the dark brown eyes so much like her own.

"You're late, Savannah." Both her tone and expression indicated her displeasure.

"Yes, Mother, I'm late. But I did come home."

"Yes, you did. This time."

No other words passed between them. There was nothing left to say that hadn't already been said.

A nervous cough broke through the awkward silence, switching Savannah's focus to the place that housed her father's favorite lounger, where her uncle Bill now stood. "You sure do look good, Savannah," he said. "Real productive."

Savannah smoothed the sleeves of the tailored blue suit. "Thank you, Uncle Bill. You're looking as sharp as ever."

He hooked his thumbs in the suspenders he'd worn for as long as she could remember. "Still have that storybook imagination, do you, gal? That's okay." He patted his belly. "I appreciate your kind words."

Just as well as she knew the well-worn loomed rug beneath the coffee table, Savannah recognized that few kind words would be thrown around this evening, at least when it came to her mother.

"There's lots of food in the kitchen, darlin'," Aunt May said, nervously kneading the handkerchief. "The neighbors have been real nice, bringing in casseroles and desserts and I just made a fresh pot of coffee. Why don't you grab a plate and come sit so we can all catch up."

Savannah slowly surveyed the area to see if any other visitors had crouched in the corner, hiding away from the tension that filled the room like Uncle Bill's pipe smoke. She released the breath she'd been holding when she discovered no one else was around. "I thought maybe I'd go by the funeral home."

"The visitation was over an hour ago," her mother said, more disdain in her voice. "I called you and told you the time."

Just one of her many shortcomings as far as her mother was concerned. Ruth hated tardiness as much as she hated missing her Monday night bridge game. Since it was Monday, that could account for her irritable mood. But had she ever really needed a reason?

In the interest of peace, Savannah answered, "I'm sorry. I had to take care of a few last-minute briefs and postpone two court dates before I could get on the road." Suddenly she'd become the apologetic daughter again. Always ready to please, but never quite able to do enough. "I think I'll grab that coffee," she said as she dropped her purse onto the piano bench. "Can I get anyone anything?"

Her mother turned away as May raised a trembling

hand to her plump neck. "No, honey, we've eaten enough to kill a moose. Just help yourself."

Savannah couldn't get away quickly enough. She'd surely suffocate if she had to stay two days, much less the planned two weeks. But she'd promised to remain for the reading of the will. Settle whatever needed to be settled, at least from a legal standpoint. She supposed her status as an attorney had as much to do with that as her role as a family member.

Traveling down the corridor past the gallery of photos hanging on the knotty pine walls, Savannah stopped at the small table in the center of the hall and ran a hand over the age-yellowed lace covering. Everything was the same, including the vine-covered vase centered below her parents' wedding photograph. In a fit of anger, she'd broken that vase, right after her mother had insisted Savannah stop hanging out with Sam because he only wanted "one thing." She could see the veins where it had been glued back together, still carried the scar on her knee from a cut she'd gotten while trying to pick up the pieces, remembered her mother's disapproval. Yes, some things never changed, and apparently her mother had been right—Sam had only wanted "one thing."

Making her way into the deserted kitchen, Savannah took the silver pot from the counter and poured a cup of coffee. She sat in one chair positioned around the small dinette, thankful for some time alone. The reality of her father's death coupled with seeing Sam again was almost too much to handle, but she wouldn't cry. At least not yet. Not until she was safely in bed, alone with her grief.

A few moments later, May breezed into the room carrying two empty glasses that she set in the sink before regarding Savannah. "It's been over five years since you've been here, honey. You should try to get along with your mama for both hers and your daddy's sake."

She'd given up on that prospect in her teens, and it had been seven years, not five, since her last trip home, something she didn't care to point out. "I know, May, but she doesn't seem to be willing to call a truce. I just wish I knew what I did to cause her to hate me." Aside from the typical teenage rebellion.

May's gaze snapped to hers. "She doesn't hate you, honey. She loves you more than you realize. She's just a hard woman to understand, but she's a good woman."

Savannah couldn't remember when she'd witnessed that goodness. On second thought, she did recall a time when Ruth Greer had been more affectionate, more like a real mother. Yet that had all come to an end not long after Savannah passed into puberty. "I've tried to understand her, Aunt May. Even now, I'm having trouble with that. She doesn't seem to be at all upset that Dad's gone."

May rinsed the glasses, set them on the drainboard and then wiped her hands on a dish towel. "People deal with their grief in different ways, Savannah. Ruth has seen a lot of loss and hardship in her lifetime. First, our daddy died when she was only ten and I was just a baby. Then Mama had only been married to Papa Don a couple of years before she went to be with the angels."

Oddly, Savannah had never met her stepgrandfather and her mother had rarely mentioned him at all. She didn't even learn about his passing until her parents announced they were moving back to the farm in Placid. "I agree, losing two parents at such a young age is more loss than any child should have to endure." But as far as she was concerned, that didn't excuse a mother's unexplained hostility directed at her own child.

May claimed the chair across from Savannah and folded her hands on the cloth-covered surface. "Ruth practically raised me all by herself until she turned seventeen and married Floyd. When they decided to move to Knoxville, she took me with them. Lord knows she didn't have to do that when she could've foisted me off on Granny Kendrick, God rest her soul, and that's if she made it into heaven."

Savannah couldn't help but smile when she thought about all the legendary stories involving her eccentric great-grandmother. "Why didn't you stay here with Don?"

May shook her head. "It was a sad state of affairs. To hear Ruth tell it, he took to the bottle after Mama died. He spent most of his days drunk and he wasn't fit to take care of me, not that I remember much about him or that time since I was so young. I'm not sure he would've kept me around even if he had been sobered up. He never paid me much mind, both before and after we moved away. In fact, I spoke to him maybe twice in the years before he died. If I asked about him, your mama refused to say anything one way or the other."

Savannah suspected there could be a lot more to the stepfather story. "I realize how much you appreciate

Mother, May, and I do understand why you would. But that doesn't explain her attitude toward me."

May straightened and sent Savannah a disapproving look. "Like I said, she's been through a lot. She had to get me raised before she even thought about having a baby of her own. That didn't happen until years after I was grown and gone." Her expression softened. "She was so happy when you were born, and so was your daddy. They'd waited so long for you."

How well Savannah knew that. She'd been the only girl in Placid High who had parents in their mid-fifties. But that didn't really matter, especially where her father had been concerned. He'd always seemed so young for his age, and that made his passing even more difficult to accept.

Feeling a sudden onset of fatigue as well as utter sorrow, Savannah feigned a yawn. "It's been a long day. I think I'll go up to my room and read awhile before I turn in." And attempt to check her cell phone, although coverage in the area was sketchy at best. That was okay. She hadn't had a real vacation from work in years. They could do without her for a couple of weeks.

May reached across the table and patted Savannah's hand. "Tomorrow will be another long day, too, because I'm sure you'll see your old friends. Rachel and Jessica are still around and, of course, there's Sam—"

"I've already seen him," Savannah said abruptly, before adding, "I stopped by the diner for something to drink and he was coming in when I was going out."

"I hear he's making a good living with the farm,"

May continued. "In fact, he just bought a brand-new truck with all the bells and whistles."

As if she should care what Sam was driving these days. Besides, she'd already seen that new truck, and she hadn't been impressed. "How nice."

"Did you know he married the Clements girl?" May asked, as if determined to cram Sam's life down Savannah's throat.

She'd come by that knowledge after she'd left Placid, and it had hurt more than she'd cared to admit. Darlene Clements had been the girl from one county over whom Sam had taken to the prom instead of her. The same girl who'd relentlessly pursued him throughout their high school years. Obviously she'd caught him. "I'd heard that."

May sighed. "And their little girl is as precious as a puppy."

That she hadn't heard. "I didn't realize he had a daughter."

"She's about six now," May added. "And it's such a shame that she comes from a broken home. Divorce is a terrible thing for a child to go through."

Divorce?

Savannah didn't know which shocked her more—that Sam and Darlene's marriage had ended, or that he'd fathered a child. "When did they split up?"

"A couple of years ago, maybe longer. Didn't your mama tell you?"

"She never tells me anything, May." And neither had her old girlfriends, but she'd only sporadically spoken to them over the past few years.

Savannah scooted back from the table and stood before she had to endure any more unexpected news. "Tell Mother I'll see her in the morning."

May looked completely dismayed. "You should tell her."

Yes, she should, and she supposed she could make it brief. "You're right."

After giving her aunt another hug, Savannah left the kitchen and returned to the living room, where she found her uncle watching a sitcom rerun. "Where's Mother?" she asked when she discovered Ruth had disappeared.

Bill put down the television remote and smiled. "She's in her room, sugar. She said she has one of her sick headaches."

Savannah had no doubt she'd contributed to that headache. "Before I retire for the night, do you and Aunt May need anything? Extra towels or linens?"

"Your mama saw to that when we came in yesterday. Now you scoot along and get some rest. And just so you know, the weatherman's calling for storms tonight."

An appropriate ending to a perfectly dreadful evening, Savannah decided.

As soon as she doled out a hug for her uncle, she grabbed up her bags, scaled the stairs and entered her old bedroom at the end of the hall. She closed the door behind her before turning to survey the place where she'd spent many a night during her teen years, talking on the phone for hours with her girlfriends, and Sam. Everything still looked much the same as it had when she'd left for college. The pink-and-blue patchwork quilt still covered the double bed. The shelves flanking the floral-cushioned window seat still held all the mementos of her youth—withered corsages, movie ticket stubs, debate trophies.

After setting her bags on the cedar chest at the end of the bed, she walked to the bureau and removed a favorite snapshot from the mirror. The photo—taken on the beach in Gulfport—featured the inseparable group of friends known to their fellow students as "the six-pack." Best buddies Chase Reed and Jessica Keller sat side by side on the sand in the middle of the group. Childhood sweethearts Rachel Wainwright and Matt Boyd had claimed the spot on the right, Rachel's head resting on Matt's shoulder. And of course, she and Sam sat to the left, holding each other tightly, Sam's beat-up guitar at their feet. They'd easily assumed the role as Placid High's designated "hottest couple." But it hadn't been a farce. It had been real.

How young they all looked. How hopeful and ready to take on the world. Forever friends, they'd vowed. Then everything had changed after graduation. Still, the picture signified that she'd seen more than her share of good times in Placid. But those fond reminiscences were all a part of the distant past, and that's where they would stay. Yet at the sound of rain pelting the window, another memory came back to Savannah, as bright as the flash of lightning on the horizon.

A surprise midnight visit one misty fall evening. A few well tossed pebbles to garner her attention. A trellis perfect for climbing. One love-struck girl who still believed in happily-ever-after. One teenage boy driven by raging hormones. An easily removed screen and a kiss so hot it could have set the roof on fire.

Sam had begged her to come inside, but she hadn't allowed it. At least not that particular night....

All in the past, Savannah kept reminding herself as she hauled her suitcase onto the bed and began to unpack. No good ever came of rehashing old history, her mother had told her time and again. She couldn't agree more, but that didn't keep her from remembering. That didn't prevent the sudden sense of sadness when she turned her attention to another framed photograph resting on the nightstand, the one of her and her father at the Tennessee State Fair when she was eight years old.

Remorse hit her like a blow to the heart. She should have come home more often. She should have insisted that he come to visit her in Chicago even if her mother had refused to make the trip. She should have known something was wrong during their last conversation when he'd told her several times how proud he was of her, how much he loved her and then asked her to forgive her mother. She should have been there to hold his hand when he'd died.

Savannah couldn't contain the sorrow any more than she could stop the storm. With the photo clutched against her chest, she stretched out on her back across the bed and released all her pent-up anguish. The tears fell hot against her cheek as she mourned the loss of her father and her inability to earn her mother's love. She grieved the innocence she no longer possessed. She even allowed herself to cry for all the promises Sam had broken, and most important...for what might have been.

CHAPTER TWO

THE CROWD OF MOURNERS gathered around the gravesite was as thick as the Delta humidity, leading Sam to believe well over half of Placid's population had come to say goodbye to Floyd Greer. If things had turned out differently all those years ago, he might've been sitting with the family with his arm around Savannah, comforting her. Instead, he stood several feet away, on the outside looking in.

Not long after the minister delivered the final prayer, Savannah appeared from beneath the green funeral tent, flanked by her aunt and uncle. When he noticed Ruth Greer trailing behind the trio, Sam figured the problems between mother and daughter hadn't disappeared, and that was a damn shame. His own mother hadn't stuck around long enough to build any kind of relationship with him, good, bad or indifferent. At times like these, people needed someone to lean on—except maybe Savannah.

She held her head high as she accepted condolences from the townsfolk, forcing a smile every now and then. Although she looked composed on the surface, Sam knew better. She'd always been inclined to keep her emotions bottled up inside so no one could see her suffering. Not that he was one to talk. But with Savannah, things had been different. He had been different. They'd served as each other's sounding board and leaning shoulder from the moment she'd arrived in Placid.

And that had all ended a long time ago....

"Done any fishin' lately, Mac?"

Only one person ever called him Mac. Sam turned to find Chase Reed standing behind him, dressed in a civilian suit instead of the Army-issue uniform he'd been wearing the last time he'd seen his best friend over a half-dozen years ago.

Sam grinned and offered his hand. "I'll be damned, Reed. I heard they'd finally let you out, but I didn't believe it."

Chase shook Sam's hand and smiled, but it didn't form all the way. "I'd had about all the active duty I could take."

Sam imagined he had. Three tours in a war zone would be more than most men could take, and the stress showed in Chase's features. He had a definite edge about him now, unlike the kid who'd been the happy-go-lucky golden boy.

Sam felt damn guilty that he hadn't stayed in touch nearly enough during Chase's absence, but he'd never been great at correspondence. "How long have you been back?" he asked.

"For a couple of weeks."

Looked like his friend was punishing him for that lack of communication. "And you didn't call and let me know you were in town?"

"I had to help Dad clean out the old sharecropper cabin behind the house so I'd have a place to stay."

Chase shook his head. "Pretty sad, living at home at the age of thirty-one."

Sam could relate. "I've been living at home since I left college and even after I married." Just one more thing that hadn't set too well with his ex-wife.

"Sorry to hear it didn't work out between you and Darlene," Chase said.

"It was just one of those things." One of those things that Sam sometimes regretted because of the impact on his daughter. "When you get a chance, you need to stop by and see my kid. She's going to be with me all week."

Chase barked out a laugh. "I'm still trying to picture you with a kid. Is she here now?"

A funeral was no place for a six-year-old, as far as Sam was concerned. "She's back at the farm with Hank Anderson's girl."

Chase frowned. "Hank's got a kid that's old enough to babysit?"

Sam shrugged out of his sports coat and draped it over his arm, finding little relief from the midmorning heat. "Yeah. Hank's two years older than us and his daughter was born right after he graduated."

"Man, that makes me feel old." Chase shook his head and studied the ground. "Time passes way too fast."

Sam dealt with that issue every time he looked at his child. "I know what you mean. One minute, Jamie's in diapers and the next, she's a hell-on-wheels kinder-gartner and a natural-born flirt. No telling what I'll be facing when she's sixteen and she discovers boys."

"That serves you right, Mac," Chase said. "Now

you'll know firsthand why Savannah's parents used to give you hell when you dated her."

Sam suddenly remembered where he was and why. "It's going to be tough, not having Floyd around. He was one of the good guys."

"Yeah, he was." Chase remained silent for a time before he added, "I heard Wainwright's bank has been calling in loans on some of the farms. The greedy bastard."

That was a subject that made Sam as angry as Chase sounded. Edwin Wainwright was the biggest SOB in three counties, and a rich one at that. "You heard right. That's why I took my banking business elsewhere when I started upgrading the farm."

Chase's expression turned to stone as he focused on some point behind Sam. "Speaking of bastards," he muttered.

After facing the mourners again, Sam immediately caught sight of the reason for his friend's caustic tone. Dalton Wainwright, the son of the man who'd dubbed himself the king of Placid, had stopped to visit with Savannah. And Dalton's wife, the former Jessica Keller, stood by his side.

Not everything had changed, Sam decided. During their high school years, Chase had always despised Dalton Wainwright. Obviously he still did.

"I can't believe she's still married to him, and I can't believe she has a kid by him, either," Chase said, more malice in his tone. "He didn't deserve her back then, and he doesn't deserve her now."

Yep, his friend's hatred still burned bright as a

bonfire. "Have you talked to Jess since you've been back?"

Chase kept his gaze trained on Dalton in a menacing glare. "He won't let her out of his sight, and if I came less than two feet from him, I'd kill him."

The comment caught the attention of Pearl Allworth, who was standing nearby. She scowled at Chase but Sam noticed a gleam in the town gossip's rheumy eyes, like a starving woman who'd just been tossed a prime steak. He also noticed the glare Dalton leveled on Chase as he led Jess away. A look that said, "She's mine."

Sam decided it would be best if he diverted Chase's attention before he took off after Dalton and started a scene to feed the rumor mill for months. He centered his attention on Matt Boyd, who'd stopped to speak with Savannah. "Too bad Rachel's not here. Matt said she wasn't feeling well this morning. I suspect I know what ails her. She's got a bun in the oven."

Chase continued to stare at Jess as she headed away. "Nah. Not after all these years. Matt's too busy playing the county cow doctor instead of breeding his wife."

Sam grinned. "That might be the case, but I've still got a gut feeling Rachel's pregnant."

"And I think he's more concerned about Gabe Wooley's band of heifers than making his own baby," Chase said. "Twenty bucks says she has a virus."

Sam took Chase's offered hand and shook on the deal. "You're on."

They shared a laugh before Sam noticed Savannah heading toward the black limousine parked at the curb. When their gazes briefly met, she immediately looked away, but he continued to watch her until she disappeared into the car.

"Savannah still looks good, Mac," Chase said.

Time to play ignorant. "I hadn't noticed."

"You're lying."

Yeah, he was. "Okay, maybe she hasn't changed much, but neither has her attitude toward me. Not that I give a damn. I have just as much right to resent her, too."

"Give it a rest, McBriar," Chase said. "We were all kids back then. You need to get over the past."

Savannah wasn't inclined to bury their past any more than he was. She'd proven that yesterday when she'd run out on him again at the diner. She was proving it right now by pretending he wasn't there. Not a problem. He wasn't in the mood to reconnect with her, either. But he did have to admit she still looked great. Really great. He could admire her from a distance, and leave it at that.

Chase patted him on the back. "Why don't you come with me to the Greers' to pay our respects. That way you can get a better look at her."

So much for not being obvious in his admiration. "You go ahead without me. Right now I need to get back to Jamie. I'll make a point to look in on the family later this evening."

Just for grins, he also planned to have a talk with Savannah to satisfy his curiosity. To learn if she'd gotten what she'd wanted all along—a life that hadn't included him. And he knew exactly when and where he'd find her.

SAVANNAH LOVED THIS TIME of day, right after the sun had set over the fields and the summer air had cooled to a tolerable temperature. Initially when they'd moved to Placid, she'd despised the flat plane of the land that seemed to go on for miles. She'd hated that so many trees had been cut down and plowed under for the sake of agriculture. She'd detested everything about the area, until the day she'd discovered the small bridge rising over the dried-up creek bed that separated her parents' farm from the McBriars' acreage. A welcome break in the barren landscape where the live oaks had been spared. Her very own private oasis, both then and now.

Nothing had really changed, except for the new wooden planks beneath her feet. Most likely Sam had taken it upon himself to make sure the bridge remained solid and stable with his own two hands. He'd always been good with his hands.

Savannah ran her palm over the message that she'd carved into the railing years ago—Sam and Savannah Forever. A typical and foolish teenage pronouncement of love. Or maybe for Sam it had simply been lust. Without warning, the image of their secret meeting place hidden by the nearby copse of woods filtered into her mind. A place where she and Sam had learned so much about each other, both physically and emotionally. Especially physically. Many times they'd lain together on a blanket, experimenting and exploring each other eagerly, but not quite going "all the way" for a solid two years. Then came the night of her seventeenth birthday when, alone in her bedroom, he'd said "Please" and she'd said "Yes."

After she heard the rustle of leaves followed by footsteps, Savannah turned her attention to her left to discover Sam emerging from behind the curtain of trees, as if she'd somehow psychically summoned him. Yet he wasn't the lanky boy of yesterday. He'd matured in body with a broader chest and more bulk. Instead of T-shirt and jeans, he wore black dress slacks and a white tailored shirt. He carried a brown paper bag, not the age-worn guitar he'd oftentimes brought with him in their youth. But those cobalt blue eyes still held the power to reel her in like a hummingbird to sugar water.

As Sam approached with a self-assured gait, a sudden, sharp sense of awareness caught Savannah off guard. Her frame went rigid, as if she needed to physically brace against the impact of his presence. She had imagined this moment, dreaded it in some ways. Hoped for it. For years she'd avoided it.

He paused at the end of the bridge and sized her up, much the same as he had the day before in the diner, his expression unreadable. And as he continued on, Savannah struggled for words. Maybe she should offer an apology for being so abrupt yesterday, in spite of the fact he still owed her one for the way he'd treated her years ago. Then again, maybe not. She would be adult, coolly polite, but she wouldn't grovel.

"Hello," she said as soon as he stood a few feet from her.

Sam offered her the sack but no greeting. "I've been instructed to give you this."

She took the bag and asked, "What is it?"

"Gracie's pecan pie."

Savannah fondly remembered the housekeeper who'd treated her like one of the family. "I can't believe you still have Gracie."

"Yeah, I still have Gracie," he said without even a hint of a smile.

Now what? Bid him goodbye and leave? If she had any sense at all, that's exactly what she would do. Yet curiosity overcame common sense. "Aunt May told me you had a daughter. What's her name?"

He streaked a palm over the back of his neck. "Jamie."

"Congratulations." If only she could sound more sincere, but the shock over Sam choosing the name they'd planned to give their own child reflected in her tone.

"Still practicing law?"

"Yes," she said, ignoring the obvious disdain in his tone. "It's hard work but it has its rewards."

"I can't imagine keeping corporate CEOs out of hot water would be all that damn rewarding, so it must be the money."

Clearly he'd learned she'd chosen corporate law, and apparently he didn't approve. Not that she cared what he thought about her career choice. "I've represented struggling small businesses as well, sometimes pro bono, so it's not all about the money."

"If you say so."

His overt sarcasm drove her need to get away from the bitterness that was almost palpable. "I better go. Mother's probably wondering where I am." Then again, probably not. "Give Jim and Gracie my love and let them know I miss them. I didn't have an opportunity to speak with them at length after the funeral."

His expression turned stoic as stone. "You could tell them before you run back to Chicago."

Obviously he wasn't going to do her any favors or cut her any slack. "I'll try to stop by for a visit before I leave." In spite of the possible emotional upheaval, she also wanted to see Sam's daughter.

"Fine." Without further hesitation, he turned and headed away, as if he had nothing else to say to her. As if he had no use for her.

She shouldn't be surprised, nor should she feel anything but relief. But as she started across the bridge toward home, Savannah experienced an overwhelming sense of emptiness, just as she had that day in the diner when they'd ended a close-knit relationship with hurtful words neither could ever take back. She hated the feelings. Hated that he could still strip her emotions bare. Hated him for acting as if nothing had ever existed between them. Hated herself for still caring.

Just as Savannah stepped off the last wooden plank, Sam called her name, stopping her progress. She faced him again and simply answered, "Yes?"

He kept perfectly still while he kept his gaze locked into hers. "Do you regret it now?"

She frowned. "Regret what?"

"Leaving town to get what you wanted, and staying away from your family when they needed you most."

They meaning her father. She couldn't disregard the dagger he'd thrust right into the heart of her guilt. Obviously he wanted to hurt her again, and he was doing a fairly good job. "I did what I had to do to make a life for myself, Sam. Maybe you never understood it, but my dad always did."

"You're probably right about that," he said. "But you might want to ask yourself if it was really worth it."

With that, Sam spun around and strode away, leaving Savannah alone to ponder his words and the questions whirling around in her mind. Questions she didn't dare ask him…or herself.

HE'D NEVER SEEN A SWEETER sight—except for maybe the one he'd seen earlier on the bridge. Sam immediately pushed thoughts of Savannah from his mind to concentrate on his daughter dressed in a pink polka-dot gown curled up in his dad's lap, her thumb stuck in her mouth, her eyes closed against the overhead light. Her hair was as dark as his dad's was gray.

Sam raked the baseball cap off his head and dropped down in the chair across from his dad. "How long has she been asleep?" he asked in a near-whisper.

Jamie's eyes popped open and she raised her head. "I'm not asleep, Daddy. I'm just restin' my eyes."

Exactly what he'd told her several times when he'd drifted off in front of the TV during one of her favorite cartoons. "You looked pretty asleep to me, Joe. If you didn't have your thumb in your mouth, you would've been snoring like your grandpa."

She looked more than a little perturbed. "I don't snore, Daddy."

"Neither do I," his dad added.

"Oh, yes, you do, Jamison McBriar," came from the

direction of the kitchen. "Like a steam engine about to blow."

Sam chuckled. "Guess Gracie would know."

Jamie worked her way off Jim's lap and climbed into Sam's. "Did you see Ruthie?" she asked.

Lying was out of the question, but he'd have hell to pay if he told the truth. Vague would probably work best. "No, sweetheart," he said as he pushed a curl from her forehead. "I just dropped off the pie and left."

"Did you see Ruthie's daughter, Daddy?"

So much for avoiding the truth. "Yeah, I saw her. I gave her the pie."

She grinned and said, "Papaw says she used to be your girlfriend," followed by a giggle.

Sam sent Jim a nasty look. "That was a long time ago."

Jamie yawned and rested her head against his shoulder. "I'm gonna miss Floyd. He used to let me ride on the tractor."

Sam had always felt that Floyd considered Jamie the granddaughter he'd never had. "We're all going to miss him, kiddo. He was a good man."

"The best," Jim said. "He would've given you his last pair of jeans if you needed 'em."

Jamie raised her head and looked at Sam straight on. "Is Ruthie sad?"

"Yeah, I imagine she is."

"Kind of hard to tell with Ruth," Jim added. "She's as strong as a barbed-wire fence."

Jamie glanced at her grandfather before turning back

to Sam. "I want to see Ruthie in the morning, Daddy. I want to tell her I'm sad, too."

He could think of several reasons why that might not be such a good idea. "Maybe we'll see her in a couple of days."

Jamie shook her head. "I want to see her tomorrow. We can go after we feed the cows."

She looked so determined, Sam couldn't refuse. "Okay, but we'll only stay for a little while." Otherwise, Savannah might decide to boot him off the premises.

Jamie put on her "old soul" face, as Darlene always called it. "Why do people have to die, Daddy?"

A question he wasn't sure how to answer. "It's just a part of life, sweetheart."

Fortunately, Sam's stepmother entered the room with a book in hand before he had to offer a more lengthy explanation. As far as he was concerned, Gracie hadn't changed much since the day she'd become their housekeeper. Maybe her hair was a little grayer. Maybe she had a few more wrinkles. But overall, she was still Gracie, the godsend. "You don't need to worry your pretty head about that, sugar pie," she said as she tossed her braid back off her shoulder. "Now let's get you to bed so we can finish reading the penguin story."

Seemingly satisfied to leave the question be for now, Jamie slid her feet onto the floor and started toward the hall. Sam halted her progress when he asked, "Are you forgetting something, Joe?"

She ran back to him and kissed his cheek. "'Night, Daddy."

"'Night, sweetheart. Watch out for those bitin' bed-bugs."

Jamie flashed him a dimpled grin. "There ain't no bedbugs, Daddy."

Sam started to correct her bad grammar, but he'd save that for later—right before he gave her back to her mother.

After Jamie kissed her granddad good-night, she took Gracie's hand and tugged her toward the bedroom, chatting all the way down the hall about visiting Ruth and meeting "Daddy's old girlfriend."

Sam tilted his head back against the sofa and momentarily closed his eyes. He opened them to his father's "you're in trouble, boy" stare, reminding him of other times when he'd had to face Jim McBriar's wrath for something he'd done wrong. For the life of him, he had no idea what he'd done now. He imagined he was about to find out.

Jim stretched his legs out before him and rested his palms on his slightly bulging belly. "Did you have a nice talk with Savannah when you went to the Greers'?"

He should've seen this coming. "I didn't go to the house. I met her on the bridge, handed over the pie and had a two-minute conversation with her. End of story."

"Was there water under the bridge?"

Sam knew exactly what his father was getting at, and he refused to take the bait. "That gully's been dried up for years."

"That's too bad because a bridge without water can be pretty useless."

A few more moments of silent scrutiny passed before

Jim added, "You know, the word *grudge* rhymes with *smudge*. And that's exactly what a grudge is—an ugly smudge on the soul that needs to be cleaned away."

If there was one thing Sam couldn't stand, it was beating around the bush. "What's your point, Dad?"

"My point is that at one time, you and Savannah meant the world to each other. A little forgiveness goes a long way."

"I have forgiven her." But he sure as hell hadn't forgotten the way she'd left, or why.

Jim leaned forward, hands clasped between his parted knees. "No, you haven't forgiven her, just like you never forgave your mother. And let me tell you something, son. Savannah isn't your mother. Your mother was running to something—a new life. Savannah was running away."

Man, he didn't want to hear this. "You mean from me."

His dad released a rough sigh. "It was never about you, boy. There was a lot of hurt going on in that house."

"Yeah, and Ruth was doling out most of it."

Jim pinned him with a harsh stare. "Ruth's reasoning is not for us to judge, Sam. Not unless we've lived in her shoes."

Sam only knew that Ruth's behavior bordered on cruelty where Savannah had been concerned. Ruth hadn't been too keen on him, either, at least back then. "Can we just move out of the past and onto another subject?"

"Fair enough," Jim said as he leaned back against the couch. "I hear tell that Ruth's selling the farm to Wainwright."

The course of the conversation wasn't much better than the previous one. "That's what I hear, too."

"My guess is he'll probably tear the house down and build something on it."

"I don't know what he'll do with the house, but he's going to lease the land to me."

Sam didn't think his dad's face could get any redder. "What in the hell were you thinkin' when you climbed into cahoots with that SOB?"

Gracie entered the room and nailed her husband with a glare. "Lower your voice, Jimmy. You granddaughter's trying to sleep. And must we use such crude language when an impressionable child's in the house?"

Jim pointed at Sam. "Our boy just told me he's going to lease the Greer land from that snake Wainwright."

Gracie's gaze snapped to Sam. "What in the hell are you thinking, Samuel Jamison McBriar?"

So much for the crude language and lower your voice warning. "I'm thinking I might as well lease it or someone else will. Maybe even someone who wouldn't treat the place the way Floyd would've wanted it to be treated. Wainwright could sell it to some corporate operation that'll set up shop right next door to us. Not to mention we could use the extra money to hire hands from a whole slew of people who need jobs."

Jim came to his feet. "You could use some horse sense, son. Deals with the devil come with a price."

Maybe so, but Sam was willing to take his chances. "I'll handle Wainwright."

Gracie smirked. "And I'm going to fly over the fields tomorrow without the benefit of an airplane, too."

"Does Savannah know about this?" Jim asked.

That was one obstacle he didn't care to consider at the moment. "I don't know what she knows, Dad, and honestly, I doubt she cares unless she has some fool notion to keep the place in the family. That's about as likely as Gracie taking flight in the morning."

He exchanged a smile with Gracie before his dad said, "I guess you know what you're doing, Sam. I just hope it doesn't come back to bite you on the butt."

Sam was too tired to argue the point. Besides, the deal with Wainwright was all but done, and he almost never went back on his word. Not in the past few years. "Yeah, I know what I'm doing, Dad. You didn't waste your money on my college education."

"You definitely have smarts, son," Jim said. "At least when it comes to running this farm. Now, as far as your personal life goes, you might have been behind the door when they handed out the common sense."

Gracie slid onto the chair's arm. "Leave the man alone, Jimmy. He's just had some bad luck in the relationship department."

That was the last thing he cared to discuss. "If you're finished lecturing me, Dad, I'm going to tell my kid good-night and get some sleep." He rose from the sofa and turned his attention to Gracie. "Since Jamie has her mind set on seeing Ruth tomorrow, do you mind taking her by the house?"

"She's got to start baking for the summer festival," his dad answered for her. "Lots and lots of cakes and cookies."

Yeah, right. "Unless someone changed the date, the festival doesn't start until Saturday."

"True, but Gracie likes to get things done early." Jim winked at his wife. "Isn't that right, honey?"

After the confusion left Gracie's face, she said, "That's right. Besides, you should take Jamie by and check on the family. Ruth might need a hand with something."

"Plus, we've already paid our respects and actually made it into the house," his dad added. "And while you're there, mind your manners and be nice to Savannah."

Okay, he'd mind his manners. As far as being nice to Savannah, well, that was a stretch. He could play at being civil for his family's sake but he sure as hell wouldn't be her best friend. She gave up that right the day she walked out of town and never looked back.

CHAPTER THREE

MUTED VOICES FILTERING IN through the open bedroom window pulled Savannah out of a deep sleep. After glancing at the clock and noting the time, she practically vaulted out of bed. She rarely slept past dawn, much less 9:00 a.m., even on weekends. Her dad used to say that life was too short to snooze it away, and she'd never forgotten it. For a few moments she allowed the loss of her father, the ever-present grief, to subside before she faced the day—and her mother.

Savannah dressed in a faded purple T-shirt and a pair of tacky white knit shorts before heading to the hall bath to complete her morning ritual. Her unruly hair was a hopeless cause, thanks to going to bed with it wet, so she piled it into a ponytail and padded down the stairs in desperate need of caffeine. She found a fresh pot of coffee on the kitchen stove and blueberry muffins on the counter, but not a soul in sight. Then she recalled the earlier sounds of conversation and decided her aunt, uncle and mother had opted to enjoy their breakfast on the front porch.

Savannah ignored the muffins and grabbed a cup of coffee to take outside. The moment she opened the front door, the summer scent of fresh-mown grass assaulted her senses and resurrected more memories.

Good memories of walking barefoot in clover and chasing fireflies at night.

When she stepped onto the porch, Savannah pulled up short. Not only did she find May, Bill and her mother seated on the chairs scattered around the weathered wooden decking, two others had joined them. A little girl with dark, dark hair and cobalt blue eyes stared at her from her perch on the porch swing. And next to that little girl, the man who had occupied her dreams more nights than she could count.

"Have a seat, young 'un." Uncle Bill stood and gestured toward the only unoccupied chair, which happened to be much too close to Sam. If he were in the next county, that would be too close.

Savannah refused to give in to the urge to sprint back into the house. Instead, she took the offered chair, coffee mug gripped tightly in her hand. "Good morning," she managed, relieved that her voice didn't give away her nervousness.

Her mother, in typical fashion, nixed the greeting to ask, "Where are your shoes, Savannah Leigh?"

She hadn't even realized she was barefoot. She never went without shoes outside the house these days—under normal circumstances. Nothing about this little morning soiree seemed normal. "They're inside," she muttered, wishing she could crawl into the nearby well. She could only imagine how she looked—wild-haired, wild-eyed, worn-out and shabby. Not that she should care one whit what Sam McBriar thought about her appearance.

"You're pretty," the little girl said, followed by a

toothless grin. Then she turned to Sam and said, "Isn't she pretty, Daddy?"

Oh, Lord. This child was looking for confirmation from the wrong person.

"Yeah, she is," Sam responded, surprising the fool out of Savannah.

She took a sip of coffee to soothe her parched throat. "You're very pretty, too, and you must be Jamie," she said, offering up a smile.

"You're Savannah and you used to be Daddy's girlfriend."

Luckily she hadn't taken another drink of coffee, otherwise it might have ended up all over the front of Uncle Bill's overalls.

"That's right, Jamie," May answered when Savannah didn't. "But that was quite a little while ago."

"Before he met my mommy?" Jamie asked.

"A few years before," Savannah said, although that wasn't quite accurate. Darlene had had her eye on Sam since junior high.

Seemingly satisfied with the explanation, Jamie scooted off the swing and climbed into—of all people— Ruth Greer's lap. And Ruth, who only moments before looked as if her face might crack if she moved her lips, gave Jamie the sweetest of smiles. "Are you sad, Ruthie?" Jamie asked.

"A little," Ruth said. "But Floyd wouldn't want us to be sad. If he were here, he'd tell us to wake up—"

"And enjoy the day," Jamie finished. "I bet he's saying the same thing in heaven."

Ruth brushed a stray hair from Jamie's forehead. "I'm sure you're right."

Jamie slid from Ruth's lap and took her hand. "Can we go work on the quilt, Ruthie?"

Savannah recalled the wedding-ring quilt she'd worked on with her mother when she was a little older than Jamie. The quilt she'd refused to work on after they'd moved to Placid.

"Maybe we should go home and let Ruth rest, Jamie," Sam interjected.

"Nonsense," Ruth said. "You come on in the house with me, sweet girl, and we'll cut out a square or two, as long as your dad says it's okay."

"Can I, Daddy?" Jamie pleaded in a voice designed to persuade a resistant parent. Savannah had used that tactic with her own father and it never failed to work wonders.

"For a while," Sam said. "Gracie needs you to help her bake some cookies when we get home, remember?"

Jamie rolled her eyes. "I can do both, Daddy."

And just like that, Savannah's mother led Sam's child through the screen door without a second glance at her own daughter.

Savannah didn't know how to feel. Sad? Yes. Memories of a better time brought about some serious melancholy. Envious? A little, but not of Jamie. The envy came from the thought of what could have been between mother and daughter if their relationship hadn't gone sour.

Bill shoved out of his chair and offered his hand to

May. "Guess we better get to town before lunchtime, darlin'."

May stood and sent her husband a smile. "That sounds like a plan."

Not to Savannah. If they left, she'd be all alone with Sam. "I could go for you, Aunt May."

From the appearance of Sam's cynical grin, he'd noticed the desperation in her tone.

May flipped her hand in a dismissive gesture. "We'll take care of it, honey. We just need to pick up your mother's headache medicine and a few groceries at the market."

Groceries? They still had a mountain of food left from the wake. "Are you sure? It wouldn't be any bother."

Bill fished a set of keys from his pocket. "You just stay here, little britches, and visit with your friend."

She would if she had a real friend present. Unless she found an excuse to make a hasty departure, she had no choice but to be stuck with Sam since her relatives had already made it halfway to the car before she could say another word. If she didn't know better, she might believe this little private time between ex-lovers had been planned.

Tension as stifling as the humidity hung on the air as Savannah drummed her fingers on the table's surface. She supposed going into the house was an option, but she didn't want him to think she couldn't handle a few minutes in his presence. After all the times they'd talked for endless hours about nothing—or everything—she couldn't thing of one blasted thing to contribute to a decent conversation.

Fortunately, Sam broke the silence by saying, "Gracie wants you to stop by before you leave."

"I will," she said. "And I still can't believe Gracie hung around after the grief you gave her."

He rocked the glider slightly with one heel. "She's still around because she married Dad a couple of years ago."

Just one more monumental event she hadn't been aware of. "I'm really glad for them." And she was. No two people were better suited for each other. At one time, she would have said the same thing about her and Sam.

He leaned forward and dangled his arms between his parted knees. Another span of silence passed before he asked, "How's your mother holding up?"

Savannah shrugged. "Okay, I guess. You know Ruth. She's not one to share her feelings. Me, on the other hand, I still can't believe he's gone…." The nagging lump in her throat captured her words for the time being. She didn't care to cry in front of Sam. In front of anyone, for that matter. Not that she hadn't cried in his arms before. Many, many times. But that was then, and this was now, and she didn't need his solace, nor did she expect him to offer it.

"Floyd talked about you all the time," Sam said, his voice surprisingly absent of animosity.

Savannah could only imagine how thrilled Sam must have been to hear regular accounts of her life. "I didn't realize you spent so much time with my father."

He leaned back against the swing. "We had our share of discussions about farming and the latest fertilizer, that sort of thing, but your name came up a lot. He thought you could do no wrong."

"We both know that's not true, don't we?" When he didn't bother to argue the point, she added, "He didn't particularly care for you, at least when we were growing up, especially that time he caught you climbing up the trellis. I still can't believe you handed him that 'cat caught in a tree' excuse when we didn't even own a cat." She couldn't believe she was playing the remember-when game with a man who clearly had no intention of participating, evident by his lack of response.

He just sat there, studying her with narrowed eyes as if preparing to take his best shot. "Floyd wanted you to be happy, so are you?"

Savannah heard no genuine concern in his tone, only mild curiosity. In fact, he'd probably like to hear that her life was a mess just so he could say he'd told her so. "I have a great condo and a great job."

He came to his feet, pulled out a chair and sat across from her. "No boyfriend? Or do you have several?"

Savannah hadn't expected he'd ask such a leading question or that he would come so close to her. Then again, most likely he'd traveled into her personal space and private life to throw her off balance. In a way, it was working. She wrapped her arms tightly around her middle as if she needed protection from him. Maybe she did. "I really don't think you should be so concerned about my dating habits." Which were basically nil at the moment, a little tidbit she didn't dare toss out.

"Then the answer is no boyfriend." He looked much too pleased with himself.

She'd rather eat red dirt than admit four years had passed since she'd had a serious relationship. "The answer is, it's none of your business."

"Sorry to hear you don't have someone to keep you occupied."

No, he wasn't, and why did so many people believe she needed a man to be content? "I have a lot to do to keep me occupied, thank you very much. Chicago is a very exciting place. Lots of things to see and do."

"Unlike Placid."

"Definitely not like Placid," she said. "I don't have to travel far to shop for a decent pair of shoes."

He barked out a cynical laugh. "I still remember the day we met. You were hoppin' mad because there wasn't a mall nearby."

She'd been angry over leaving her friends behind in Knoxville and moving to Podunk, Mississippi. "I was barely fourteen, Sam. At the time, hanging out at the mall was my life."

"You were spoiled, that's for sure."

Savannah's ears began to ring. "I wasn't spoiled. I just happened to be a typical teenager, not some hayseed who thought riding around in the back of a pickup through the town square constituted a good time on Saturday night."

Sam didn't look the least bit ruffled by the insult. In fact, he seemed smug. "I'd rather have clean air and good neighbors than rush-hour traffic and strangers living next to me."

Savannah lifted her chin in indignation. "I have neighbors."

He sent her a skeptical look. "Oh, yeah? What are their names?"

She'd strolled right into that one. "Nancy and Phil." Or maybe it was Janice and Will. She'd spoken to them twice since she'd moved into the condo three years ago.

Way past time for a subject change, and to restore some modicum of civility before they really started going at it. "Jamie's a beautiful little girl, Sam. You and Darlene should be very proud of her."

"We are." Both his tone and expression verified that.

"And she's so friendly," Savannah said. "I've never seen my mother so taken with a child." Not even her own child. Especially not her own child.

"Just a word of warning," he said. "Dad told her the story about you chasing the sow."

Great. Jim McBriar could have gone for an eternity without sharing that tale with anyone, much less a six-year-old. "Did he tell her that you let the pig out on purpose just so you could see me slip and slide through the mud while I was trying to get her back into the pen?"

"Probably not, because I never told him about that."

Of course he hadn't. "Good. I wouldn't want her to know exactly how conniving her father can be."

He narrowed his eyes into a glare. "That's a little of that old 'pot calling the kettle black' behavior, isn't it?"

So much for friendly conversation. In an effort to avoid more conflict, Savannah asked, "Are you still raising pigs?"

"Cattle. Last year I bought the Miller place so I could have extra pasture."

One more shocker among many. "That land has been

in the Miller family for years. I never thought I'd see the day when they'd give it up."

Sam's expression turned suddenly somber. "They're not the only ones, Savannah. The Delta is economically depressed and people are suffering. Whole towns have closed up shop and family farms are being bought up by vultures like Wainwright. It makes me sick to see it happening and not be able to do a damn thing about it."

"Then why do you stay?" she asked, though she already knew the answer.

Anger called out from his eyes and in his voice when he said, "Because my family helped build this town. Because if I don't stay, then Placid might not survive. I'll spend my last dying breath trying to prevent that from happening. Maybe you had no trouble walking away without looking back, but I never would."

Sam's loyalty to the town wasn't new to Savannah, nor was his continued condemnation of her choices. Many times in the past he'd echoed the same sentiments. Still, she couldn't fathom why anyone would want to champion a possible lost cause, or choose to permanently reside in a place with so few opportunities. Then again, she'd always known that Sam had wanted nothing more than a simple way of life. "I guess we both got what we wanted. I have my law career, and you got the farm, wife and child. Congratulations on meeting your goals."

"Minus the wife," he corrected, his gaze now fixed on some unknown focal point in the front yard.

"I'm so sorry to hear it didn't work out with you and

Darlene." She couldn't seem to mask the falseness in her tone.

He finally looked at her again. "We tried to make it work, but some things aren't meant to be. I learned that lesson a long time ago."

So had Savannah, and she'd never forgotten it.

The crunch of gravel beneath tires drew their attention to the driveway and the truck approaching the house in a cloud of dust. A truck she didn't recognize until the driver exited the cab.

Matthew Boyd strolled up the path to the porch sporting a wide grin. To Savannah, he looked much the same with his light brown hair and eternally tanned skin that made him seem more surfer than veterinarian.

He walked right up to the table and stared down on her feet. "I swear, Savannah Leigh, you haven't changed a bit. You still hate wearing shoes."

Savannah stood and gave him a tight hug. "And you still love pointing that out, don't you?" She looked around him toward the truck. "Where's Rachel?"

"Buried in the clinic's bookkeeping," he said as he shook Sam's hand. "She's been under the weather, so she's behind."

Savannah reclaimed her chair and thankfully Matt took a seat between her and Sam. "I heard you mention Rachel's not feeling well at the funeral," she said. "Is it summer flu?"

Matt raked his cowboy hat off his head and swiped his arm across his forehead. "Could be. She's been feeling better the past few days, which is why I'm here. She sent me by to invite you to join us at Barney's tonight."

Talk about a past-blast. "That old bar's still open?" she asked.

"Yeah, it's open," Sam said.

"And Barney even serves food now with the beer," Matt added.

Savannah laughed. "He's always served food. Box pizza and cold hot dogs, or so I've heard." She'd only been to the place once, but she'd never gone inside. She'd waited in the car with Sam and Rachel while Matt retrieved his drunken father one weekend.

"Wednesday night is all-you-can-eat-ribs night," Matt said.

"Sounds interesting." Not that she was overly fond of ribs or beer.

"Anyway," Matt continued, "we thought it might be nice to get the gang back together while you're in town. Chase has already agreed to come and so has Sam."

She couldn't believe Sam hadn't mentioned the little get-together during their conversation. Oh, yes, she could. He probably didn't want her to go. "What about Jess?"

Matt shook his head. "Rachel's going to call her, but don't get your hopes up. Dalton keeps a pretty tight rein on her these days. We sure as hell don't want him around, not that he'd show up. But he's probably not going to let her come, either."

Savannah was appalled to learn that her good friend Jessica—the former gregarious cheerleader—would let her husband dictate her every move. "I hope she does show up, because I'm really looking forward to seeing her. But if she doesn't, I planned to stop by her house in the next few days anyway."

"So are you game?" Matt asked. "It's way past time to have a proper reunion of the original six-pack."

For some stupid reason, she glanced at Sam as if she needed his permission. Worse still, he just sat there in silence, looking completely noncommittal. She could probably list a hundred reasons why she shouldn't accept, but only one immediately came to mind. "I don't remember how to get there."

Matt pushed back from the table and stood. "You can ride with us. Is seven okay?"

"Seven sounds fine, if I decide to go. I'll need to check with my mother first." Apparently coming home had turned her into a child again.

"I imagine Ruth won't care if you spend a couple of hours with old friends," Matt said, then pointed at Sam. "Talk her into it, McBriar."

Sam's smirk turned into a frown. "She's a grown woman. She can make up her own mind. If she doesn't want to do something, then I sure as hell can't make her do it."

In Savannah's opinion, he'd all but confirmed he would rather she not show up. That alone served as a good enough reason to attend the little soiree. "I'll take you up on the ride."

Matt grinned. "Great. We'll pick you up around seven-thirty."

"Didn't you say seven?" Savannah asked.

"Yeah, but you know Rachel. She's always late." Before Matt started down the steps, he turned and looked at Sam, then back at Savannah. "Hope the two of you get along for a change. I don't want to deal with a barroom brawl and risk throwing my back out."

Sporting a wily grin, Matt spun around and walked away, leaving Savannah without any retort. She could tolerate Sam for a few hours. Besides, she truly wanted to connect with her old friends, even if she didn't count Sam among them.

"Are you sure you want to do this, Savannah?"

She turned to her left to find Sam leaning against the railing, arms folded across his chest, looking much like he had when she'd left the diner the other day. "Of course. Why wouldn't I?"

"It means spending an entire night with me."

An entire night? "It's just an hour or two, Sam. We don't have to communicate at all or even come near each other."

His smile formed only halfway. A somewhat skeptical smile. "Yeah, you're right. As long as you don't have more than one drink."

Another series of flashbacks ran through Savannah's mind like a long-ago slide show. Memories of one night beneath the stars in his arms after she'd had her first wine. She shook off the recollections and firmed her frame. "Believe me, I can handle myself much better these days."

Truth be known, she was a little worried and it had nothing to do with booze. Having a somewhat tense conversation with Sam on a porch in the sunlight seemed innocuous enough. But being in the presence of a former lover in a dim bar after a couple of drinks could wreak havoc on her common sense.

Not a chance. She didn't intend to have more than one drink, if that. And she certainly wasn't going to re-enact the mistakes of her youth.

She would go to see old friends. She'd have a good time, even if she had to fake it, and she was pretty darn good at faking it.

SHE DIDN'T WANT TO BE there. Sam could tell that about Savannah the minute she walked into the bar with Matt and Rachel. He could tell because she started wring-ing her hands like an old-time washer and her shoul-ders were about as stiff as Gracie's old clothesline. She looked even more uncomfortable when a couple of people called out greetings as she worked her way through the rows of tables.

But damn, she still looked good. He'd almost forgot-ten how well she could fill out a pair of jeans. She filled out the black thin-strapped shirt pretty well, too. With her blond hair curling around her bare shoulders, those man-killing high heels, she'd make the grade as most men's dream-girl fantasy and wish for reality.

He wasn't the only man who'd noticed her, either. A group of young bucks seated at the bar gawked when she passed by, and so did a few guys who had come with their wives or dates.

In a country place full of country folk, in a bar with rough-hewn wood walls, a tin roof and seen-better-days furnishings, she stood out like tar against snow. But if those guys really knew her like Sam did, they wouldn't give her a second look. And if they did, they ran the risk of getting burned.

Once the group reached the round table in the corner that Sam had claimed an hour earlier, Rachel and Matt moved ahead of Savannah and took the two high-back stools opposite him. That left only one option—Savannah was going to have to sit next to him, whether she liked it or not. He figured she wasn't going to like it any more than he did.

Savannah confirmed his theory when she moved the stool as far from him as she could without landing in Rachel's lap. She did turn to him to say, "Hello, Sam," with a little too much formality for someone who once knew him better than anyone.

He returned her greeting with a less formal nod of acknowledgment, then followed with, "Where's Chase?"

Matt hooked a thumb over his shoulder. "We saw him at the pool tables with a group of women probably ten years his junior."

No sooner had Matt finished the sentence than Chase walked up to the table and wrapped his ham-hock arms around Savannah. Sam couldn't stop the harebrained thought "Hands off" when Chase looked her up and down like she was his favorite hot rod. "You're looking mighty fine tonight, darlin'. Where have you been all my life?"

Savannah didn't seem the least bit put off by the come-on and even grinned, which for some reason didn't sit too well with Sam. "I've been avoiding silver-tongued devils like you, Chase. But it's still good to see you even if you haven't changed a bit."

Sam disagreed with Savannah on that count. Chase was just trying too hard to convince people he was the same.

Chase took the empty stool on the other side of Sam and set it between Savannah and Rachel, causing everyone to have to shift position. That also meant that Savannah had to move closer to Sam. He might have found that amusing if her damn perfume didn't smell so good.

"Has anyone ordered anything yet?" Chase asked as soon as he was seated.

Sam raised his hand to signal the sixty-something waitress who'd been a Barney's fixture since the Confederacy rolled up the carpet. "Maybe she'll be by to take our order before midnight."

Savannah looked around before saying, "It's sure crowded for a Wednesday. Must be the ribs."

"It's the band," Chase added. "They come in from Memphis every Wednesday."

Rachel rolled her eyes. "And they let anyone who thinks they can sing have a shot. Nothing quite like spending the evening with a bunch of yahoos who erroneously believe they have talent."

Matt nodded toward Sam. "He's been known to sit in with the band every now and then."

His friend could've gone all night without mentioning that. "Not in a while."

Rachel rested her cheek on her palm and stared at him. "But you *can* sing, and I think you should give us a song tonight, just like in the old days."

Sam held up his hands, palms forward. "No, thanks."

"Come on, McBriar," Chase said. "Do it for the six-pack."

Luckily the waitress arrived to take their orders, halting the conversation. Normally he might perform a song or two, but he didn't see any reason to take time away from his friends, except maybe Savannah.

She picked that moment to lean over, surprising the hell out of him. "What are you having?"

The urge to get the hell out of Dodge. "I ate before I left the house."

"Why?"

"Because I was hungry." He still was and she was looking pretty damn appetizing. Obviously he hadn't had a decent meal in a while.

"Then what do you recommend other than the ribs?" she asked.

"The burgers are okay."

She wrinkled her nose. "Do they have salads?"

He pointed to the chalkboard hanging on the far wall. "That's the menu."

"Oh." Thankfully she straightened to study it, giving Sam some room to breathe.

After they placed their orders, the waitress returned with their drinks in record time. Chase and Matt each had a beer, while Rachel opted for iced tea and Savannah settled for a glass of cheap red wine. Sam had requested a cola, and he figured he was going to catch hell for it.

Chase was the first to notice. "Why aren't you drinking tonight, Mac?"

"Because I had a beer before you showed up and that's my limit."

"Since when?" Matt asked.

"Since I had a kid."

Savannah looked more amazed than anyone. "I'm impressed."

At least he'd done something to impress her, not that he gave a damn what she thought of him. "People tend to change as they get older and have more responsibility."

She rimmed her fingertip around the wineglass and looked away. "I suppose they do."

Matt surveyed the group and shook his head. "Man, does this bring back some good memories, having us all back together again."

Rachel hid a yawn behind her hand. "I still remember all those weekends we spent at Potter's Pond."

Matt chuckled. "I remember when Savannah and Sam got caught parking at the pond by that idiotic deputy. What was his name, Chase?"

Chase scowled. "Gordon. I never understood why my dad hired him. Not only was he a screwup, he had that brownnosing son named Brady."

Savannah rubbed her forehead as if the recollection had brought about a serious headache. "Ah, yes, Brady. He told everyone at school Sam and I were 'doing it' that night when we weren't doing all that much."

Sam had been glad they hadn't been doing much more, otherwise he would've been in worse trouble.

"Didn't the two of you get grounded after your folks got wind of it?" Rachel asked.

"For a week," Sam admitted before Savannah had the chance.

But the punishment hadn't stopped him from seeing her. He'd prefer not to remember the details, but he did. Late at night, he'd sneaked out of his back door and right into her bedroom window. The thrill of getting caught had only stoked their ongoing fire. He'd never forgotten those nights, all the more reason to steer clear of her now.

Matt draped his arm around his wife. "We can't forget the time we sent Rachel into the field house on the guise that the coach needed to see her about the cheerleading squad—"

"Shut up, Matthew," Rachel snapped. "That wasn't the least bit funny, walking in on all those half-naked guys in the locker room. I'm still angry."

"Angry because she didn't have a camera," Savannah chimed in, causing a loud outburst of laughter.

The stories kept flowing while Sam stayed stuck on the memories involving his and Savannah's former time together. He'd never had a relationship that intense before, or since. But when she left, he'd begun to realize that he'd never been more to Savannah than a temporary diversion and a teacher when it came to sex. She'd only intended to hang around town long enough for the ink to dry on her high school diploma. If he'd only been able to see back then what he knew now, he would've saved himself a lot of sleepless nights and second-guessing.

When the conversation and laughter quieted, Savannah sighed. "I just wish Jess could've been here."

Rachel folded her hands atop the table. "I tried to convince her to come but she made up some excuse about Danny's baseball game and that Dalton was too busy to pick him up."

Chase looked as if he'd eaten something sour. "He's probably too busy screwing around with some gullible woman."

Savannah leaned forward. "You mean he's cheating on her?"

For Jess's sake, Sam felt the need to set the record straight in spite of his suspicions. "No one's confirmed anything yet, and I hope like hell Jess's boy doesn't get wind of the rumors. He's got enough troubles having Dalton as his dad."

Rachel scooted closer to the table. "Speaking of that very thing…" She took Matt's hand into hers and added, "We have some news."

Matt looked to Sam as if he might bolt. "Yeah, we do."

Sam stared down Chase, letting him know he was about to be twenty dollars richer, before he stated, "You're going to be parents."

Rachel's mouth opened for a minute before she snapped it shut and swatted her husband's arm. "I thought we were going to wait to tell everyone together, Matthew."

Matt raised his hands above his head, like he was set to surrender. "I swear I didn't say a thing, Rachel."

"He didn't have to," Sam said. "I went through all the symptoms with Darlene. No drinking, sick in the morning, yawning every five minutes."

Savannah stood, rounded the table and hugged Rachel. "I'm so thrilled for the two of you."

In the meantime, Chase pulled out his wallet and handed over a twenty to Sam. "You win."

Matt didn't look too pleased. "You two were betting on my wife?"

Sam leaned back and grinned. "Yep. Chase didn't think you had it in you after thirteen years of marriage."

Chase chuckled. "Hell, I didn't think anyone had sex after thirteen years of marriage."

Once again, the group joined together in laughter, including Savannah. Sam had forgotten how much he liked her laugh. He'd always been able to make her laugh, even during some fairly rocky times. He'd also been good at making her cry, like he had that day in the diner. Right or wrong, at the time he'd figured she'd deserved it. He'd wanted her to feel as bad as he had, punish her for leaving him behind. But the past was long since dead and buried and didn't deserve a resurrection. Once he left this hellhole, and Savannah, he swore not to give it—or her—a second thought.

After the food arrived, Sam tried to focus on the conversation but found himself watching Savannah eat her measly salad. He'd taught her to kiss, and she'd taken to his instructions pretty damn well. She'd been a willing student, even if she had made him work for the ultimate reward for almost two years. And if he didn't keep his mind on the present and his eyes to himself, he could forget using a poker face to hide his fascination with her mouth, especially if she caught him with his guard down.

But as the talk once more turned to old times, Savannah seemed more relaxed around Sam, so much so she started to lean toward him whenever he tried to speak above the din. And when no one was paying him any mind, he'd inch his chair away from her. If he moved clear across the room, that wouldn't be far enough away. He'd still know she was there, and he'd still be tempted to return to the past even if he'd sworn not to go there.

During a lull in the conversation, Chase slid out of his seat and stood. "Anyone up for a game of pool?"

Sam pushed away from the table so fast he almost knocked over the stool. "I'm in."

"Count me in, too," Matt said. "As long as you concentrate on the game, Reed, and not the kind that involves finding a willing woman while pretending to play pool."

"Well, now that you mention it." Chase leaned down and draped his arm over Savannah's shoulder. "You wouldn't happen to be willing, would you, sweetheart?"

She removed his arm, much to Sam's satisfaction, even if he shouldn't care what the hell she did and who she did it with. "Not on your life, Chase," she said. "That would be like kissing my brother."

Chase grinned. "Just let me know if you change your mind."

Matt came to his feet and said, "While we're gone, you two girls can talk about us all you want."

Sam had no doubt he'd be the prime topic of discussion, especially if Savannah had a mind to rake him over the coals with Rachel for his less-than-friendly attitude.

Once they reached the tables, Sam grabbed a cue from the wall holder and turned to discover that the couple currently playing pool didn't appear to be in a hurry to complete their game. When they kept kissing and touching each other, he almost suggested they give up and take it into the parking lot.

Matt came to his side and said, "You and Savannah looked kind of cozy back there at the table."

He shouldn't be surprised by the comment. To any casual observer, they might have looked "cozy." "Your imagination's out of control, Boyd."

Chase joined them to add his two cents. "I don't know, Mac. Are you sure you're not hankerin' to take a little trip back in time with Savannah?"

Sam battled the images the comment created and the urge to curse his friends. "You two don't know what in the hell you're talking about."

Fortunately, the couple had finally cut out, providing a diversion. "Looks like it's our turn," he said.

While Matt gathered the pool balls, Chase leaned back against the table and regarded Sam. "Twenty bucks says you and Savannah will end up in bed together before the week's over."

Sam didn't like the bet or the bedroom images running through his mind. "Go to hell, Reed."

Matt offered his hand to Chase. "I say three days."

"You're on," Chase said as they sealed the wager with a shake.

When they both looked at Sam expectantly, he picked up a cue and took his first shot, missing the pocket by a mile. "No good ever comes from repeating history," he muttered as he straightened. "You can both make a hundred bets and neither of you are going to win." If he considered what they were suggesting, he'd also be in line to lose.

"You never know," Matt said. "Second chances don't happen too often, bud. Maybe you and Savannah just might realize what you've both been missing."

Sam stepped aside for Chase to take his turn, all the while thinking Matt could be on to something. He had no intention of getting tangled up with Savannah, between the sheets or otherwise, even temporarily. No way in hell would he put aside all the emotion for sex, just to get soul-punched by her again. But he wasn't above letting her know exactly what she'd been missing.

No real risk involved, just a little revenge.

CHAPTER FOUR

SAVANNAH LEANED OVER TO Rachel and practically shouted, "Kitty with tail caught in the radiator."

"Rooster on crack," Rachel replied with a sneer.

For the past hour, they'd been playing this game when each wannabe singer took to the stage. They'd laughed long and often, but the amusement had begun to fade. Savannah wasn't sure how much more of the bad music she could stand or how long her voice would hold from trying to converse with Rachel. Unfortunately, it didn't appear the karaoke would end anytime soon, or that the guys were even close to finishing their pool game. Maybe that wasn't such a bad thing. Being seated next to Sam had been disconcerting, especially when anyone made an offhanded comment about their former relationship. Correction. Their former sex life. She'd tried to turn a deaf ear, but the images had bled through despite her resistance.

As the crowd grew more boisterous, Rachel grew more tired by the minute, apparent by her yawning. Savannah wouldn't be surprised if her friend nodded off right where she sat. At least the screeching woman had ended her questionable performance, putting their ears temporarily out of their misery while the band took a five-minute break before resuming their open-mike sessions.

Rachel checked her watch and frowned. "Ten more minutes and I'm going to drag my husband out of here so we can go. Unless you want to stay longer. But then, I'm sure Sam would be glad to give you a ride in every way possible." She topped off the comment with a grin.

"No, thanks," Savannah said with conviction, even though the innuendo did produce a few inadvisable thoughts. "Taking me home is the last thing on Sam's mind."

Rachel rolled her eyes. "Come on, Savannah. I've seen the way he looks at you even though he's trying to hide it. And you've been looking at him the same way, too, when you don't think anyone's paying attention. But I've noticed."

Savannah frowned at her friend's conjecture. "That's ridiculous. We've barely said two words to each other tonight."

Rachel smiled. "So what? I still remember a time when the two of you couldn't keep your hands off each other."

"Those days have long since passed," Savannah said, maybe a little too adamantly. "We're adults now, not lustful kids."

"Savannah, you're in complete denial if you think that given the opportunity, the two of you wouldn't jump at reliving that past. Time doesn't always alter chemistry between former lovers. Take me and Matt, for instance. I still get those nice little chills every time he gives me *that* look."

That might be the case, but Rachel and Matt had destiny on their side. She and Sam didn't. "Speaking of Matt, how's he handling the whole fatherhood thing?"

Rachel leaned back and sighed. "He's still a little shell-shocked, but he's getting used to the idea."

She tried to hide her surprise. "This wasn't a planned pregnancy?"

Rachel's gaze slid away. "Not exactly. We've been talking about having a baby for ages but the time never seemed right. First, we had college and then we had to build the practice and then came the house. I decided if we didn't just take the plunge, we'd both be too old and tired by the time Matt finally realized it was the right time."

She couldn't quite get past Rachel's assertion that *she'd* decided to get pregnant, which led Savannah to wonder if Rachel hadn't taken matters into her own hands. Regardless, it wasn't her business to know all the particulars, and she couldn't fathom her friend doing anything even remotely deceptive, especially when it came to her marriage.

As soon as the rowdy applause died down, the band's lead singer walked up to the microphone, hopefully to spare them more audible torture.

"Ladies and gentlemen. We've got someone in the house who can sing the hell out of a song. So let's see if we can encourage him to come up here and serenade us."

Finally, Savannah thought, someone who might not make her want to stuff paper napkins in her ears. But she nearly choked on the last sip of wine when the lead man called, "Sam McBriar, where the hell are you?"

Regardless of what Matt had said earlier about Sam sitting in with the band, she couldn't quite believe that he'd actually perform in front of such a large crowd. After they'd met, a whole year had passed before she'd discovered he could sing, and only because she'd stumbled upon him one afternoon in his barn playing his guitar. Little by little, he'd become more comfortable with her after some gentle coaxing. She'd been so taken by his talent back then. All his talents, for that matter, and he'd had many....

"Do you think he'll actually do it?" Rachel asked after she stopped clapping as fervently as the rest of the masses.

"I have no idea." And she didn't. However, so far, no Sam.

Just when Savannah assumed he wasn't going to answer the call, Sam appeared on stage. The patrons grew even louder when a band member handed him a guitar as he moved the barstool near the microphone.

Savannah was torn between disbelief and eagerness—until he said, "This is a song for someone special."

If he sang *their* song, she'd leave. Or at the very least, escape to the ladies' room, as if she could really run from the reminiscences that particular tune evoked. As if she would ever forget those sultry Mississippi nights when Sam would sing softly while she sat on the porch swing, absolutely smitten.

Yet as Sam played the first few chords, Savannah

realized she'd been wrong in her assumption, but she did recognize the tune. Anyone who'd cut their teeth on country music would know the musical story about a rodeo cowboy traveling to the Texas Panhandle in hopes of arriving by morning. An extremely popular song.

Her dad's favorite song.

Every time it played on the radio, he'd turn to her and say, "Now, that's good country music, Savannah."

Surely Sam's choice was a coincidence, not calculated. She'd never mentioned her father's fondness for the number because at the time it had seemed insignificant.

Regardless, Sam sang it well. Very well. His baritone was as deep as he was tall and he hit each note with clarity as his strong hands steadily strummed the guitar. She scanned the crowd to find several women, both old and young, looking as if they might swoon. Who wouldn't be completely reeled in, not only by his voice but also by his looks? The black T-shirt he wore conformed to his lean body, enhancing the broadness of his chest and the noticeable bulk of his arms. And those jeans looked as if they were tailor-made to accommodate his long legs. He categorically fit the bill as a gorgeous country crooner.

In that moment, he became the boy again—the one that she'd practically worshipped. She became the gullible girl who would have given him anything. She had—heart and soul—and her complete trust, before he'd proved to be untrustworthy. She needed to keep that in mind, yet she couldn't deny he could still mesmerize her with his voice, just as he had years before.

After he finished, Sam leaned into the microphone and quietly said, "I hope you enjoyed it, Floyd," shattering Savannah's theory that the whole thing had been a fluke. Somehow, someway, he'd known about her dad's love of the legendary song.

Savannah decided then and there to set aside their differences and thank Sam for his thoughtfulness. Apparently she would have to postpone voicing her gratitude since he'd been sidetracked by a rather endowed waitress wearing painted-on jeans and a cut-down-to-there, tight white top.

When the young woman tucked a piece of paper into Sam's front pocket, Savannah inherently knew what it contained—a phone number. She was suddenly caught up in a sudden surge of jealousy when Sam leaned over and whispered something in the waitress's ear.

She found it absolutely absurd that she would resent the flirtation so much. Sam was free to do whatever or whomever he pleased. They hadn't come there together. They weren't a couple. She had no reason whatsoever to envision pulling every strand of shiny brown hair out of the harlot's head....

"Savannah?"

She looked up to find Rachel watching her with concern. "Yes?"

"Are you okay?"

"I'm fine." A patent falsehood. She wasn't fine at all. She was ticked off at Sam for being attentive to another woman. Mad at herself for feeling as if she had a right to be angry. "Why do you ask?"

"You look a little distracted."

"I'm just running out of steam." Another untruth. She was fuming like a boiler.

Rachel nodded toward Matt, who stood nearby sporting an impatient look. "As soon as I dance with my husband, we'll go."

"Take your time."

Once Rachel and Matt left the vicinity, Savannah closed her eyes and pinched the bridge of her nose. How could she be so foolish that she couldn't control those latent feelings for Sam? She'd moved on with her life. Nothing he did or said should make a difference now.

She decided to thank him later and at the moment, avoid him completely. Not an issue. He'd probably left with the waitress, even if they'd only made it as far as the parking lot. More power to them. Good riddance and goodbye.

"You're still here."

The overtly masculine voice drifted into her ear, indicating Sam hadn't left the building after all. Savannah could never mistake that low, sexy drawl—she'd known it intimately in the dark of night and the light of day. She stared up at him as he hovered above her, looking way too good to ignore. But ignore him she would. "Yes, I'm still here, but I'll be leaving as soon as I pay my check." Provided Matt and Rachel only danced one dance.

He reclaimed the stool beside her. "I settled up with one of the waitresses a few minutes ago."

Perhaps she'd overreacted after all. Then again, probably not. He might have settled more than only the bill.

"You didn't have to take care of my tab. I'm more than able to pay my way."

"Damn," he grumbled. "Wish I'd known. That salad and glass of wine set me back six months. I'm not sure I'll be able to buy my kid a pair of shoes. Good thing she doesn't wear any when she's with me."

At one time Savannah would have smiled over his wry wit, another aspect of his personality she'd grown to know and once loved. But she wasn't quite in the mood for sarcasm. Nevertheless, proper etiquette dictated he deserved some credit for his consideration and the musical tribute. "Thanks for taking care of it. And thank you for dedicating the song to my father. He would have appreciated it a lot. But how did you know it was his favorite?"

He leaned forward and rested his folded hands on the checkered tablecloth. "When he was having a bad day, I'd go see him and bring my guitar. We'd sit on the front porch drinking your mother's sweet tea and I'd play for him. He always wanted to hear that particular song."

She was beginning to think Sam had been closer to her father than she had been in the past few years. "I'm sure he appreciated that gesture, too."

"I didn't mind and he didn't seem to care if I hit a bad note."

Feeling somewhat magnanimous, Savannah shifted slightly toward him so he could hear her over the band. "I can't imagine you ever hitting a bad note. Your performance tonight was exceptional, although I admit I was surprised you actually sang in front of this many people. You were always so shy when it came to your music."

He didn't appear as if he appreciated her pointing that out. "Believe it or not, people do change, Savannah. I've learned the hard way that life doesn't last forever, so I might as well do what I want while I still have time."

He sounded as if he were sixty, not thirty. "Have you ever thought about singing for a living? You're good enough."

He shook his head. "That would take all the enjoyment out of it."

"You don't feel like you've given up on a dream?"

His features turned stony. "Running the farm has always been my dream. It might seem simple to you, but that's the way it is. Some people don't need fame and fortune. Others do."

A dig at her ambition if Savannah had ever heard one.

They both fell silent, the remnants of resentment hanging between them. Sam evidently still took exception to her decision to build her future out of state, and she still took exception to his disapproval of that decision.

No doubt they would remain at an impasse for the rest of their lives. Again, it shouldn't matter, but sadly on some level it did.

Savannah turned her attention to the once-packed floor, where the masses had definitely thinned out. Rachel and Matt danced by, oblivious to everything but each other. Their devotion brought about Savannah's wistful sigh. "I wonder how they do it."

"Easy. They hang on to each other, put one foot in front of the other and walk around in circles."

She glanced at Sam and ran head-on into his cynical half smile. "I meant how can they still be so committed to each other after all these years?"

"Just lucky, I guess," he said. "And I imagine they work at it."

Yet it had always seemed to come so easily for Rachel and Matt. Savannah couldn't recall witnessing the slightest argument between them in all the time she'd known them. "I suppose you're right."

When Sam raked the chair back and stood, Savannah asked, "Where are you going?" as if she really cared.

"Onto the floor."

Savannah swallowed hard. "You mean to dance?"

He looked altogether put out. "Yeah, since no one's recruiting me to sprinkle sawdust."

That seemed much safer than polishing his belt buckle. "Thanks, but no thanks."

Savannah's refusal was lost on Sam, who'd already made his way to another table and another partner, proving he hadn't intended to ask her. Instead, he'd chosen a fresh-faced blonde who had to be at least twenty-one but she'd wager not much older. Without hesitation, the young woman allowed Sam to lead her onto the floor while the band played a romantic ballad designed with lovers in mind.

Savannah watched the blonde stare at Sam with blatant adoration before she rested her head against his shoulder. She remained transfixed when Sam held the young woman's hand against his heart as he moved in time with the music. She tried to tear her gaze away, but couldn't. She tried to ignore another nip of jealousy, repulsed that she would give in to those absurd emotions. Yet she couldn't help recalling a time when she'd been Sam's only partner. When he'd taught her how to dance.

After the couple moved almost directly in front of the table, Savannah decided she'd seen quite enough. If Sam gave her even a momentary glance, she'd send him a look that could very well give away her shaky emotional state.

Savannah grabbed her purse and headed for the restroom, a refuge where she could gather her wits and touch up her makeup. She muttered a few unflattering comments directed at Sam and wished she could snap off her tongue when a spiral-curled redhead stepped out of one stall.

Savannah smiled briefly and hoped to leave it at that. No such luck, she thought when the girl grinned and said, "Hi, I'm Junie," and without taking a breath added, "Is Sam McBriar your boyfriend?"

When she missed her lips with the gloss she'd been applying, Savannah inspected her teeth for coral smudges. "No, he's not my boyfriend."

"Then he's a friend?"

She was in no mood for twenty questions. "He's an acquaintance. Why?"

"Because my friend Bethany, she's the one dancing with him, and if he was your boyfriend, I just wanted you to know they're not hooking up or anything. Her dad works for him. Besides, he's too old for her anyway."

Savannah tucked the gloss away in her bag and gave

the persistent pixie her full attention. "How old are you?"

Junie lifted her chin, looking somewhat indignant that Savannah would dare ask, a sure sign she was probably about to lie. "Twenty-one. How old are you?"

"Older than twenty-one."

With that, Savannah grabbed her purse and marched out of the bathroom, thankful to be free of the inquisition, yet reluctant to return to her seat to witness Sam and Bethany dancing, even if they didn't intend to "hook up." But if Junie knew Sam the way Savannah did, anything was possible.

At least maybe by now Rachel and Matt were ready to leave. Yet when she reached the table, she found only five empty chairs and a note jotted down on a napkin, tucked beneath the fake-crystal salt shaker.

> We're calling it a night. I'm sure Sam won't mind giving you a ride (wink, wink) since he's going your way… Hugs and kisses…

Savannah recognized Rachel's handwriting long before she'd read the signature, as well as a ploy to throw two former lovers together. She perused the dance floor in search of Sam, but he'd clearly disappeared. Maybe Blonde Bethany or the buxom waitress had already claimed him for a ride home and a nighttime of fast fun. Now what?

Savannah dropped onto the stool and began shredding the napkin while she weighed her options. She could seek out Chase and request a ride, but when she looked toward the back of the bar, she noticed he seemed pre-occupied with some brunette. She could call a cab. Oh, wait. This was Placid, not Chicago. No cab company. She could go by foot, but walking home six miles in the dark didn't seem advisable, and that's if she could actually find her way. Surely she could locate some charitable, familiar soul and beg.

"Let's go."

Apparently she'd been wrong about Sam making a quick exit. "Go where?"

"I'm giving you a ride home."

She slid off the stool and faced him. "Then you knew about this little note?" she asked as she gestured toward what was left of the napkin.

He afforded the paper pile a fleeting look before bringing his attention back to her. "I ran into Matt right when they were leaving. He asked if I'd take you home since Rachel wasn't feeling well. I said okay, so you're stuck with me."

Lovely. "Fine. I'll go with you, but only because I don't have a choice."

He released a low, skeptical laugh. "I don't know about that. You could probably get a ride with any of the guys at the bar. They've been staring you down all night."

"Really? I hadn't noticed." And she hadn't because Sam had earned most of her consideration for the past few hours.

He inclined his head slightly. "So what's it going to be? The devil you know, or the devil you don't?"

Savannah almost said "Neither," but thought better

of it. She'd rather go home with Sam than with a stranger. *Ride* to her home with Sam.

She picked up her purse, threw the strap over her shoulder and said, "Just keep your horns and pitchfork to yourself."

"You used to like my pitchfork."

Some things never changed. "Shut up or I'll reconsider and walk home."

Without further commentary, she started toward the door to a chorus of whistles and catcalls from the aforementioned bar dwellers. She wouldn't be a bit surprised if Sam had paid them to prove his point.

After she pushed her way through the exit and walked into the welcome night air, Sam trailed behind her as she scanned the rutted parking lot—and immediately located his truck. Not the shiny black one she'd seen at the diner, but the red single-cab 1968 Chevy that he'd driven in high school. "Manny," short for Manly Truck.

Savannah turned around and paused in her tracks. "You still have Manny?"

He walked past her and opened the passenger door that squeaked like a rusty gate. "Yeah," he said. "If you take good care of something, it can last a lifetime."

She immediately thought of Rachel and Matt's marriage. "You're right."

"Man, I'm actually right about something? It's a miracle." His tone was dry and somewhat accusatory.

"Yes, it is a miracle," she said as she climbed onto the black cloth seat.

While Sam rounded the truck to the driver's side, Savannah studied the familiar surroundings as a host of memories tried to force their way into her overly tired mind. How many times had she sat in this truck snuggled up next to Sam? Many more than she could count. But tonight she would remain on her side of the cab, not parked in the center next to a man who'd probably prefer she ride in the truck bed.

Sam slid into the driver's seat and slammed the door shut, jarring Savannah out of her momentary stupor. He switched on the ignition, turned to her and said, "You can stop choking the door handle. I'm not going to jump you."

Irked by his observation, Savannah rested her hands in her lap. And just when she thought she could relax, Sam draped his arm over the seat as he backed out of the parking spot, his fingertips practically brushing her shoulder. She immediately recalled the day his dad had given him this truck. She remembered how proud he'd been when he'd come to pick her up to show off the gift. Remembered the times they'd sat in the cab while she'd cried on his shoulder after arguing with her mom. Remembered other times when they hadn't talked at all.

She mentally stopped short, wondering how on earth she'd climbed on board that train of thought. Evidently reason had briefly left her, thanks to a patently tempting man. A man with whom she'd shared a bittersweet history.

After Sam pulled out of the lot and onto the rural road, Savannah rolled down the window, allowing the breeze to blow across her face. The smell of fresh-cut hay and damp air thrust her memories back into overdrive. She'd forgotten how dark the nights could be in the country, how bright the stars. Wishing stars that shot across the sky in plain sight, only most of her wishes failed to come true, including her wish that she and Sam would have a future together. Marriage and children together, like Matt and Rachel. She'd been a child back then, with a child's view of the perfect life. Now she was grown, and she'd come to learn that some things simply weren't meant to be, exactly what Sam had said earlier that day.

They didn't speak for the next few miles, the low hum of the engine the only sound breaking through the quiet until Sam asked, "Do you remember what's around the next bend in the road?"

"What's left of the old drive-in," she muttered without much thought.

"Beyond that."

She knew where he could be heading, yet she wasn't sure why. She did know she didn't dare play along. "My house."

"The road to Potter's Pond."

The name that had been bandied about during dinner. The private piece of land where the town's youth went to park. A rite of passage, some would say. The place where kids had been "necking for nearly a century," according to Sam's dad, although she always thought that to be an embellishment.

"We spent some pretty hot nights there," he said when she didn't bother to respond.

Very true, and very unwise to discuss it in detail. Feigning ignorance would be her best course. "Summers are always hot in Mississippi."

"That's not what I meant and you know it."

Oh, no, no, no.... She wasn't going there. "It doesn't matter what you meant. I'm not going to talk about it."

"Calm down. I was just seeing if you remembered."

Savannah didn't buy his innocent act one bit. She also couldn't forget the sins of her youth, though heaven knew she'd tried. "I really don't see the point in remembering a time when we were both incredibly ignorant."

"Ignorant or not, we couldn't get enough of each other."

And she couldn't get out of the conversation fast enough. "Like I said, we were ignorant. Let's just leave it at that."

Another brief span of silence passed, steeped in tension and turned-back time while they approached the well-worn path that had led to Savannah's teenage downfall.

"I wonder if the place still looks the same," Sam said when the rusty rail fence surrounding the pond came into view.

"I'm sure it's exactly the same since not a lot changes around here." That included Sam, who'd always been fond of teasing her without mercy. That seemed to be his goal tonight—doing his best to shake her up with the unwelcome nostalgia. Unfortunately, that ploy was beginning to work. She started to feel as if each breath she drew took great effort, exactly as it had been on those long-ago nights when she'd been high on anticipation and low on wisdom.

He sent her a fast glance and a somewhat sinister—

albeit sexy—smile. "If Manny could talk, he'd have more than a few stories to tell."

"Could you just keep your eyes on the road and your mind on the present?"

And your foot on the accelerator, she wanted to say when he appeared to slow down. She'd be surprised if Manny was chugging along above ten miles per hour while her heart had to be going at least a hundred.

One more minute and they would be at the gravel drive. One more minute and he could choose to make a turn that would lead them right down memory lane and straight into trouble. Just when Savannah prepared to protest loudly, Sam sped up and passed by the turnoff.

Savannah mentally compiled a laundry list of insults directed at him as she released the breath she'd been holding and unclenched her fists. Obviously he'd been bent on taunting her just to get a reaction from her, and she hated that she'd played right into his hands. The best way to thwart his attempts would be to not react at all, and that's precisely what she planned to do from this point forward.

Yet by the time they reached the farm, her legs were so weak when she climbed out of the cab, she felt as if she'd run a marathon with forty-pound weights strapped to her ankles. Adding to her angst, when she closed the door and turned around, Sam was right there, maybe a foot away.

"Thanks for the ride," she muttered, determined to get in the house before he could sense her discomfort and celebrate his victory.

Sam braced a palm above her head, halting her departure. "It's still early."

If she wasn't careful, it might be too late. "Why are you doing this?"

"Doing what?"

There went the old innocent act again. "Dredging up old times as if I'd be interested in taking up where we left off."

"Aren't you curious?" he asked.

"Curious about what?"

"About how it would be between us now?"

Unfortunately, yes. "No."

"Are you sure about that?" he asked, his unwavering gaze trained on hers.

Savannah was only sure about one thing—she needed to leave now. Yet as she maintained contact with his dark, pensive blue eyes, her feet felt as if they'd been cast in cement. The sudden desire to relive the past, to satisfy that unwelcome curiosity, commandeered her common sense. An overpowering desire derived from a place she so wanted to ignore.

When he leveled his gaze on her mouth, she knew it could be only a matter of time before she crossed a line she'd sworn to never, ever cross again.

CHAPTER FIVE

HE KISSED HER. ON THE cheek. Like someone would kiss their sister.

Savannah stared at him for a long moment, poised between disbelief and ridiculous disappointment. "What was that?"

"Just trying to be friendly."

Yeah, right. "The way you looked at me a minute ago, friendship was the last thing your mind."

"You looked at me like I was your last meal, sweetheart."

He had a lot of nerve, acting as if that near-miss kiss was somehow her fault. As if this whole falling-into-the-past predicament was her fault. "Just when I decided to make the effort to get along with you while I'm here, you take advantage of the situation."

He leaned closer, his mouth only a whisper away from her ear. "Lady, if I was going to take advantage of you, we'd be parked underneath that old oak tree at the pond and we'd both be naked about now."

Savannah experienced a full-body shiver that she hoped he hadn't noticed but most likely had. She took a step back, away from all that outrageous magnetism.

"Don't look so worried, Savvy," he said. "I'm not any

more interested in reliving the past than you are. But it sure was fun seeing your doe-in-the-headlights look."

And it sure would be fun to haul off and slap that arrogant smile off his face. "Sometimes you can be a royal jackass, Samuel McBriar."

He had the audacity to laugh, which prompted Savannah to ask, "Do you really find this so hilarious?" She didn't see one iota of humor in the situation.

"Yeah, I do. I can count on one hand the times you said a curse word."

She could think of one instance when she'd cursed him in a public place. "Technically speaking, a jackass is a donkey, so that doesn't exactly meet the curse-word criteria."

"Is that donkey comparison aimed at my attitude or my anatomy?"

"Your ego."

"Whatever you say, Savvy."

She detested the dreadful nickname he'd given her in high school when she'd landed on the honor roll the first time. "Please stop calling me that. I'm not a child."

He streamed his gaze down her body and back up before returning his attention on her face. "Nope. You're all grown up."

In view of her rather heated reaction, he might as well have used his hands instead of his eyes. "Go home, Sam."

"Not a problem, Savvy." And just like that, he rounded the truck to leave. No argument. No protest. No real kiss good-night, which was a blessing in disguise.

As soon as Savannah had enough wherewithal to move, she started toward the house, with each step deriding herself for almost falling into his trap. After all her talk of maturity, she was still behaving like that infatuated girl of long ago.

And he became the rebel again when he shot out of the drive, stirring up dust the way he used to do after they'd had some silly, insignificant argument. She managed to make it to the porch in time to watch his taillights fade in the distance. Regrettably, she couldn't say the same for her lack of composure.

Savannah dropped down on the glider and attempted to analyze exactly what kind of game Sam was playing and why. She did know she would be a fool to play along. But isn't that exactly what she'd done? And isn't that exactly what Sam had hoped she would do?

Right then she was too tired to scrutinize her actions or his motives. She needed to get some sleep, or at least try.

Once in the foyer, Savannah glanced to her left to discover her mother seated in her favorite chair in the living room, dressed in a faded pink housecoat, a book resting facedown in her lap while she sported a typically stern demeanor.

She instinctively wanted to ignore Ruth and run to her room, but as she'd previously mentioned to Sam, she wasn't a child any longer. "Why aren't you in bed?" she asked as she stepped inside the parlor.

Ruth came to her feet slowly, reminding Savannah that her mother's advancing age had begun to take its toll. "I waited up so I could tell you that the attorney from Jackson will be by to go over your father's will tomorrow afternoon."

That information could have been held until morning, which led Savannah to believe the proverbial other shoe was about to drop. "Okay. Is that it?"

"No."

Great. She was thirty years old and about to be lectured by her mother—or grounded for the duration of her visit. And like an adolescent, she felt the need to defend her actions. "If you're going to scold me about going out so soon after Dad's funeral, I needed to be around my friends so I wouldn't feel so sad."

Ruth clutched the book against her chest. "You're a grown woman, Savannah. It makes no difference to me how you spend your time. I just wanted to say that dredging up the past isn't always wise."

"You mean hanging out with old acquaintances?"

"I mean you and Sam."

Had her mother been spying on them? Of course she had. The curtain shielding the front window was wide open, giving Ruth Greer a bird's-eye view of the front drive illuminated by the yard light. Although there hadn't been all that much to see, Savannah could imagine how it might have looked. "We're just friends." A bit of a stretch, but she was too exhausted to go into more detail.

Ruth shook her head. "You're so caught up in your own little world, you can't see what's right in front of you."

Anger as sharp as a carving knife sliced through Savannah. "What is that supposed to mean?"

"Sometimes it's best to quit running away from the truth, or one day you'll wake up to find you've run out of places to go."

She was too tired to decipher her mother's riddles. Too rattled by the night's events to argue. She clung to self-control only long enough to say, "I'll see you in the morning."

Without waiting for a response, Savannah headed into the hall and sprinted up the stairs. She'd be damned if she let her mother get to her again. The same held true for Sam, although tonight she'd almost lost that battle.

She did agree with Ruth on one count—dredging up the past wasn't necessarily a smart thing to do. In fact, if you let it sneak up on you, it could be downright detrimental to the heart.

"You trying to sneak out, boy?"

After only two hours' sleep tops, Sam had been so preoccupied, he hadn't noticed he wasn't alone when he walked into the kitchen. He also wasn't in the mood for a chat. But out of respect, he turned from the back door to find his dad seated at the breakfast nook wearing a white T-shirt and light blue boxers, a cup of coffee in hand. "I thought I'd get an early start."

Jim glanced at the clock on the wall. "It's not even close to dawn. Are you gonna work by candlelight?"

"Last I checked, we had electricity in the barn. I need to fix a couple of stalls." Hammering a few nails might alleviate some of his frustration. "What are you doing up so early?"

"You were making a lot of racket in the bathroom and I'm a light sleeper, thanks to you."

Nothing like being blamed for a parent's poor sleeping habits. "What have I got to do with that?"

Jim scooted his chair closer to the table. "I had to learn to sleep with one eye and both ears open to make sure you didn't leave the house after your curfew."

Yeah, he'd managed to do that a time or two, and he'd almost always been caught. Almost. "That was a lot of years ago and in case you haven't noticed, I'm a grown man. I should be able to come and go as I please at this point in my life."

"Yep, you should at that."

Someday soon he'd build a house of his own so he wouldn't have to deal with the hassle of living at home. "If you're finished playing watchdog, I'm leaving now."

"Gracie won't like it if you don't have your breakfast first."

"I'll come back in for breakfast."

Jim gestured toward a chair. "Have a cup of coffee first. We need to chew the fat a bit."

No use in trying to fight the man when he had a bone to pick, Sam decided. He strode to the kitchen counter, poured a cup of coffee from the pot and took the seat across from his dad. Might as well get to it so he could get to work. "Talk."

Jim leaned back and rested his hands atop his belly. "Darlene called looking for you last night."

He predicted his ex might have taken exception to him leaving Jamie at home for the evening, but it wasn't as if he'd completely abandoned their daughter. "What did she want?"

"After I told her you were out with the old gang, she told me to tell you that since it's festival weekend and the kiddo wants to be there, she'll pick Jamie up on Saturday instead of Friday."

He hadn't really planned to attend the annual event, but if his daughter wanted to go, he'd suffer through it. "Fine. Anything else?"

"Yeah." His dad stretched his arms above his head and stacked his hands behind his neck. "She asked if Savannah was going to be at the get-together last night, I told her yes and then she said something about you following her advice."

"I don't know what she's talking about." Oh, yeah, he did.

Jim took a drink of coffee and smacked his lips. "At first I thought maybe she was pleased to hear you've been with Savannah, but I can't quite wrap my mind around the ex-wife encouraging the ex-husband to make time with the ex-girlfriend."

Sam couldn't imagine where that was anyone's business. "Darlene told me to get out more, and I did. End of story."

"But did you get reacquainted with Savannah?"

"No, and I don't intend to." After what he'd done to her last night, he'd pretty much guaranteed that wouldn't happen. "Now if you're finished with the questions, I need to get started."

"Just one more thing. Ruth called and said the attorney's coming by this afternoon to read the will. He'll drop off the lease paperwork from Wainwright in the next couple of days for you to go over before you sign it."

At least Sam could move forward on that front. But he couldn't help but wonder how Savannah would react once she learned that the old home place was about to sell, and that he was going to be the one working the land.

He figured she'd do one of two things—accept the inevitable, or raise holy hell. He would lay down money on the last one.

"EXCUSE ME, MR. FARLEY, could you please repeat that?" Not that Savannah really needed to hear the attorney's words again. She'd understood exactly what he'd said— she just didn't quite believe it.

The balding, bespectacled lawyer smiled as if repeating the will's terms didn't bother him a bit. "Since the property is jointly titled, all proceeds from the sale of the house, equipment and land will go to Ruth."

She stared at her mother, who sat on the floral sofa, stiff as a skateboard. "But you're not going to sell the farm now, correct? This clause is in case you want to do that in the future."

"I've already sold it."

"Who bought it?" Savannah asked.

"Edwin Wainwright," Farley said.

Savannah could barely contain her shock. "Mother, you have got to be kidding."

Ruth sent her a quelling look. "We'll discuss it later.

I'm sure Mr. Farley would like to finish up so he can go back to Jackson."

"I do have one more appointment," Farley said. "But as soon as we go over the last of the details, feel free to look over the will, Miss Greer, and then call if you have any concerns."

Oh, she had some concerns, all right, but most had to do with her mother's decision to sell the farm to Wainwright, not her father's last wishes.

To that point, her aunt and uncle had been standing against one wall in the parlor, observing the proceedings. Savannah had all but forgotten their presence until Farley said, "Mr. Taylor, Mr. Greer bequeathed you his autographed baseball collection. And Mrs. Taylor, he wished you to have his stamp collection." He leaned over and handed Bill a document. "This is the appraised value of the items."

From the way her uncle raised his eyebrows, she assumed they were of some monetary as well as sentimental value. Many an evening Savannah had sat at the dining room table and listened as her dad talked about those collections. And several times she'd regretfully cut him off to join her friends or finish her homework.

"Ruth and Savannah, you are to divide any remaining keepsakes how you see fit," Farley added. "But there is one item your father specifically designated you be given, Savannah. The wooden cradle made by his great-great-grandfather."

Savannah recalled the beautiful spindled cradle stored safely in the attic. No matter how long or hard she'd begged as a child, her mother hadn't allowed her to play with it. With adulthood came insight, and she now understood why that rule had been established. Her father had hoped to one day see his own grandchild occupying that treasured heirloom, something that would never happen now. That fact alone threatened to send Savannah into an emotional tailspin and with great effort, she stopped the urge to cry.

Farley then handed her an envelope. "He also left you this."

Savannah wanted to wait to open it, but it seemed everyone expected her to reveal the contents right away, especially her mother. She lifted the flap and withdrew a five-thousand-dollar life insurance policy naming her as the beneficiary. And attached to the certificate, she found a personal note.

Dear Savannah,
I know it's not much and you probably make more money than this in a week, but I wanted you to have something to put away for your children. Just let them know that their old granddad loves them, even if he never had the pleasure of knowing them.
Love, Your Dad

Savannah stared at the letter through a mist of tears she'd tried so hard to keep at bay, her emotions battered by the realization that her offspring would never know how wonderful her father had been. They would never know how much he had influenced her, how much he had adored her.

Then and there, she silently vowed to keep his legacy

alive by sharing the stories he'd told her, the lessons he'd taught her, provided she decided to have children.

She bit the inside of her cheek to keep from sobbing, raised her chin and said, "Thank you, Mr. Farley. Is there anything else?"

"No, ma'am." The attorney came to his feet and hitched up his pants. "Again, if you have any questions, just get in touch with my office. Your mother has my number."

While Ruth saw Farley to the door, and Bill and May left the room, Savannah sat quietly clutching the envelope in her grasp. She wanted to take shelter in her old bedroom for another long cry, yet she had too many burning questions, and she didn't want to wait a minute longer for the answers.

Once she heard the front door close, Savannah called to her mother in case she, too, decided to escape the inquest. Ruth entered the living room, head held high, and reclaimed the chair she'd been occupying a few moments before.

Savannah decided to get right to the point. "Why are you selling the farm?"

Ruth focused on some unknown point across the room. "Because I got a good offer and those are hard to come by these days."

She didn't buy that for a minute. "But this place has been in your family for at least three generations. How could you let it go to someone like Wainwright?"

Ruth raised a thin brow. "Do you plan to live here?"

"Well, no, but—"

"Then why would I want to keep it if I have no one to pass it on to?"

Obviously her mother didn't believe her daughter would produce any offspring. "Where are you going to live?"

Ruth twisted her wedding ring round and round her finger. "I'm moving back to Knoxville. Bill and May are heading home tonight and they'll be back first of next week with a trailer to get what furniture I plan to take. I'll move in temporarily with May until I find a place of my own. I have enough money to buy another house in Knoxville, or maybe I'll just rent an apartment in a retirement community."

Savannah couldn't fathom her mother residing in senior-citizen housing with no garden to tend to. Yet she saw no use in arguing with Ruth Greer. Once she had her mind set on something, no one could persuade her to do otherwise. "Fine. By the way, what does Wainwright plan to do with the house?"

"He's probably going to tear it down since he's already leased the land."

The hint of satisfaction in Ruth's voice, the thought that the place that held many good memories would soon be gone, rendered Savannah momentarily speechless. "How can you be so unaffected by that? You and Dad made a life here. It's as if you're okay with destroying all the memories."

Her mother's expression went bitter as brine. "He can burn it down, for all I care. Not every memory tied to this place is a good one."

Savannah recalled her aunt's assertions that life had

been hard on the farm following their mother's death. But she couldn't imagine it had been so terrible that Ruth would want to demolish the place. "I can certainly understand how horrible the memories of Grandmother's and Dad's illnesses must be, but surely you have some good ones, too. I remember you talking about playing hide-and-seek with May in the attic and Dad courting you on the front porch."

"I see no need to live in the past," Ruth said.

"I see no need to raze a perfectly good house," Savannah countered. "And what if you change your mind and decide to come back?"

Ruth raised her ever-present emotional wall and stood. "I would never do that. The faster I can get away from this place, the better. It's poison."

Poison?

May breezed into the room, interrupting the uncomfortable conversation. "Ruth, can you tell me where Floyd kept his collections? I thought we'd go ahead and take them back with us now and anything else you'd like us to take."

Ruth avoided making eye contact with Savannah as she said, "I'll show you where everything is."

The opportunity to prod her mother further might have escaped Savannah now, but before she left for Chicago, she was determined to have some answers to Ruth's cryptic statement. But she did have one more question she needed answered immediately.

She hurried into the hall and found her mother climbing the stairs behind May. "Any idea who'll be leasing the land from Wainwright?" she asked, although she suspected she already knew the answer.

Her suspicions were confirmed when her mother glanced back and simply stated, "Sam McBriar."

HE COULD HEAR THE ECHO of rapid footsteps in the metal building, but he couldn't see who was about to pay him a visit since he was on his back beneath a truck. More than likely, he was about to be summoned by his child.

As soon as the steps stopped, Sam asked, "Is it time for supper, kiddo?"

"It's time for us to have a talk."

That voice sure as heck didn't belong to Jamie, but he recognized it all the same. He turned his head slightly to see a pair of strappy high heels exposing pink-painted toenails. And above that, some really nice ankles. Unfortunately, he couldn't see the legs attached to those ankles unless he came out from under the truck. From the sound of Savannah's tone, he might better stay put. But if he made up some lame excuse and sent her on her way, he'd still have to face the music at some point in time. Besides, he wanted to see her, even if she had her panties in a twist.

"Sam, are you coming out here or am I going to have to drag you out by your boots?"

Like she was strong enough to do that. And speaking of panties… "I have to ask you something first. What are you wearing?"

"This is no time for sex talk."

"That wasn't what I had in mind, but now that you mention it—"

"I'm running out of patience."

And he was running out of excuses. "I'm just saying that if you're wearing a dress, you might want to walk backward a ways if you value your modesty."

A few seconds ticked off, she muttered, "Oh," and took his advice.

Sam slid from beneath the truck, stood and grabbed a rag from the nearby workbench before facing her. While he made a futile attempt to wipe the grease from his hands, he managed a quick look at her clothes. She had on a pale blue sleeveless dress that hit her right above the knees and highlighted her curves like a neon sign that flashed Touch Me. Most would consider the outfit decent enough, except to a guy who was having some pretty indecent thoughts.

"How did you find me?" he asked.

"One of your workers pointed me in the right direction. I didn't realize you employed so many men."

"Do I need to call them all in here as reinforcements?" When she glared at him, he decided to test the stormy waters. "Look, if you're still pissed off at me about last night—"

"That's not why I'm here, although I'm still not too thrilled with your game-playing."

Little did she know, this wasn't a game. Not in the way she assumed. "Then what did I do this time?"

She wrapped her arms tightly around her middle. "You lied to me."

Here it comes. "About what?"

"My mother's decision to sell the farm."

"It wasn't my place to mention it."

"Even though you're going to lease the land from Wainwright?"

No way out except to tell the truth. "It doesn't matter one bit to you what I do, so I saw no reason to say anything about it. And that means I didn't lie."

She pointed an accusing finger at him. "You lied by omission."

"Not really. The farm is your mother's business and leasing farmland is my business."

She rolled her eyes. "Haven't you heard of common courtesy? Oh, wait. I forgot you don't know the meaning of courtesy."

He was on the verge of getting as riled as she was. "When have I ever not been courteous to you?"

She tapped her fingertip against her chin and pretended to think. "Aside from last night, I believe I remember something about a scene in a diner twelve years ago when you treated me like dirt."

No surprise she would hurl that little bit of history in his face. "Oh, yeah? I recall you failing to tell me you decided to leave Mississippi to go to college, which makes you a hypocrite, *Savvy*."

He could see pure fury building in her dark eyes. "I didn't lie to you, Sam. I couldn't find the time to tell you I was going out of state before that day in Stan's. I wasn't even sure I'd been accepted to Northwestern until the day before."

"And that's lying by omission," he said, throwing her own words back at her.

"That didn't give you the right to talk to me the way you did. I still remember every horrible thing you said in front of half the town."

So did Sam, and he regretted a lot of it, but not enough to take all the blame. "After you waltzed into the diner and dropped one helluva bomb on me, how did you expect me to react?"

"Like someone who cared for me, but apparently I'd been wrong about that. If you care for someone, you don't call them a selfish bitch."

Damn, he had said that, and at the time, he'd meant it. At the time, he'd been an eighteen-year-old kid with some seriously wounded pride. "I apologize for the bitch part."

She looked exasperated. "But not the selfish part?"

He tossed the rag onto the workbench. "You didn't care how anyone felt about you leaving, including your father, so I'd say that made you fairly selfish."

She balled her fists at her sides like she wanted to slug him. "You knew I had to get away from this place. I was drowning."

And I was holding you down, he wanted to say, but that same old pride prevented him from doing so. "Right. You were drowning. You had bigger dreams than a place like Placid could handle. I might not have gotten it then, but I get it now. And don't forget that you called me a heartless bastard."

"I apologize to your dad for the bastard part."

Okay, maybe he deserved that, but she had no idea what her decision had done to his heart. And he'd carry that secret to his grave, because fact was, she'd leave again, just like before, no matter what he confessed. "Glad we cleared that up. Anything else?"

She nailed him with another defiant glare. "Yes. Tell Wainwright you changed your mind about leasing the land."

That came as no surprise. "Sorry, can't do that."

"Yes, you can. It's my understanding you haven't signed the papers yet."

"That's right, but I will sign them."

"Just to punish me?"

Time to set her straight. "To keep a promise I made to your dad."

"Promise?" She sounded doubtful.

"Yeah. He asked me to take care of the place after he was gone."

She looked more than a little confused. "I don't understand why he would entrust it to you of all people. I remember a time when he didn't think all that highly of you."

That was just enough to set him off. "There's a whole hell of a lot you don't know about your dad."

Savannah looked madder than a wet hen. "And you don't know what you're talking about."

He was just the man to enlighten her. "Did you know that Floyd's folks never owned one acre because they didn't have a damn dime to their name? Did you know they spent their whole lives working for someone else, your dad included, until he married your mom? All he ever wanted was a place to call his own. That farm meant more to him than anything aside from his family. He needed to know that someone would take good care of the place. Like it or not, sweetheart, that some-one is me."

"No, I don't like it but—"

When he took a step toward her, she took a step back. "If you weren't so pigheaded you'd realize that your fa-ther's dying wish is more important than your hatred of me."

She turned from steamed to sophisticated in about two seconds. "I suppose it's not my place to question my father's decision. But you're very wrong about one thing. I don't hate you."

"What did you say?" He asked not because he hadn't heard her, he just didn't trust his ears.

"I said I don't hate you. Hate, like love, requires com-mitting to strong emotions. I personally don't feel one way or the other about you."

He wasn't sure which was worse—her hating him or not caring at all. "You felt something last night. Maybe it wasn't hate or love but I'd bet the farm it had a lot to do with lust."

She propped one hand on her hip, reminding him of Miss Ellie Wagner, his second-grade spinster school-teacher, only a lot better looking. "*You* talked about the pond and no, I didn't feel anything other than embar-rassed when I remembered what a fool I'd been. But I'm not that malleable teenager anymore, Sam. You can't mold me into being that starry-eyed girl who used to jump whenever you called."

He released a rough laugh. "Mold you? I could just as soon mold a feather pillow out of a cinder block. Besides, I've never forced you to do anything you didn't want to do."

"You're trying to make me be happy that my father, for whatever reason, decided to declare you his surrogate son. You're trying to make me admit that I'm still somehow attracted to you when all I want to do is get out of here."

He hooked a thumb behind him. "There's the door. No one's tying you down. But first, I have one more thing to say."

"Go for it. Just make sure you say everything because I don't intend to have another real conversation with you again."

And that was probably best. The more they talked, the more they risked wounding each other with words. He didn't want or need that misery again. But he wouldn't let her leave before he called her bluff. "You know what your problem is, Savannah? You're afraid."

"Afraid?" This time she laughed. "Of what? You? That's ludicrous."

"Then why the hell are you backed up against the table?"

She looked around like she hadn't realized where she was at the moment. When she moved her hands from the death grip she had on the edge of the bench, she knocked over a bottle of tire cleaner. And when she tried to right it, she knocked it over again. After finally setting the bottle straight, she studied the cement floor and said, "Are you through interrogating me?"

"Not yet." He moved right in front of her, leaving only a few inches between them. "Maybe you're not afraid of me, but you're afraid of being around me because you know there's still something going on between us. I don't like it any more than you do, but it's there."

"Speak for yourself."

She asked for it, she was going to get it—the truth. "Okay, I'll be the adult here and admit it. The minute I laid eyes on you a few minutes ago, I wanted to run my hands up that dress."

That got her undivided attention. "Stop it, Sam."

Her mouth might be saying stop, but the fire in her eyes said go. "What's the matter? If you don't feel anything, then you shouldn't give a tinker's damn what I want to do to you."

"I don't care about your fantasies as long as you don't try to act on them."

"Sure, Savannah. Right now you're shaking like a leaf. You can lie to yourself, but I know you better than you think I do." He brushed a wisp of hair away from her cheek. "And I'm thinkin' you want to kiss me. *Real* bad."

She blew out a shaky breath. "You wish."

More than she realized. "I *know*. And I've got to tell you, Savvy, I'm disappointed in you. I remember the girl who never ignored a challenge. That girl didn't stop until she got what she wanted. Guess the Windy City's made you soft."

Realizing he might've gone too far, Sam backed up and leaned against the truck. He shouldn't be all that worried. Just because he'd thrown down the gauntlet didn't mean she'd actually grab it and run. Or that's what he'd thought until she strode toward him.

Sam saw his plan to avoid this very thing go up in smoke the minute Savannah took his mouth in an all-out assault. His fault for striking the match and lighting up an old flame. Not that he was complaining. He was fairly uncomfortable in a real nice way with her body rubbing against his and her arms draped around his neck. Good thing the truck was offering some support, otherwise he might have dropped to the ground—and taken her with him.

Many a night he'd fantasized about kissing her again, but nothing beat the reality. She could give as good as she got and he was giving her his best effort. He didn't see any sign of this little make-out session ending any-time soon, unless he found some superhuman strength.

Instead, he found her butt with his palms and nudged her closer, letting her know exactly what she was doing to him. What she'd always done to him, like it or not.

When Savannah released a moan against his mouth, he ran his palms up the backs of her thighs, taking the dress with him while ignoring all the reasons why they shouldn't be doing this. If he had any consideration for what was best, he'd come to his senses and back off. But the way he was feeling right now, that would probably take a miracle.

"Daddy! Where are you?"

CHAPTER SIX

THE CHILDISH SHOUT COMING from somewhere in the distance was as effective as a bucket of snow on Sam's libido. They simultaneously broke the kiss and while Savannah turned her back on him, Sam ran both hands over his face in an attempt to recover—and then let go a loud laugh when he opened his eyes to one hell of a humorous sight.

Savannah spun around and scowled. "This is not a laughing matter. Stupid on my part, but not at all funny."

"Oh, yeah, it is. My hands are on your butt."

She looked like he'd taken complete leave of his senses. "You mean they *were* on my butt."

He rubbed a palm over his jaw. "Well, seeing as how you're an attorney, let me put this in legalese so you'll understand. The evidence that my hands *were* planted on your backside is imprinted on the dress in question."

She glanced over her shoulder, then gave him a fairly fierce look that said he was going to have hell to pay. "I can't believe you did that."

He held up both hands, greasy palms forward. "Hey, you started it."

"And you didn't try to stop me."

"Do you blame me?"

She propped both hands on her hips. "Let's just say we're both to blame and leave it at that."

"Daddy!"

Jamie was definitely getting closer, and so was Sam to the heart of the matter. Savannah had come down with a serious case of lust, and he'd definitely caught it. "In here, sweetheart," he called to his daughter now that he was sufficiently calm, at least on the outside.

Savannah's eyes went wide as wagon wheels. "How am I going to hide the mess you made?"

In two strides, Sam grabbed her by the waist, turned and sat her on the truck's hood. "Don't move and she'll never notice."

Jamie rushed into the shop and pulled up short when she spotted their guest. "Hi, Savannah!"

Savannah put on her best smile but to Sam it looked forced. "Hi, sweetie. It's good to see you again. I'm just watching your dad work on the truck."

Jamie looked at Sam, then Savannah, and started giggling. "No, you're not. You were kissing my daddy."

Sam exchanged a what-the-hell look with Savannah before he asked, "Why would you think a thing like that, Joe?"

"'Cause you've got lipstick on your lips, Daddy." Jamie rocked back and forth on her heels, like she couldn't quite contain her excitement over the discovery.

Sam immediately wiped his mouth with the back of his hand. No need in offering up an explanation because knowing his kid, she wouldn't buy it. "What do you want, Jamie?"

"Grandma Gracie told me to come get you for dinner. She wants Savannah to come, too, and so do I."

Sam saw a little desperation in Savannah's eyes before she gave Jamie a smile. "Honey, I wish I could but—"

"Please, Savannah?" Jamie pleaded. "You've gotta stay for dinner because Grandma Gracie's making her famous ham and sweet potatoes and the banana pudding you like and she's already set a place for you at the table."

Sam noted a moment of indecision in Savannah's eyes before she said, "I would need to go home and change first."

Jamie frowned. "Supper's almost ready and I'm hungry."

Patience wasn't his daughter's strong suit. At the moment, politeness wasn't, either. "Mind your manners, kiddo."

Jamie looked as contrite as a scolded puppy. "Sorry, Daddy. I just think Savannah looks pretty and she doesn't need to change clothes. That's all."

When Savannah gave him a help-me look, Sam turned his attention back to his daughter. "Tell Gracie we'll be at the house in a minute."

"Okay." Jamie backed toward the door, grinning. "You gonna kiss some more?"

Not if he wanted to save himself from another huge error in judgment. "Get out of here, Joe, or I'm going to make you shovel manure all day tomorrow."

"No way, Daddy-o." Jamie turned on her heels and left the shop at a dead run, leaving Sam alone with

Savannah, who didn't look at all grateful for the dinner invitation.

She proved that when she said, "You shouldn't have told her to expect me for dinner. I can't very well go to the table with proof of your evildoing to my person all over the back of this dress."

"Your *person* enjoyed my evildoing, just like I expected. And consider yourself lucky. If Jamie hadn't interrupted, you might've had two more handprints on your top."

She picked up the rag, balled it up and launched it at him like a cloth missile. "Wet this and see if you can undo the damage. And while you're at it, wipe that smug look off your face."

"Sweetheart, that ain't smugness. That's pain."

She sent a quick look downward at the source of his distress, blushed like a fire engine and muttered, "Sorry."

So was he. Sorry he hadn't sent her on her way sooner. Sorry he'd provoked her. Real sorry he couldn't do a damn thing about his pain.

Sam walked to the utility sink and soaked the towel before returning to Savannah. "Turn around."

After she complied, he put one hand on her waist and rubbed at the stains with minimal pressure. He didn't make much headway with the grease, but he did enjoy the effort. At this rate, he'd have to make up some reason to miss dinner.

She glanced back at him with an aggravated expression. "Is it working?"

"It's worse."

She abruptly faced him and snatched the towel from his grasp. "You'll have to apologize to Gracie because I am not going in your house like this."

Sam came up with a quick plan that might satisfy her, even if he couldn't. "I'll take you through the outside entrance of my bedroom and you can put on a pair of jeans and one of my T-shirts." As long as he didn't imagine her wearing only his shirt, he might get through the meal with his dignity intact.

She ran both hands through her hair. "In case you haven't noticed, I'm about nine inches shorter than you and I weigh less, too. How do you expect me to wear your jeans?"

This admission probably wasn't going to go over too well, but he didn't have much choice. He didn't want her to think that his bedroom had a revolving door welcoming every woman in the county. Why that mattered at all, he couldn't say. "They belonged to Darlene."

"I see."

No, she didn't. She probably thought he'd kept those old clothes because he didn't want to let go of his ex-wife. Wrong. He just hadn't bothered to toss them out. "Which is it going to be? My plan or going home and explaining my greasy hands on your butt to your mother?"

After a slight hesitation, she sighed. "I'll agree to your plan, but I have to go right after dinner. May and Bill went home and I don't want to leave Mother alone much longer. I also told her we could sort through some of Dad's things this evening."

"Not a problem." Actually, it was. He really wanted to get her alone again after dinner to set her straight on a few things, namely that what had happened wasn't all his doing, even if he had egged her on.

Hell, who was he kidding? If he got her alone, which was about as likely as Jamie keeping quiet about the lipstick, he couldn't be sure that he wouldn't want to kiss her again, and not stop there. Better to leave well enough alone.

Sam pushed off the truck and gestured toward the open garage door. "After you."

When she moved in front of him, he patted that grease-covered, knock-'em-dead butt, proving old habits died hard, even after a decade.

She turned and walked backward, just like his daughter had a few minutes ago. "What are you doing?"

"Just thought I'd try to remove some more of the mess." Now he was lying. Big-time.

"You're still that same old bad boy, aren't you?"

When she reluctantly smiled, Sam saw the girl she used to be. The girl he'd come to rely on to save him from his rebel ways. The only girl he'd let close enough to hurt him. The woman he still wanted after all these years.

Savannah could cut him to the core again if he let her. And he'd literally be damned if he did.

THE WELCOME SCENT OF good old Southern cooking permeated the dining room like a pleasant morning mist. The same yellow floral print cloth covered the table and the weathered wooden plaque that read God Bless Our Home still hung over the back door. The camaraderie of old friends sharing a meal provided a welcome change for someone who'd spent most of their time away from work in the confines of a sterile condominium. Yet even in the familiar surroundings and in the presence of people she dearly loved, Savannah felt uncomfortable.

She'd barely been able to make a dent in the pile of food Gracie had set before her, probably because she was too busy choking down her guilt. She kept wondering what she'd been thinking in the shop. Actually, she hadn't been thinking at all. She'd run solely on impulse, completely reeled in by a sexy devil in denim.

Yet Sam had been surprisingly silent throughout the meal. He'd also been remarkably controlled even when they'd walked into his bedroom earlier. He'd simply tossed her the clothes and waited in the hall until she'd changed out of the dress. She, on the other hand, had recalled all the times they'd been alone in that bedroom. Back then, propriety had dictated they never close the door. But the converted room that had once been a garage was tucked away in the back of the house, allowing for a few stolen kisses during what should have been study time.

No more kisses for her today. She'd done too much of that already for reasons that defied logic. Not that logic had ever come into play when Sam was involved. He'd presented a challenge, and something primal had driven her to act the fool that she'd always been around him. He certainly hadn't been wrong on one point—desire was a powerful motivator—and she refused to give in to it again.

Fortunately, Jamie had been seated between them during the meal, providing Savannah with some much-needed separation from Sam. More important, Jamie had made it through the meal without mentioning her suspicions about the kiss. Accurate suspicions. And since the little girl had disappeared with Gracie a few minutes ago, it appeared they might actually be in the clear.

"I hear the two of you were swapping gum out in the shop."

Savannah nearly spewed iced tea all over the table after Jim's sudden proclamation. She dabbed at her mouth with a napkin and sent a panicky look at Sam.

And like the cad he could be, he grinned as if he found the situation quite amusing. "Who told you that, Dad?"

"Your kid."

"She's always had one heck of an active imagination," Sam said without looking at Savannah.

Jim snorted. "She's got enough smarts to realize that country boys don't wear lipstick."

Savannah pondered how on earth she would escape this predicament. Leaving would be too obvious. Crawling beneath the table would, too. Fortunately, Gracie picked that moment to breeze into the dining room. And even better, she didn't return with Jamie, saving the little girl from some questionable conversation. At least Savannah could count on Sam's stepmother to be the perfect portrait of decorum, no matter what Jamie might have revealed.

Gracie stood behind Jim's chair and rested her palms on her husband's shoulders. "I've hung your dress up to dry, Savannah. But I'm afraid Sam's hands aren't going to come out unless I wash it again and use bleach, and that would ruin it."

So much for decorum. And so much for Sam taking care of it himself. "Don't worry about it, Gracie," she said. "I have other dresses."

"But not with Sam's mark on 'em, I bet," Jim added with a smirk.

Both Gracie and Jim chuckled at Savannah's expense. Worse, Sam chimed right in. Clearly not one of them recognized her mortification.

Savannah desperately wanted to turn the conversation away from anything having to do with grease or lipstick. "By the way, where is Jamie?"

Gracie pulled up a chair and sat next to Jim. "She's on the phone with her mama. And she told me to tell you that you have to stay and listen to her play the guitar in a bit."

Savannah wanted to bow out and go home, but she couldn't in good conscience disappoint a child. Not to mention she no longer had a valid reason to go home. When she'd called to say she was staying for dinner at the McBriars', her mother informed her that she was too tired to sort through the keepsakes anyway.

As wary as she was of spending more time with her former lover, as much as she didn't trust herself around him, Savannah saw no reason not to be sociable with his family. A half hour longer wouldn't matter in the grand scheme of things—as long as she didn't end up alone with Sam. "I wouldn't want to miss hearing Jamie play, so I'd be glad to stay for a while."

"She's pretty good," Jim said. "Sam's been teaching her since she was knee-high to a cricket."

Savannah gave her attention to Sam, who was turning his fork over and over. "Jamie must come by it honestly," she said.

Sam didn't bother to look up from his current preoccupation with the utensils. "She's going to be a lot better than me if I have any say in the matter. I want to make sure she knows enough while I still have the opportunity."

He sounded almost despondent, as if for some reason spending time with his child might be coming to an end. Savannah couldn't fathom Darlene taking Jamie away from him. Or maybe Sam just assumed that someday Jamie would choose other activities over her father. He had his mother's abandonment to thank for that concern.

Jamie rushed into the room like a miniwhirlwind, guitar in hand, and declared, "We all have to go in the backyard. That's where I can get my muse."

This time everyone laughed, followed by Sam asking, "Do you even know what a muse is, Joe?"

Jamie shrugged. "Nope. I heard it on TV. What is a muse, Daddy?"

"I'll explain it to you some other time," he said. "It's late and Savannah needs to get home to her mom."

Sam was obviously intent on getting rid of her as soon as possible, which only spurred her desire to stay longer. "Don't hurry on my account. I'm not afraid of the devil or the dark."

She sent Sam a pointed look and he responded with a noncommittal expression.

Gracie pushed back from the table and stood. "Y'all go on outside while I clear the dishes. I'll be out in a jiffy with the pudding."

Savannah saw a prime opportunity and grabbed it. "I'll help you, Gracie," she said as she practically jumped out of the chair.

Gracie seemed rather pleased by the offer. "I'd enjoy the company, Savannah."

Jim stood and kissed Gracie on the cheek. Sam, on the other hand, remained rooted to his seat.

After Jim and Jamie filed out of the dining room and headed toward the back door, Gracie picked up the serving dishes while Savannah walked around the table gathering plates. When she leaned over to take Sam's, her nerves were strung as tight as a guy wire. But he didn't move, didn't speak, didn't touch her. In fact, he shifted slightly to prevent any contact.

Without even a passing glance at Sam, she followed Gracie into the kitchen that was more familiar than her own. She'd spent hours there with Sam's then-housekeeper, chatting nonstop while she honed her cooking skills. Skills that she rarely used these days.

The area had remained much the same with butcher-block counters and an oversized white farm sink that she began to fill with hot water. She lost all semblance of concentration when Sam sauntered into the kitchen, hands in pockets. But he didn't give her a look as he left out the back door.

Savannah blew out a breath of relief as she opened the lower cabinet and fumbled around for a minute, knocking over several items before she finally found what she'd been searching for. She'd been fumbling like an imbecile all day, thanks to Sam.

When Savannah straightened and set the dishwashing liquid on the back of the sink, Gracie moved to her left and smiled. "No need to do anything but rinse off the dishes, sweetie pie. Jimmy gave me a brand-new dishwasher for a wedding gift."

Savannah kneed the cabinet closed and looked to her right to discover the shiny stainless appliance that Gracie so deserved. "It's about time."

"But not so romantic," Gracie said as she rinsed off the utensils and set them aside on the drainboard. "I told Jimmy that if he'd go out to the workshop and get a tow chain, I could wear it around my neck and maybe then I wouldn't be so disappointed that he hadn't bought me a necklace."

Savannah laughed yet internally cringed over the "workshop" reminder. "I suppose it's the thought that counts, huh?"

"Yes, and I count my lucky stars that I finally got him to the altar after twenty some-odd years. Did you know it took him five whole years to kiss me?"

"No, I didn't know that." Savannah opened the drawer to the washer and lined the top rack with glasses. "I've never even heard all the details about how you came to be Jim's housekeeper, only that you just showed up one day, according to Sam."

This time Gracie laughed. "Dumb luck or fate sent me here, I'm not sure which. I was twenty-one years old and working at the feed store. Someone told me about the job and I was so sure it would be easier than standing on my feet all day. So I applied and Jimmy hired me. Grandpa Mick, Jimmy's dad, was still alive then, so that made three males in this house, and after seeing the state of the place, I almost left and never came back."

Savannah could picture Gracie way back when, before time had painted silver in her dark hair and fine lines above her brow. "But you did come back. Why?"

Gracie wiped her hands on a dish towel and leaned a hip against the cabinet. "Because I took one look at that lost little five-year-old boy who didn't know why his mama had left him behind, and I couldn't leave."

When Savannah had met him, Sam still possessed some of those lost-boy traits—a risk-taker and border-line troublemaker. Had it not been for his father's iron-hand influence, he might have turned out differently considering his mother's careless disregard. "Your feelings for Jim didn't play a role?"

Gracie smiled. "Actually, not in the beginning. Jimmy was an old grump all the time. But deep down I knew his bad attitude had to do with getting his heart stomped. I just hung in there until he finally came around." She sighed. "Finding forever with your first love is worth all the trials and tribulations. And the waiting."

Finding forever with your first love…

Since she'd wised up in adulthood, Savannah had begun to believe that concept was only a fantasy. Rachel and Matt were the exception, and so were Gracie and Jim. Not everyone could be quite that fortunate.

She rinsed off a plate and handed it to Gracie. "There wasn't anyone special before Jim?"

Gracie leaned over and slid the plate in the dishwasher.

"Not really. I dated a couple of boys in high school, but they didn't hold my attention that long. Of course, for years I had this fear that Linda would show up one day and take Jimmy and Sam away from me."

A justified concern, in Savannah's opinion. "Speaking of Linda, does Sam ever hear from her?"

Gracie shook her head. "Up until a few years back, she sent birthday and Christmas cards, but that's about it. Then a year after Jamie was born, she called Sam. I don't know what she said to him, but I do know he was upset for days afterward. Everything stopped the following year. No cards or calls. That's when we discovered she'd passed away from cancer."

Steeped in shock, Savannah went momentarily silent. "I had no idea."

"Not many people know," Gracie said. "You can count on Sam not to say anything. And it's really very sad. She'd remarried and had a daughter who should be in her early twenties by now."

Just one more thing Savannah hadn't been aware of. "Then Sam never met his sister?"

Gracie took a large blue bowl from the refrigerator and placed it on the counter. "No, and I doubt he ever will. As far as I know, Linda never told her husband or the girl about Sam. At least that's what she said to Jimmy that time she called. I can't imagine living a lie all those years and carrying it to the grave."

In some odd way, Savannah did understand why someone might keep that secret, right or wrong. When life rocked along smoothly, many wouldn't want to upset the applecart.

The screen door creaked open followed by Jim calling, "Gracie and Savannah, the concert's about to start and I'm ready for my dessert."

"Hold your horses," Gracie called back. "We'll be out in a minute."

Savannah grabbed one of the bowls from the counter and helped Gracie dole out the banana pudding. They worked in companionable silence until Gracie said, "Just so you know, I didn't mean to embarrass you over what happened between you and Sam earlier."

Savannah could issue a denial, but Gracie would see right through her. "It was just one of those things." One of those things that she would probably live to regret.

Gracie patted Savannah's cheek. "I know, honey. I imagine it's hard to control that attraction to each other, even though that could create a bushel of problems for you both."

Before Savannah could respond, Gracie was halfway out the kitchen with three bowls of pudding balanced in her grasp. Before she could insist that she wasn't rediscovering anything with Sam. Clichéd animal lust was one thing—caring was another altogether. As she'd told him in the shop, she didn't feel anything for him. She didn't dare. And she sure as heck wouldn't kiss him again.

After she'd had some time to regroup, Savannah carefully walked down the three steps leading to the backyard to join the group. She set the two remaining bowls on the picnic table, then slid onto the chair next to Gracie. Sam was seated in a green metal lawn chair across from the table with Jamie standing next to him.

As he tuned the guitar, Savannah centered her attention on his hands. Hands that she'd always found so strong and appealing, calluses and all. She thought about the men in Chicago, the pretty boys whose idea of manual labor consisted of pounding a computer keyboard. She couldn't recall one who had hands as strong as Sam's.

After offering Jamie the guitar, Sam said, "Okay, Joe, it's all yours."

The little girl looked suddenly shy. "I want you to sing with me."

Sam frowned. "This is your show, kiddo."

"Please, Daddy?"

"Go ahead and sing with her, son," Jim prodded.

"Yes, do," Gracie added before turning to Savannah. "You have to see this."

Jamie took the guitar from Sam and climbed into his lap, her brow furrowed in concentration as she began to strum the guitar. Together father and daughter sang a simple, familiar and beloved lullaby about mockingbirds and gifts.

As Savannah witnessed the tender scene, a host of emotions bore down on her. The pride in Sam's eyes and the gentle way he treated his child reminded her that she'd known he had a great capacity to love, virtually untapped until he'd been given this precious little girl.

She also thought of her own father, how close they'd been. How she'd always been able to count on him during troubled times, except when it came to battling her mother. But then she'd once relied on Sam as well, before everything had fallen apart.

Savannah summoned every ounce of strength to maintain her composure until the song ended. But when Jamie looked at Sam and said, "I love you, Daddy," and he replied, "I love you, too, kiddo," she could no longer trust herself not to break down.

She joined Gracie and Jim in a round of applause before she rose from the chair. "That was beautiful, Jamie," she said around the knot in her throat. "And I really have to go now."

Gracie sent her a concerned look. "You haven't touched your pudding, Savannah. And your dress is still drying."

"I'll finish the pudding and Sam can drop the dress off tomorrow," Jim said. "If the girl needs to go, we should let her."

After Jamie slid from Sam's lap, she walked to Savannah and gave her a hug and a sweet, sweet smile. "Floyd liked that song, too. Do you think he can hear us in heaven?"

She softly patted Jamie's cheek. "I'm sure he can, and I know he enjoyed it as much as I did."

When Jamie let her go, Savannah clung to her last scrap of self-control. "Thank you for dinner, everyone. I'll see you soon."

She barely made it up the steps before the tears began to flow like a country stream. A rogue sob slipped out as she opened the back door and she prayed no one had heard it. As she made her way through the house, she tempered her steps though she dearly wanted to run. Run from the feelings hovering just beneath the surface. Run from the realization that she did still have some latent feelings for her first love. Run from Sam.

It's best to quit running away from the truth, or one day you'll wake up to find you've run out of places to go....

As Savannah walked out the front door, she acknowledged that for once her mother could very well be right.

CHAPTER SEVEN

WHEN GRACIE STOOD AND announced, "I'll go see about her," Sam immediately came to his feet and said, "I'll go."

"Can I go, too?" Jamie asked.

He bent and kissed her cheek. "You can go to bed. I'll tuck you in when I get back."

Before his daughter could object to the order, Sam sprinted up the cement stairs, Gracie dogging his steps. He didn't make it past the kitchen before she called to him to wait. He didn't want to wait. He wanted to get to Savannah and find out what was wrong, even though he had a few theories.

Out of respect, he turned to his stepmother. "What is it, Gracie?" he asked as he unsuccessfully tried to keep the impatience out of his voice.

She grabbed a couple of tissues from the box on the counter and handed them to him. "She's going to need these and your kindness."

Like he didn't realize that. "I don't plan to treat her with anything but kindness."

"She also doesn't need you toying with her feelings right now. So don't go thinking you're going to take advantage of her vulnerability by charming her back into your bed. And don't forget that no matter what you do, she'll be leaving again."

He didn't need that reminder, and he didn't need the guilt trip, either. He opened a kitchen drawer and removed a flashlight. "If you're done with the sermon, I've got to go. She could be halfway to Chicago by now."

She waved him away. "Fine, but don't forget your manners."

If he didn't leave right away, he would.

Sam rushed out the front door and jogged down the path that led to the Greers' farm. Since Savannah had a head start and seemed to be in a big hurry, he doubted he'd catch up to her before she made it back to the house. But when he emerged from the break in the tree line a few minutes later, he discovered he wasn't too late after all.

For Sam, the bridge had been the means to get to her. For Savannah, it had served as a refuge for as long as he'd known her. The three-quarter moon provided enough light to outline her silhouette and although he couldn't make out many details, he figured she'd been crying. Maybe she still was.

When he reached the bridge, Sam approached her slowly so he wouldn't startle her. But the rasp of wood beneath his boots drew her attention and she began swiping beneath her eyes with her fingertips.

Classic Savannah—trying hard to hide the tears. Sam wasn't sure what to offer first, the tissue or a talk. He handed her the tissue and decided to let her talk when she was ready. He turned off the flashlight, set it on the railing and then took his place beside her.

They stayed that way for a time, the occasional croaking bullfrog and hissing locust the only sounds interrupting the country quiet.

After a few minutes, Savannah finally broke the silence. "Have you ever gone through something so heartbreaking that you're not sure you'll ever get over it?"

Yeah. The day she walked away. The unexpected thought jarred him, but he didn't want to analyze it now. "You mean losing your dad."

She glanced at him before turning her attention back to the landscape. "Yes. Seeing you and Jamie together brought it all back. I wonder how long it will take before I can remember him without becoming an emotional mess."

"You give yourself some time to grieve, then you go on. Eventually it gets easier."

She faced him and rested an elbow on the rail. "How long did it take for you to get over your mother's death?"

Obviously someone in his family had enlightened Savannah. Probably Gracie, who always had good intentions, even if she couldn't leave well enough alone. "I barely knew my mother."

"I know, Sam, but it still had to hurt. Especially learning she'd died after the fact."

She was trying to lead him into forbidden territory and he didn't care to take that trip. "I don't want to talk about her."

Savannah showed him her famous sympathetic look, the one that never failed to make him want to confess to his crimes. "You've been carrying this burden around for as long as I've known you. It might help if you did talk about her."

He recalled what she'd said in the shop and that provided a way out. "Why do you care? Best I recall, you told me earlier you didn't."

She lowered her eyes. "I don't like to see anyone suffer."

Now he was just anyone. But if she wanted the sorry facts, he'd give them to her, if only to make her understand why he'd always avoided the topic. He'd begin by telling her something he'd never told another soul. "I knew all along she was sick."

Even in the dim light, he could see the shock in her expression. "When?"

"She called one day and asked if she could come for a visit. I didn't see much point in it. When I told her that, she said that she wasn't sure how much longer she'd be around. I told her I didn't believe her and hung up."

Savannah shook her head. "I know you hated what she did to you, but I can't imagine why you'd think she'd stoop low enough to make up an illness."

No, she wouldn't understand, unless he revealed everything. "My last memory of my mother was the day she left the farm. She told me that as soon as she had a nice place to live, she'd come back for me. And we all know how that turned out."

She laid a hand on his arm. "I'm so sorry, Sam."

He didn't want her compassion. He wanted to move past this point in their conversation. "I learned long ago that sooner or later everyone leaves, by choice or by death. It's just a part of life."

"Do you regret not seeing her?"

He'd avoided those feelings by not thinking about it. "It doesn't matter. It's done, and I can't go back and undo it."

"You're right about not being able to change the outcome, but I still have a difficult time believing the sadness magically goes away."

How well he knew that. "At least you had some good memories of Floyd. I imagine that helps ease some of the pain."

"It does," she said. "But when I realize how much I've missed over the years because I stayed away, I feel so guilty."

Sam wanted to ask if she'd ever missed him. If she regretted leaving him behind. He refrained for fear he might not care for the answer. "Like I've told you before, Floyd was proud of your accomplishments. And like you said, he understood why you didn't come home."

"I suppose so. But it still doesn't seem like real justification for not visiting him more often."

Sam would have to agree, but he wouldn't kick her while she was down. "Again, you can't wind the clock backward. You just have to live with it and learn from your mistakes."

"That's a lesson I'm having a hard time learning, especially where you and I are concerned."

Not once had he ever thought of her as a mistake, even after the bad ending to their relationship. "Are you talking about then or now?"

"I'm talking about my behavior in the shop." She turned back to the view, both palms braced on the railing like she needed support. "I thought I knew all the stages of grief. I had no idea sexual acting out was one of them."

He should cut her some slack but he didn't like feeling used. "And I thought you just couldn't resist my charms."

She sent him a solid frown. "Your sarcasm isn't justified since your actions were a contributing factor."

He put up both hands, palms forward. "Hey, you kissed me, not the other way around. I only reacted like any man would."

"You challenged me and you knew I couldn't resist. I wish I had a nickel for every time you pulled that on me. I could buy my whole condo building with that fortune."

"I was just seeing if you were still the same Savannah." And wondering if she felt the same spark that he did. According to her, that hadn't been the case. She'd only been navigating some weird stage of grief. Sam still wasn't quite buying that speculation.

"I am still the same in that respect," she said. "I don't like to back down, which makes me good at what I do. Unfortunately, that trait didn't work in my favor today. I should never have kissed you and I'm really sorry I did. It won't happen again."

No one was sorrier than Sam that it had happened, and that it wouldn't happen again. "Believe it or not, I know where you're coming from. I've been known to use sex as a means to forget."

She sent him a sideways glance. "Is that what you did after the divorce?"

That's what he'd done after she left town. "Sometimes you just need someone to hold to help you make it through a loss. At least that's what you think you need. Meaningless sex is a sorry substitute for having a real friend to lean on."

"Real friends can be hard to come by in my world."

That was an acknowledgment he'd never thought to hear coming out of her mouth. "I've always known you to have a slew of friends, Savannah."

She tugged at the hem of the too-big T-shirt. *His* T-shirt. "I've been too busy building my law practice to socialize that often. And when I do attend the occasional cocktail party with colleagues, it's hard to tell a prospective friend from someone who's just playing you to get ahead."

Nothing like a cutthroat career. "That's pretty sad, not having friends."

"That's the price you pay for being in my line of work." She hid a yawn behind her hand. "What time is it?"

Sam turned on the flashlight and checked his watch. "It's nearly eleven."

She stretched her arms above her head and faced him again. "It's getting late. I need to go home and you have a little girl waiting for you to say good-night."

For some strange reason, he didn't want to leave Savannah just yet. "Since Jamie's probably already asleep, I'll walk you home."

"I can make it on my own."

He was well aware of that. Deciding not to push, Sam

grabbed the flashlight and tried to hand it to her. "Then take this, just in case."

She waved the offer away. "That's not necessary, either. The moon's bright enough to light the way. Besides, I could walk this path in my sleep."

"You could, but I don't want you to fall and break something."

"If that happens, I'll yell loudly and you can send out a rescue party. Have a good night."

"You, too."

She started away, then turned back to him again with a smile that went straight to his soul. "Oh, and I forgot to say thanks for listening to me. Believe it or not, you've really helped."

Sam had a hard time believing that anything he'd said had been beneficial. Then he suddenly realized he'd been going about this all wrong. Great sex hadn't been the only major aspect of their shared past. Honest-to-goodness dialogue had been the cornerstone of their relationship. "Feel free to call me if you need anything."

She laid her palm against her chest like a practiced drama queen. "Why, Samuel McBriar, you're actually being nice to me. What's the catch?"

He couldn't blame her for being suspicious. "No catch. I just thought you might need a friend while you're here, in case you end up on the wrong side of Ruth."

And he thought she couldn't look more amazed. "You're actually suggesting friendship?"

Yeah, he was in a sense. "Stranger things have happened. Now, I'm not saying we have to pal around. I'm just saying I'm willing to listen if you want to talk."

"Do you really think we can do that, Sam? We've said some fairly hurtful things to each other. I'm not sure we'll ever be able to get past that."

Neither was Sam, but he was willing to try for her sake. Maybe even for his. "We just had a fairly decent conversation and I don't remember more than a couple of flying insults."

"That doesn't mean we won't slide back into bitterness mode again. Perhaps we should just end it on a friendly note and leave it at that."

That might be a sensible course of action, but solid sense hadn't always come into play when it came to Savannah. "If that's what you want, then I'll abide by the decision. But the offer still stands if you change your mind." And he could come up with a few ways to help her change her mind, all involving his mouth, but only in the talking sense.

"I'll think about it," she said as she headed for home.

As Sam watched Savannah start across the bridge, he realized that if he wanted to show her what she'd been missing, friendship was the best way to go. He just wished he'd thought of it before she'd kissed him. Of course, spending more time with her meant he'd run the risk of getting his heart pounded again just to prove a point. He could handle it. Hell, he was raising a daughter and running a farm. Remaining emotionally distant couldn't be any tougher than either of those responsibilities.

Problem was, he'd originally thought a little revenge would taste mighty sweet. Now he realized that after all the things she'd said to him today, he had something to prove. He needed to prove he wasn't that cruel kid who hadn't been able to swallow his pride in order to wish her well. He needed to prove that the man had moved on without her, and he could do it again. More important, he needed to prove it to himself.

Life would be much easier if he made peace with the past, and that's what he planned to do before Savannah left in the next few days. Only this time, he'd be the one to walk away.

As she entered the darkened house, Savannah tried to be as quiet as possible in deference to farm-life rules—in bed by nine, up before dawn. Yet as she scaled the stairs, the wood protested her weight with a series of creaks. The same noises that had gotten her into trouble when she'd stayed out too late with Sam.

Sam...

Even now, he continued to invade her mind like a favorite poem. Even years later, she'd fallen into old behaviors that should have been erased from her life long ago. Maybe those behaviors *had* stemmed from grief. Perhaps she had needed someone to turn to for comfort and he'd simply been available. If only it were that easy. If only that were true.

More important—and extremely surprising—he'd confided in her about his mother, hard secrets she wagered he'd kept from his family. She questioned why her and why now, but the answer seemed fairly obvious. They'd been confidants from the beginning. The fact that they'd so readily taken up where they left off tonight did disturb her, but not enough to completely rule out his proposal.

For a moment she considered turning around and walking back to the McBriars' house, knocking on Sam's door and telling him she'd accept his friendship offer and lay out the terms. Yet giving in to impulse had never served her well. She needed time to think, to weigh the cost. To listen to her head and tune out her heart. First, she needed to sleep, or at least try.

After she reached her bedroom, Savannah paused when she noticed an illumination shining from beneath the narrow door at the end of the hall. Odd, since her mother never left one single light on in the house unless absolutely necessary. Either Ruth was currently in the attic, had been in the attic and forgotten to turn off the staircase light, or she was letting her daughter know that she'd suffered through the task of sorting through her husband's mementos alone. Option three seemed the most logical. Ruth Greer had always enjoyed her role as patron saint of passive-aggressive.

Savannah padded down the corridor to turn off the light before retiring, yet something called to her to confirm that the upper floor was in fact unoccupied. As she scaled the steep steps slowly, the rickety wood groaned like worn-out bedsprings. Darkness greeted her when she opened the main attic door and an eerie feeling settled over her. She felt blindly along the wall for the switch and after a few seconds, finally located it, flipped it on and washed the room in a welcome golden glow.

After she surveyed the area, Savannah's anxiety eased somewhat. Nothing in the musty space looked particularly scary. A few hodgepodge items lined the cedar walls, from old lamps to an ancient sewing machine, the cherished solid pine cradle resting in the corner. Yet her attention was soon drawn to an unmarked cardboard box set out in the middle of the plank floor.

Savannah moved quietly into the room and peered past the partially open lid. She had no right to investigate, at least not without her mother present, but sheer curiosity stripped her of all hesitation. Just a peek, she told herself. Just a quick inventory of its contents, she thought as she knelt before the carton and opened the flap.

She withdrew the item on top, the familiar photo album that depicted her family's life in pictures. After lowering herself onto the floor, she crossed her legs and turned to the first picture of her father, looking so tall and stately in a dark suit, his arm around her mother, who wore a simple white cotton dress and a smile that didn't quite reach her eyes. Even on her wedding day, Ruth looked almost forlorn, an observation that had been lost on Savannah to that point.

She then came to the photo of the house on Carroll Street where she'd spent her childhood. Yet the details of that place had all but disappeared through the years, substituted by recollections of the farmhouse where she now sat. Good memories so closely tied to her relationship with Sam.

She refused to think about him now. Reviewing the album would serve as a diversion, at least temporarily. With that in mind, she studied the assortment of photographs of her youth, including the day they'd moved to Placid. The scowl on her face illustrated exactly how unhappy she'd been about leaving Knoxville. After that, she discovered only empty spaces awaiting more photos that had never been taken, symbolizing the decline in her relationship with her mother, who'd always served as the family photographer.

After setting the album aside, Savannah rummaged through the rest of the objects that included a lace handkerchief tied with a blue ribbon and several postcards from various locations throughout the country. Beneath her father's fatigues from his army days, she came across a sketch pad.

The memory of her mother drawing for hours seeped into Savannah's mind. An era when Ruth's love of art was something she readily shared with her husband and daughter. Yet she couldn't remember the last time she'd seen her mother pick up a pencil for anything other than writing down a phone number or composing a grocery list. But she did recall that Ruth had seemed to lose interest in her artistic endeavors as soon as they relocated to Mississippi, much the same as she'd lost interest in her daughter.

"What are you doing, Savannah?"

The angry voice sent Savannah's heart on a dash and her gaze to the door where she discovered her mother glaring at her. She battled the urge to cower and forced herself to her feet for the explanation. "You left the light on, so I came up to see if you were in here. Of course, you weren't, so I decided to look through this box. I hope that's okay."

Her mother's icy expression said it wasn't. "That box is none of your concern."

So much for diplomacy. "Why? Did you start staking your claim on Dad's things without me?"

"That's my right. He was my husband."

"And he was my father." Savannah drew in a calming breath to avoid a late-night argument. "I thought we were going to go through everything together."

"You were too busy, like always."

Savannah barely maintained a grip on her anger. "I'm not going to fight with you tonight, Mother." In fact, she decided to make another effort to defuse the situation. Holding up the sketch pad, she said, "I'd almost forgotten how much you used to love to draw. If it's okay, I'd like to take a look at your work."

Ruth held out her hand. "I'd rather you not. Those are my private drawings."

Private drawings? Savannah questioned exactly what her mother might be hiding. Nudes? A portrait of a covert lover? Both of those theories seemed utterly ludicrous. Perhaps Ruth was simply self-conscious about her talent.

She was too worn-out to worry about it now and for that reason, she relinquished the drawings to Ruth. "If you change your mind, let me know. Believe it or not, I'm only interested in seeing what gave you joy in the past because heaven knows, nothing seemed to make you happy in the last two decades."

Clutching the drawings to her chest like a lifeline, Ruth executed an immediate turn and said, "I'm going to bed," before she left the room.

Unwilling to throw in the towel, Savannah managed to make it down the stairs and into the hall before her mother made it into her bedroom. "Talk to me, Mother."

Ruth continued to face the door. "I'm tired."

"So am I. Tired of trying to figure out what I did that made you hate me so much."

"I've never hated you, Savannah."

Exactly what May had said a few days ago. Exactly what Savannah had told Sam earlier, a partial lie. But she still had a difficult time believing her mother. "You acted as if you couldn't stand the sight of me most of my teenage years. I don't know where we went wrong, and more important, I don't really know you at all. But I want to know you. I want to know what you were like when you were younger. What your life was like."

Ruth paused with her hand on the knob and pinned Savannah in place with a hard look. "Like I told you before, the past belongs in the past, and that's where I intend to keep it."

She stepped inside her bedroom and closed the door, in turn closing out her daughter. Savannah firmly believed she might never break through the emotional barrier her mother had built. Dredging up old history could be painful, but sometimes the past wouldn't go away unless you invited a full-out confrontation. Perhaps she should learn to follow her own advice.

CHAPTER EIGHT

SAM WISHED HE HAD A CAMERA to capture Savannah's appearance when she strolled into the kitchen. She wore a gray nightshirt that hit her midthigh and from the looks of her tangled blond hair, she'd just crawled out of bed. She also looked sexy as hell.

In all their time together, they had never woken up together. They'd never made love before dawn. He'd never watched her sleep. The moments they'd spent alone had been in the cover of dark. Hot and hurried moments in the usual teenage places, with only a couple of occasions when they'd actually been in a bed.

He didn't need to think about that now. Not when he'd come over here with only one goal in mind—to show her he could be a friend. That wouldn't happen if he let his urges enter into the mix.

For safety's sake, Sam waited for Savannah to retrieve a mug from the cupboard and set it safely on the counter before he made his presence at the breakfast table known. Otherwise, he might end up with a coffee cup concussion. "Mornin'."

She spun around, hand to her heart, and once the shock left her eyes, she drew in a deep breath. "What are you doing here?"

He leaned down, picked up the brown paper sack by

his feet and set it on the table. "Just thought I'd bring your dress back, but I'm sorry to report that Gracie said you can still see my handprints." He wasn't really sorry at all. She'd be carrying a reminder of him back to Chicago, and that somehow seemed fitting considering all the reminders of her that he'd had to live with for years.

She looked around, then held her finger to her mouth. "Would you mind being a little quieter? Explaining that to my mother is the last thing I need this morning."

He leaned back and propped his heels on the seat of the opposite chair. "She's gone to town to help Rosie Blankenship set up the volunteer fire department's booth for the festival. She also told me to tell you that Jess called and said she'll meet you at Stan's around eleven."

Savannah poured a cup of coffee and leaned back against the counter. "Since when did you become my personal secretary?"

"Since you decided to sleep in."

She glanced at the clock on the wall. "I had no idea it was so late."

He had no idea he'd be so fascinated with that damn nightshirt. "Didn't sleep well last night?"

"You could say that," she said.

"I was up most of the night, too." Literally.

"What kept you awake?"

If he told her the truth, then he'd probably ruin the opportunity to visit with her for a while. If he told her she'd been on his mind and in his dreams, she'd most likely send him on his way. "I had a couple of cups of coffee when I got back to the house, thanks to Gracie.

She wanted make sure I was fully awake while she grilled me."

"About what?"

"About you. When I didn't come home immediately last night, she was convinced I talked you into doing the deed right there on the bridge. I told her to give me some credit. If I'd wanted that to happen, I would have brought a sleeping bag along with the flashlight."

She blushed just like she had the very first time he'd kissed her, back when they were both wet behind the ears and way too eager. "So sorry we didn't accommodate Gracie."

Sorry? That gave him serious food for thought. "Yeah, I am, too. I hate disappointing Gracie." So much for keeping a tight rein on the innuendo.

He could tell she was trying not to smile, but she couldn't seem to stop. "Don't you have something to do, Sam, like maybe run a farm?"

"The soybeans are in the ground and the winter wheat's been harvested, so I'm taking a break for a few days."

When he dropped his feet from the opposing chair, she claimed it. "I wish I could take a break from my mother," she said as she rimmed the edge of the mug with a fingertip. "I had a confrontation with her right before I went to bed, which is why I tossed and turned most of the night."

Nothing new there. For as long as Sam had known her, Savannah had always butted horns with Ruth. "What did you do this time to get her all riled up?"

"Last night, I came across a box in the attic and she

came across me going through it. She was furious because there's something in that box she doesn't want me to see."

He pushed his empty cup aside. "Skeletons?"

"Maybe. I'm not sure because she's not talking."

He thought about pressing her for more answers but decided not to get caught up in the issues between mother and daughter, especially when it didn't involve him. "The way I see it, it's high time you and your mom sit down and have it out, once and for all."

"I agree, but I can't do that if she keeps avoiding me."

"You've always been pretty persistent." She'd pursued him without thinking twice back in their younger days. Not that he'd resisted. "You're going to have to be if you want to settle this bad blood between the two of you. Unless that's not what you want."

"That is what I want." She took a drink of coffee and set the mug down hard. "I don't want to leave without getting some answers from her."

She could've gone all day without reminding him she'd be leaving. "Then make her sit down and clear the air."

"That's my plan."

He leaned back in the chair and laced his hands behind his neck. "Good luck. And if you decide you need to sound off after that conversation, like I said last night, I'm available."

"Thanks, but I need to do this on my own."

That came as no real surprise. "Whatever works for you."

Savannah's gaze drifted away to some unknown focal

point across the room and then without warning, she started smiling.

Curious, Sam asked, "What are you thinking about?"

She turned her attention back to him. "Do you remember the first time you ate breakfast with us?"

Boy, did he. One of the most uncomfortable experiences of his life. "Yeah. One Saturday during that first summer after you moved here. I used to do my chores and then come over here to hang out with you."

Her smile turned into a full-fledged grin. "And that morning, my dad told you—"

"'Listen here, young man. If you're going to court my girl, you better come inside and have a sit-down with me first.'"

That brought about Savannah's laughter. "You were so nervous you barely ate my mother's pancakes, and no one ever turns down Ruth's pancakes. She makes the best in the state, maybe even the country."

He returned her smile. "Yeah, but it's kind of hard to choke down food, good or not, with a girl's father staring you down. Little did he know, courting you was the last thing on my mind at that time. I just liked the fact you could play catch."

She rested her cheek on her palm. "That was the only thing you liked about me, my skills as a catcher?"

Not hardly. "Yeah, and you were a quick study when it came to learning to drive the tractor."

"I'm so flattered."

And he was so lying. "Okay, you did look good in shorts, but I didn't notice that for a couple of months.

You were kind of skinny back then." Not that he'd ever minded.

She looked a little offended. "You weren't all that filled out, either."

"True. I didn't do most of my growing until our sophomore year. That was about the same time I started to realize you were a lot smarter than me."

"You were smart, Sam. You just took more interest in the coaches' playbook than the history books."

He had to agree. "That's me in a nutshell, the dumb jock. And if I'd known how far you'd go with all those smarts, I probably would have skipped that first breakfast and all the ones after that." The words shot out of his mouth like a bullet before he had time to pull his finger off the trigger.

Savannah's face went stone-cold, letting Sam know she hadn't taken too kindly to the comment. "You know what they say about hindsight."

Damn his stupidity. "Savannah, I didn't mean—"

"Yes, you did, Sam." She smiled as she stood, but it didn't quite make it all the way to her eyes. "As they say, you might not always say what you mean, but you always mean what you say."

Not always, Sam thought as she rushed out of the room. There were plenty of words he'd said to her that he hadn't meant, and some words that he'd never said, words that she'd always wanted to hear. Just as well. Some things were better left unsaid.

SAVANNAH ARRIVED AT STAN'S ten minutes early and when she didn't see Jess, she chose a booth next to the jukebox and farthest away from the counter where farmers tended to gather. After she slid onto the worn green vinyl seat, she looked around to see if she knew anyone among the mostly male patrons who'd stopped in for a coffee break or early lunch. A few she recognized immediately and a couple seemed familiar, but she couldn't quite place them.

As the minutes ticked down, she periodically glanced at the door and her watch. She took out her cell phone, read a few text messages from work and ignored every one. Eventually she would have to respond, but not until she was good and ready.

Just when she'd begun to believe she'd been stood up, in walked her one-time best friend, Jessica Keller Wainwright, the ex-cheerleader and former prom queen. For the most part she looked the same to Savannah, even though she'd filled out a bit and had cut her one-time waist-length auburn hair into a stylish, chin-length bob. Yet the way she carried herself, with her head slightly lowered and her hands tightly clasped together, she didn't at all resemble the outgoing girl Savannah had known. When their gazes met, Jess finally smiled, though it wasn't the vibrant grin Savannah recalled. And her hazel eyes didn't reflect the joy that had once been her trademark.

After Jess reached the booth, Savannah immediately stood and gave her a hug both for old times' sake and because she looked as if she could really use one. "It's so great to see you," she said after they parted.

"You have no idea how good it is to see you," Jess

replied as she slid into the booth opposite Savannah. "I swear you haven't changed one iota, Savannah Leigh."

Oh, but she had, and not just physically. Her instincts were much better than before, and they told her that something wasn't quite right with her friend. "Neither have you."

Jess rolled her eyes. "Always the diplomat, but thank you anyway. My butt's about as big as a double-wide trailer, in case you haven't noticed."

"You look great, so stop exaggerating."

"I'll stop exaggerating if you'll stop lying. I'm at least twenty pounds heavier than the last time you saw me."

"So what? You've had a baby."

"I had a baby nine years ago."

Savannah felt the need to bring out more logic to bolster Jess's confidence. "You're also over thirty and I know from personal experience what time can do to your anatomy. Besides, your butt was always Dalton's favorite part. Now he has a little more to love."

She released a caustic laugh. "Oh, sure. Believe me, Dalton doesn't particularly care for the current state of my hips, and he reminds me frequently. Welcome to married life."

Savannah had never liked Dalton Wainwright. Now she liked him even less. "How's your son?"

Jess's expression brightened. "Danny's great. He's also obsessed with baseball. It's fairly time-consuming, with all the games and practices. But thank heavens he's not involved in football. He's so small for his age that I'd be a nervous wreck watching him get tackled."

"That must disappoint Dalton since he was the quarterback stud in high school." Heavy emphasis on *stud,* at least in Dalton's mind.

"Not really. Dalton's so busy being the rich man's son that he doesn't have time to deal with a nine-year-old boy's extracurricular activities."

"I'm sorry to hear that." But not exactly surprised.

Jess grabbed a plastic menu from the metal holder in the middle of the table. "I could use something to eat. Do you want anything?"

"Yes, a margarita. But since Stan doesn't serve hard liquor, I'll take some iced tea."

Jess put the menu aside. "No food?"

"Actually, I had a late breakfast." If one considered a cup of coffee appropriate breakfast fare.

"Okay, then tea it is, even though I really hate to eat alone."

In response to Jess's mock pout, Savannah gave in. "All right. I'll have an order of Stan's famous curly fries."

"Great." Jess tried to catch the waitress's attention by raising her hand. When that didn't work, she put her pinkies in her mouth and let go a fairly loud whistle, drawing the attention of the server as well as several men seated nearby.

Savannah couldn't help but laugh at her friend, who'd suddenly shown some semblance of the girl she'd once known.

When the waitress didn't immediately arrive, Jess gave her attention to Savannah. "Rachel says that Sam took you home the other night. Did you two do a little horizontal lambada?"

More shades of the old Jess. "He *drove* me home. I thanked him, got out of the truck and he left. End of story."

"Come on, Savannah. He didn't even kiss you?"

It was just like Jess to want a recap of some romantic adventure that didn't exist. "We had a couple of drinks, exchanged a few words and that's it. No hugs and kisses or anything remotely resembling a mating ritual. Not that night."

Jess looked as though she'd struck gold. "That night? There've been others?"

Great. Just great. "We've been together a couple of times." Now that sounded extremely suspect. "Not that kind of together. We had dinner at his farm with the family present."

Jess narrowed her eyes. "And you're telling me that you and Sam, the hottest couple in the history of Placid High, are having a strictly platonic relationship?"

Evidently her blush had given her away. "Okay, we've had one kiss."

Jess slapped her palms on the table and nearly knocked over the napkin holder. "I knew it." She leaned forward and said in a conspiratorial whisper, "Give me details. My sex life is on life support, so I need a vicarious thrill from you."

That had Savannah questioning why Jess was still with Dalton, something she would address later. Right now she could use some advice. "Sorry, there's nothing more to tell. But there does happen to be a proposition in the works."

"Okeydokey. Now we're getting to the good stuff."

"It's not *that* kind of proposition, Jess. Sam wants us to be friends, if you can imagine that."

"Oh, sure." Jess released a grating laugh. "Sam McBriar, the Scottish stallion, only wants to be friends with his favorite little lassie. And I want to be a supermodel in my next life."

Savannah didn't blame Jess for her reaction. It did sound totally implausible. "Actually, after we moved past trading barbs, we had a nice talk last night. No hanky-panky involved. That being said, I'm worried that if we do remain friendly while I'm here, things could change. I might actually do something really stupid."

Jess raised a brow. "Like have some really nasty sex with him?"

Now the whole thing sounded sordid. "As much as I hate to admit it, I'm still attracted to him." Something she'd clearly demonstrated when she'd kissed him under the guise of being unable to resist a dare. "That's pretty crazy after all this time, huh?"

"Let me ask you something, my dear, misguided friend," Jess said. "Do you have a man in your life?"

Savannah knew exactly where this was heading. "Not presently."

"How long has it been?"

"A couple of years." Give or take four.

"Then I personally think you should do it, and I mean that in every sense of the word. Otherwise, you'll end up like me, gathering dust bunnies in your nether regions that you'll have to sweep out all by yourself."

Savannah should have expected that advice. "Hopping into bed with Sam would be beyond stupid."

"Of course you shouldn't hop into bed with him. That's not sexy. You should slink into bed and strike a pose."

Savannah responded to Jess's grin with one of her own. "Ha, ha. Sex for the sake of sex never turns out well."

Jess looked thoroughly frustrated. "For heaven's sake, Savannah, you're still in your prime. You're single. You're free to do as you please with whomever you please, even the old boyfriend. Who would know?"

If Jess didn't lower her voice, everyone. "I'd know."

"And you'll be leaving town with your secret. A dirty little secret with Sam that you can fantasize about for years to come. You should stop thinking and just go for it."

"I agree, sugar. You should go for it."

Savannah looked up to find Trudy standing at the table—a waitress who'd gone to work at Stan's before Peter was a saint. She also happened to be Pearl Allworth's best friend, the other mouth muffler who spewed gossip exhaust like a tricked-out Chevy.

Before Savannah could issue a greeting, Trudy added, "Why, half the women in town would drop their drawers for a chance with Sam McBriar, and the other half wished they were that brave."

"We need two sweet teas, Trudy," Jess interrupted through an exaggerated smile. "I'd also like a double cheeseburger with mayo, all the way. And Savannah would like an order of curly fries as well as a side of it's none of your damn business, okay?"

Trudy's expression went as sour as a lemon drop.

"Listen, missy, you should be worrying about your marriage instead of worrying about someone else's affairs. Rumor has it several women in town are dropping their drawers for your husband."

With that, Trudy spun around and headed away, leaving Savannah appalled and Jess looking oddly unruffled over the accusation.

"Then it's true about Dalton's infidelity?" Savannah asked after recalling the talk at the table in Barney's Bar.

Jess shrugged. "Probably."

"And it doesn't bother you?"

"Honestly, I don't care what he does anymore, as long as he leaves me and Danny alone. Now could we talk about something else?"

"Sure." Savannah sensed the gravity of the situation and her heart ached for her friend. But she wouldn't force Jess to elaborate.

After the drinks and food arrived, all talk of Dalton ceased, replaced by reminiscences of more carefree days. Savannah welcomed the subject change, but she didn't welcome the man who walked right up to the table, inserting himself in their catch-up conversation.

Wearing an expensive tailored navy suit and neatly trimmed jet-black hair, Savannah realized that Dalton Wainwright could pass as his father's clone, or perhaps Satan's spawn.

She gritted her teeth when he sent her a smile that was about as sincere as a politician's promises. "Good to see you, Savannah," he said.

Unfortunately, she couldn't say the same. "Hello, Dalton."

He immediately targeted Jess with a demeaning look. "I should've known you'd be here when you didn't answer the phone." He glanced at the half-eaten burger on Jess's plate with obvious disdain. "There's enough fat in that meal to hold you over for a month."

Although Jess had abandoned the sandwich several minutes before, she took another defiant bite before asking, "What do you want, Dalton?"

He slid his hands into his pockets. "Where's Danny?"

"At Jeff's house."

"You need to pick him up this afternoon."

Jess tossed the napkin aside. "You told him you'd watch his practice."

Dalton seemed thoroughly offended that Jess would question him, ruffling Savannah's feathers even more. "Dad called an investors' meeting this afternoon," he said. "As VP of operations, I have to be there."

Jess didn't look as if she were buying it. "You have a meeting every afternoon, Dalton. You could miss one for your son's sake."

"Those meetings put your food on my table. And speaking of that, I need dinner by six. I'm playing poker tonight."

Savannah had half a mind to haul off and punch him. She chose a verbal assault instead. "Which *her* will you be poking, Dalton?"

He responded with a smirk. "Still the same old smart-ass, aren't you, *Savvy?*"

Dalton tossing out the hated nickname only fueled Savannah's fire. "In your case, you can drop the *smart*."

Jess cupped her hand to her ear. "I believe I hear

Edwin calling, Dalton. You best run along before he puts out an all-points bulletin."

"Dinner by six," he demanded before turning on his heels and striding out the door like a domestic dictator.

Savannah sent Jess an apologetic look. "I'm so sorry about the poker comment. I certainly didn't mean to embarrass you, but as always, Dalton brings out the worst in me."

"Me, too," she said. "And don't be sorry for anything you said to him. I just wish I could be that quick on my feet when he starts launching the insults."

Savannah wished she could find some way to talk some sense into her friend. "You deserve so much better, Jess."

"You're right, I do." She glanced around the room before focusing on Savannah again. "That's one of the reasons I wanted to meet you here and not at the house. I want a divorce and I need you to handle it."

On one hand, Savannah wanted to cheer. On the other, she was sorry she couldn't honor the request for representation. "I wish I could help, Jess, but I'm not licensed to practice in Mississippi. I also specialize in corporate law, not family law."

Jess again looked despondent. "I hadn't thought about that. Could you recommend someone, then? Dalton has the means to hire the best attorney in the state, so I need an attorney who's equally good."

"Not if you hire the best first. I'll come up with a name, probably a firm in Jackson or Vicksburg." Savannah had one last question. "Are you sure this is what you want?"

"I've never been more certain of anything in my life."

Jess's confident tone told Savannah all she needed to know. "Then I'll help you however I can." And she pitied the lawyer who would have to come up against the Wainwrights. "Do you plan to leave town after the divorce is final?"

Jess shook her head. "I've considered moving to South Carolina to be with my folks and my brother and his wife, but there's no way Dalton would stand for me taking Danny out of state, even if he doesn't seem all that interested in his son's life."

More unexpected news. "When did your parents move and what about their feed store?"

"Edwin bought the store and provided enough money for the folks to have a real nice retirement."

With her appetite greatly diminished, Savannah pushed aside the half-eaten fries. "Of course. Your father-in-law's goal in life is to own the entire town. Did you know he's buying our farm from my mother?"

Jess frowned. "I had no idea, and I'm sorry to hear that. I can tell you're disappointed."

Oddly she was somewhat disappointed. "On top of that, Sam's leasing the land."

"How do you feel about that?" Jess asked.

"At first I was livid because I honestly believed Sam saw it as a way to get a little revenge. But then he explained that my dad made him promise to take care of the place. At least I know the farm will be in good hands. And enough about that. What are you going to do with your time as a free woman?"

"First, I'm going to take Danny to see Mom and Dad

after I file for divorce, hopefully before the end of the month. I've decided that would be a good time to explain everything to him. After that, I'm going back to work. I've been hired to teach second grade at the new elementary school in the fall."

"That's great news." Savannah was pleasantly surprised by her town's progress and Jess's return to the workforce. "I had no idea there was a new elementary school."

Jess smiled. "Things are changing here, Savannah. Nothing ever stays the same, even in a place like Placid."

Savannah held up her glass and proposed a toast. "Here's to good change, a new career and, better still, your new life."

Jess tipped her glass to Savannah's. "I'll definitely drink to that. And the next time you see me, I'll be twenty pounds lighter, unencumbered and gainfully employed."

She had no idea when she'd be returning to Placid, if ever. As of next week, she'd have no house to come home to. No real reason to return. Still, Savannah didn't want to rain on Jess's proverbial parade. Besides, she could always invite her to visit Chicago.

As soon as she said goodbye to Jess, Savannah climbed into her car, fully intending to drive home. Yet she was so concerned by her friend's situation, she felt as if she needed to locate someone who could help with the attorney reference. Someone she could count on to keep the information confidential. She could think of one person who fit the bill, and without much thought, she found herself steering the car in his direction.

CHAPTER NINE

AFTER SAVANNAH RANG THE McBriars' doorbell, she could hear the sound of tiny feet padding across wood. Jamie greeted her with a happy-girl smile as she slapped the screen open and said, "Come help us bake, Savannah!" Then she sprinted toward the kitchen while Savannah barely had time to grab the door before it closed in her face.

Jamie's wholehearted enthusiasm buoyed Savannah's spirits. Being around such an exuberant child made Jess's situation and Ruth's continued avoidance a little more palatable. At least for the time being.

Savannah entered the kitchen to find Jamie seated on a bar stool at the center island and Gracie transferring at least a dozen chocolate cupcakes onto one of several tin plates. "Wow, Gracie. I think my blood sugar just elevated and I haven't even eaten one yet."

Gracie looked up with a smile, strands of silver hair framing her oval face that was streaked with flour. "My granddaughter's been nibbling for at least two hours."

Jamie grinned. "I've been licking the bowl."

That was evidenced by the chocolate ring around Jamie's mouth. "I take it these are for the festival."

"Uh-huh," Jamie answered. "I'm gonna help make all of them. Right, Grandma?"

Gracie scooped some icing from a bowl and dotted Jamie's nose. "If you don't eat them all first. Now go and tell your dad to wash up for lunch."

"Savannah, you wanna come with me?"

"Actually—"

"She's going to stay with me, sweetie," Gracie interjected.

"Okay." Jamie climbed off the stool and rushed out of the room like a minicyclone.

"Did you come to help me bake or did you want to speak with my son?" Gracie asked as soon as Jamie was no longer within earshot.

"I do need to talk to Sam. I wanted to run something past him." She feared she'd wanted any excuse to see him.

Gracie spooned some more batter into the muffin pans without missing a beat. "Seems like you and Sam are getting along real well these days."

"We're trying to be friends again."

"It's none of my business, but are you sure that's all there is to it after what happened between the two of you in the shop?"

"If you're asking if we're intimate, the answer is no."

After slipping the pan into the oven, Gracie returned to the island and leaned a hip against it. "I already know that because he's been in a foul mood. And if he continues to take three showers a day, then the well's going to go dry. I'm tempted to tell you to put the man out of his misery."

Here came the blush again. "Maybe the hot weather's responsible for his mood."

Gracie smiled. "Oh, he's hot all right, but it doesn't have a thing to do with the weather. It's fairly obvious that sparks still fly every time the two of you are within a hundred yards of each other. You might kill the relationship but you can't always kill the chemistry."

Savannah felt the need to defend herself. "You're wrong about that. At first we held each other in low esteem, then moved on to civility and now we're going to try to be friends."

That earned her Gracie's frown. "Aren't you afraid of losing your heart to him again? You know how women can be. We're nothing if not a mess when it comes to emotions."

She had the problem pegged, and Savannah would be wise to heed the warning. "I'm a different person now, Gracie. Sam and I are both different people. We're mature enough to keep our relationship platonic." Or so she hoped.

"You may be able to handle it, Savannah, but Sam's not as strong as he seems. You're probably the only woman who broke his heart, but you broke it all the same. I don't want to see it happen to him again." Gracie patted her cheek. "I love you like you were my own daughter, but I love Sam, too. That's why I hope you'll think hard before you act, unless you have plans to stick around."

No, she didn't plan to stick around. Once she went home to Chicago, she and Sam would return to their own lives. They could agree to be friendly in the interim, which could invite more trouble in the long term.

The back door swung open, jarring Savannah from

her thoughts. Jamie breezed in, ponytail swinging like a pendulum as she hurried to reclaim her stool at the counter. "Daddy said he'll be coming in soon, but he wants Savannah to come see him in the barn first."

A timely opportunity had presented itself. Once she had Sam alone, she'd ask for an attorney reference, then lay out a few terms before they moved forward with the friendship clause.

Savannah headed out the back door and through the gate leading to a narrow gravel path. She'd walked this pebbled road many times before, on days much like today. The afternoon sun bore down on her bare neck where she'd piled her hair on top of her head in an attempt to counteract the heat. The sandals she wore did little to protect the soles of her feet from the layer of stone. But when she reached the barn, the scent of hay brought to mind why at one time she would have weathered any conditions to come here. The place had been another sanctuary, an escape from all the rigors of her strained relationship with her mother. She'd learned how to saddle and groom a horse here, how to ride in the nearby round pen, all under the watchful eye of a boy she'd so desperately wanted to impress.

Once inside the stable, Savannah spotted a green metal wheelbarrow full of pine shavings in front of one stall to her left. Then that boy—now very much a man—emerged from the open door wearing a white T-shirt, faded jeans and a pair of heavy brown work boots. Although he was dusty and damp, he couldn't look any better if he'd donned a high-dollar tuxedo.

Sam set the shovel in his grasp against the wooden

frame and smiled. "Hey," he said before he clasped the T-shirt's hem and pulled the cotton up to wipe off his face, giving Savannah a glimpse of his ridged abdomen. That sight alone ate like acid into her resolve to be only his friend, further cementing Gracie's assertion.

You might kill the relationship, but you can't always kill the chemistry....

The sound of a nicker served to divert Savannah's attention from Sam's finer features. To her immediate left, she discovered a midnight-black horse with his muzzle stuck through the stall's railing, his nostrils flaring as if trying to recognize her scent. She definitely recognized him.

"Oh, my gosh! You still have Sky." She immediately walked to the stallion and scratched the zigzag star in the middle of his forehead. "Hey, buddy. Remember me?"

She heard solid footsteps from behind her, followed by, "He remembers you."

After she glanced back to find Sam standing only a foot or so from her, Savannah turned back to the other stud. "I hope he remembers. He gave me my first ride."

"Yeah. That's something me and old Sky have in common."

Sam was clearly determined to be the bad boy today, which could make the task at hand all that more difficult for Savannah.

She faced him again, possibly at her own peril. "Jamie said you needed to speak to me."

He hooked his thumbs in his belt loops, briefly drawing her gaze where no decent female's gaze belonged in a public place, or a private barn, for that matter. Not unless she wanted to invite trouble. "Yeah. She wanted me to talk you into going to the festival with us."

"You couldn't have come up to the house to ask me that?"

"I didn't want you to have to make excuses to her in case you have other plans. She can be pretty damn insistent when she gets something in her head."

Admittedly, that made sense, and Savannah admired that in a girl, even a six-year-old female. "Actually, I planned to go through Dad's things and pack up some of my stuff. Maybe even have that talk with my mother if I can get her to sit still long enough."

"Ruth will be at the festival along with everyone else."

Sam had a valid point, but Savannah still had a lot to do. "Then I guess I'll just go through everything without her."

"You can do that on Sunday," he said. "Tomorrow, you should come with us to the festival for old times' sake. I'll buy you some cotton candy."

That brought to mind all the summers they'd spent together, the festivals they'd attended as a couple. Four, to be exact, though it should have been five. Reliving those experiences couldn't hurt, as long as Sam's daughter was present. As long as she kept the invitation in perspective—just an innocent outing, a pleasant reminder of better times.

Yet as soon as she said what she needed to say to him, he might rescind the offer. "I'll think about it and let you know."

"Fair enough."

"Now I have a couple of things to tell you." She planned to save the most pressing one for last. "First, you have to keep what I'm about to say to yourself."

"Not a problem."

Savannah knew it wasn't, otherwise she wouldn't take him into her confidence. "When I saw Jess today, she told me she's divorcing Dalton."

Sam leaned a shoulder against the stall door and scowled. "It's about damn time she left that sorry SOB."

She couldn't agree more. "Anyway, she asked me about an attorney. I was wondering if you might know one who could handle her divorce."

A flicker of discomfort passed over his expression. "I used a guy out of Jackson named Franklin. He's supposed to be one of the best. Hard to tell, since Darlene and I just about agreed on every point in the settlement."

"So the two of you had an amicable parting?"

"Yeah, you could say that. No custody or financial issues. It was fairly easy as far as divorces go."

In Savannah's experience, that was rare, but not completely unheard of. "Would you recommend him anyway?"

"Probably so. He's supposed to be a shark. In fact, I kind of got the feeling he would've rather been representing Darlene so he could go after me for what I'm worth."

First problem solved. "Good. Jess is going to need that kind of representation to battle the Wainwrights. Do you have his number?"

"Up at the house. I'll write it down before you leave."

At least she'd accomplished that goal. Now on to the next.

Savannah returned to petting Sky because she simply couldn't look at Sam without giving her uneasiness away. As the stallion nuzzled her hand, Savannah snagged the opportunity to delay the conversation a bit longer. "I see you haven't changed a bit, Sky. Always trying to woo the ladies whenever you have the chance. I bet you're still the most sought-after stallion in the county." Aside from his owner.

"He's retired from breeding duty," Sam said. "I turn him out in the evenings and let him run. The rest of the time he basically eats and sleeps. I thought about gelding him, but I decided that wouldn't be fair since I've already sold off the broodmares. No need to add injury to the insult."

Savannah shifted into avoidance overdrive. "Why did you sell the broodmares?"

"The market wasn't that good at the time and I was practically giving away top-quality foals. Wasn't worth the effort any longer."

"Sky would probably disagree." When she sensed Sam moving closer, she tried to brace herself. "I remember how exciting it was every time a new foal hit the ground. I also remember that one filly that looked just like Sky. What was her name?"

"Maggie. Is that why you're here, to discuss Sky's offspring?"

She continued to stare into Sky's stall even after the stallion had left her company for the hay bag hanging in the opposite corner. "I came to tell you I've been thinking a lot about what you suggested last night."

"And?" he asked when she hesitated.

"I have a few things I need to say." She prepared to spell them out, one by one, as she turned toward him. "First, I appreciate our conversation last night. You were very helpful."

"You've already told me that."

"True, but it bears repeating. However, I do have some concerns. I'm worried that if we continue to socialize on a regular basis while I'm in town, other things might possibly come into play."

"You're talking about sex." Sam didn't pose it as a question, only a statement of fact.

"Yes."

He lifted his shoulders in a casual shrug. "Shouldn't be a problem now that you recognize it's just a grief phase."

"I lied."

"Oh, yeah?" His cat-ate-the-canary smirk said he wasn't all that taken aback by the disclosure.

"I suppose grief could be part of it, but I realize that there's still some—"

"Chemistry between us."

"Yes." The admission and Sam's unwavering scrutiny sent her down the aisle to pace like a caged cougar. "That underlying chemistry could present major complications."

"You mean sex."

She stopped a few feet away and turned back around. "Precisely. And although I wouldn't mind having a friendly relationship with you, we would have to avoid—"

"Sex."

If she heard the word one more time, she might start screaming like a banshee. "Would you stop repeating yourself? I feel like I'm in a marketing seminar and you're trying to sell me on it."

He swiped his arm across his forehead. "According to the marketing 'rule of seven,' I'd have to repeat it four more times to sell you on it."

"How do you know about marketing strategy?"

"I'm not as dumb as I look."

He was anything but dumb. "Well, I'm not buying it no matter how many more times you say it."

"Good, because selling sex is illegal." He had the gall to grin.

"Back to the pertinent issues at hand." If she could actually remember them in light of all the "sex" talk. "I have a few ground rules I want to lay out before we go any further."

"What a shocker," he said.

She ignored Sam's sarcasm and began the countdown. "First, we can talk about the past, as long as we don't dwell on the pond, parking at the pond or necking at the pond."

"What about Manny's front seat?"

From the amusement in his expression, Savannah surmised he was so enjoying her predicament. "That's out and you know it. We have plenty more memories to focus on, such as high school football games and the six-pack. And we can certainly talk about the present, my job, the farm, your daughter."

"The price of commodities?" he asked.

His smugness was starting to wear on her tolerance. "Whatever floats your boat. Furthermore, it would behoove us not to be alone together in a place where the opportunity to—"

When he opened his mouth, she wagged a finger at him. "Don't say it."

As he pretended to zip his lips, Savannah clung to the last scrap of patience. "In summary, I wouldn't be opposed to being friendly with you as long as we have an understanding of the rules."

"Are you done now?"

Not until she turned the tables on him. "I just wanted to add that aside from your innuendo the night after the bar and what happened in the workshop yesterday, you've been rather restrained. That would lead me to believe that maybe you're the one who's afraid to—"

He moved faster than that proverbial speeding bullet and framed her face in his palms, quelling her words with a kiss. A deep, insistent kiss that didn't last long enough before he released her and stepped back.

As soon as the mental fog cleared, Savannah firmed her resolve. "You clearly can't follow the rules."

"I just don't like being called a coward."

She enjoyed a good deal of satisfaction that he wasn't quite the iron man he pretended to be. "How do you think I felt when you accused me of—"

"It's my turn to speak, Savannah."

He sounded so gruff she could only utter, "Okay."

"Like I told you in the shop yesterday," he began, "I'd be lying if I said I didn't have a few fantasies about you. Truth be told, I've wanted you from the moment I saw you in the diner. If you were wearing a burlap sack, no makeup and your hair was a freakin' mess, I'd want you. But I want a few other things more."

Sam stopped only long enough to draw a breath while Savannah patiently waited for him to continue. "I want simple. I want to wake up at sunrise and work the land and I want to go home at sundown to my family. I also want friends I can count on, not people who pretend to be my friends. But I damn sure don't want complications. So no matter how this plays out between us, I'm not going to let a little lust screw up what I want."

Savannah couldn't agree more, but she still had one burning question. "Then why did you kiss me?"

"It seemed like the only way to shut you up."

He'd done that, and quite well. She was still feeling the effects, particularly in her knees that felt as flimsy as rubber bands. "So you say, but I'm not convinced you won't do it again if given the opportunity."

A flicker of anger showed in his eyes. "And I don't like being on trial while you're playing judge and jury, ready to convict me for being untrustworthy."

The next confession could be a killer. "Maybe I don't trust myself."

"You're a strong woman, Savannah," he said in a lighter tone. "You can do anything you set your mind to. But if you don't think being friendly with me is worth the risk, then that's fine. And just so you know, I can control myself. The question is, can you?"

"Daddy! Gracie said she needs some help!"

Savannah spun back around and through the open half door leading to the outside paddock, caught sight of Jamie sprinting back to the house.

"I swear, she's a master at interruption," Sam said. "Makes me wonder how people with six-year-olds make other babies."

She didn't care to think about making babies, or at least the process of making babies. "I really have to go," she said as she worked her way around him in order to make a hasty exit.

He caught her arm before she could leave. "You haven't answered my question yet. Are you going to the festival with us or do we part ways now?"

"I need more time to think." She couldn't do that with him staring at her.

He released her and folded his arms across his chest. "I want an answer before you leave this damn barn so I know what to tell my kid."

Talk about demanding. "If we stay here any longer, Gracie's going to assume something nefarious is going on."

"Is that a fancy word for saying she'll think we've been rolling in the hay?"

Boy, did that bring back one heck of a memory. "We did that once, remember? Luckily I could hide the scratches with my clothes."

Sam streaked both hands down his face, as if trying to erase the recollection. "Kind of hard to forget those times when you're around."

Recognizing she'd sufficiently shattered one of her

rules, Savannah added, "Then maybe we should just fondly remember how it used to be between us and leave it at that."

He picked up the shovel, his expression showing a good deal of frustration. "Fine. If that's what you want. But you need to make up your mind and stick to it."

As if she hadn't been reminding herself of that same thing. "You keep confusing me."

"You're confused because deep down you know that you could use a friend. A real friend. Maybe if you keep telling yourself otherwise, you'll start to believe it."

Savannah wanted to curse Sam for his candor, for the absolute legitimacy of his words. She did want to be his friend, but she didn't want the heartache that could result from executing that leap of faith.

As far as the festival went, Savannah probably should stay home, stay away from him. But what she should do warred once again with what she wanted to do. As long as she stayed grounded, and stayed away from situations like this, she saw no real reason not to spend a little more time with Sam and his daughter before she left Placid behind, once and for all.

"Tell Jamie I'll go."

BY THE TIME EVENING ARRIVED, Savannah began to wonder if her mother would make it home. When half past eleven rolled around, she bordered on being extremely concerned—until she wandered into the kitchen for a soda and found the note attached to the refrigerator door with a magnet.

Spending the night in town with Rosie. I'll be back tomorrow evening after the festival.

No heartfelt endearment. No affectionate closing. Nothing more than a terse explanation of her whereabouts.

Savannah shouldn't be so surprised, yet she couldn't deny the little sting of hurt and a good deal of frustration. She'd planned to have the long-delayed talk with her mother, but now that would have to wait another day.

As soon as she finished eating, she decided to take a shower and begin a book she'd been meaning to read for months. But while she bathed, a thought occurred to her. She was alone, and she now had a prime opportunity to investigate the contents of the mysterious sketch pad. Provided she could actually find it.

Dressed in her favorite blue silk nightshirt and a towel turban wound around her damp hair, Savannah returned to the attic where she'd made the initial discovery. She found the box in the same spot on the floor, only this time it had been secured with two rows of tape.

If she had any decency at all, she'd leave it be. Unfortunately, she had too much curiosity to ignore the chance to learn exactly what her mother had been hiding. As soon as she was finished playing detective, she'd reseal the carton and no one would be the wiser.

Savannah dislodged the edge of the tape with her thumbnail, carefully pulled it free and opened the lid. Once more she sorted through the contents, expecting to find the drawings beneath the other items, to no avail. But when had her mother ever done what was expected?

Spent from the day and disappointment, she decided to call off the search for the time being. She resealed the box with the existing tape, headed down the attic staircase and on impulse, paused in the hallway at her mother's bedroom. If she opened the door on the off chance that she might find the drawings, she would be committing the ultimate invasion of privacy. She might also have some answers.

Not a soul would know, she told herself as she turned the knob and stepped inside. Rows of gray plastic storage bins lined the faded white walls that displayed brighter squares where pictures had once hung. The knickknacks and favorite books had been removed from the shelves and pine dresser, leaving only a lone lamp on the nightstand... and the missing sketch pad.

Ignoring the tiny bite of guilt, Savannah crossed the room, took the pad and sat on the edge of the perfectly made double bed. She studied the first drawing and noticed it carried her mother's initials and a date that indicated it had been created two months before they'd relocated to Placid. She moved on to the next sketch and the next, soon realizing that according to the descending dates, her mother had started at the back of the pad and worked her way forward.

The first few drawings depicted scenes of flowers and panoramas, a few featured farmland and wildlife. But as the drawings moved back in time, the subject matter seemed more bleak—a stark, gnarled tree standing alone in a field. A house with darkened windows. But the most startling drawing of all had been torn out yet preserved in its original place at the back of the pad.

Large hands with clawlike fingers filled most of the yellowed page. Sinister, scary hands that looked ready to strike. And most disturbing, what appeared to be a small child cowered in the corner of the remaining space, drawn right above the date that showed Ruth had only been twelve years old when she'd created the sketch.

Savannah truly believed that the drawing wasn't the musings of an imaginative child. In her mind, it conveyed a story of unspeakable abuse, perhaps the only way her mother had been able to express her terror.

Along with a queasy stomach, Savannah now had more questions than answers. Had her mother been the victim depicted in the pictures? Had she witnessed someone else being injured? Had anyone known what she'd suffered?

Savannah couldn't help but wonder if she finally found the key to her mother's emotional shutdown when she walked back into this house. Yet if she attempted to find all the answers, she would have to admit to her mother how she'd come by the knowledge. And if she did force an open dialogue, in turn reviving a past that Ruth obviously wanted to forget, she might do more harm to their relationship than good.

For the first time in a long time, Savannah had no idea what to do. She could use some advice, a solid sounding board. Someone who could guide her down the right path.

She could call Jess, but her friend had her own personal problems. The last thing Rachel needed was a late-night call when she was enduring pregnancy fatigue.

Savannah could think of only one other person whom she trusted enough to discuss the discovery.

Sam.

CHAPTER TEN

SOMETHING WAS UP.

In Sam's experience, no one called the house that close to midnight unless it involved some kind of emergency. Or it could be one of his now-and-again women claiming she had a fire that he needed to be put out, something he didn't care to deal with at the moment.

He answered with a gruff "Hello," and a soft voice answered, "It's me, Sam."

"Me," meaning the only woman who'd been on his mind of late, and the reason why he'd been restless for the past hour. He figured she was about to say she wasn't going to the festival tomorrow. Maybe even to announce she'd decided to go back to Chicago. If that happened to be the case, he'd deal with it. "What do you need, Savannah?"

"Remember when I told you something was going on with my mother?"

Something was always going on with her mother. "Yeah."

"I think I know what she didn't want me to see. I found it in her bedroom." She sighed. "I'm probably jumping to conclusions, so go back to sleep and I'll see you tomorrow."

As if he could really sleep now. "Why don't you tell me what you found and I'll let you know what I think?"

"It's a drawing. A really strange drawing. She used to sketch years ago."

He'd never pegged Ruth Greer as an artist, but nothing surprised him these days. "What do you mean by strange?"

"It's frightening and I believe it has something to do with her past."

"Did you ask her about it?"

"I can't. She's spending the night in town. I know it sounds crazy, but you'd have to see it to understand why I'm so concerned."

That was a suggestion worth jumping all over. A chance to show her the kind of friend he could be. The kind of man he was. "I'll come by and take a look."

"You don't have to do that. It's late and you have to be up early."

He tucked the receiver between his chin and shoulder and grabbed his jeans from the bedpost. "I'll be there in five minutes."

Without giving Savannah a chance to argue, Sam hung up the phone, shrugged into his jeans and a T-shirt and yanked on his boots, then headed out the door. He considered going to her place by foot before deciding to take the new truck to save time. He climbed inside the cab, turned on the ignition but not the headlights so he wouldn't wake his dad. Like the diesel engine wasn't loud enough to disturb the whole town.

Damn, if he wasn't acting like an anxious kid sneaking out of the house on his way to a forbidden rendezvous with his girl. But Savannah wasn't "his girl." She was all woman, and only a friend. On the one hand, he welcomed having her friendship again. On the other, he still worried about getting too close to her. But he'd always been willing to take a few risks, even when the outcome might not turn out the way he'd planned. And as sure as he knew every last acre of the family farm, one thing remained true—in a matter of days, he'd probably never see her again. All the more reason to take advantage of the time they had left and deal with the fallout later.

Sam made it to the Greers' place in a matter of minutes and after he pulled up to the house, he found Savannah waiting for him on the front porch. She wore a shapeless navy T-shirt and a pair of khaki shorts, but with her damp hair hanging down in soft waves, no makeup on her face or shoes on her feet, she could've walked right out of his past—or his dreams.

As Sam approached the porch, Savannah didn't move an inch. At one time she would've hurried down the steps and thrown her arms around him. Tonight, she didn't seem all that glad to see him. At least not as glad as he was to see her, something he intended to keep to himself.

After he scaled the wooden stairs, Savannah held out a piece of paper. "This is it."

Sam took the page and dropped down onto the glider to study the sketch. He agreed that it wasn't something a young girl would normally draw. "You're right. It's weird."

"It's more than weird," she said as she sat beside him.

"I think she's sending some kind of message. Either someone hurt her or she saw someone being hurt."

He handed the page back to her. "Maybe it was some kind of art project."

"More like art therapy," she said. "I just can't imagine a child creating something like this unless they had personal knowledge of the subject."

He leaned back against the glider. "Any theories as to who might have inspired her?"

She shifted slightly to face him. "What do you know about her stepfather, Don Leland?"

Sam shook his head. "Not a whole lot other than my grandfather used to say the man was a worthless drunk."

"Aunt May mentioned the drinking to me," she said. "And if he became violent when he drank, then it's possible he hurt my mother, right?"

He draped an arm over the back of the glider. "Yeah, it's possible, and so are a lot of other things. Again, you need to—"

"Ask my mother," she interrupted. "I plan to try, but I doubt I'll get very far."

"And if you don't, then you'll just have to accept it and let Ruth have her secrets, especially if they're too painful to talk about." He knew all about that concept.

She stood and began walking the length of the porch. "Painful or not, she needs to talk about it. I suspect that's been her problem all along when it comes to bottling up her emotions."

And Savannah had definitely suffered for that, something he'd witnessed firsthand. When she didn't seem to want to settle down, Sam formulated a plan that might help. "Do you want to go to bed?" Man, if that hadn't come out all wrong.

The serious glare she aimed like a rifle at him said she thought so, too. "You're just going to ignore everything I said earlier, aren't you?"

Nope, he wasn't. "I meant do you want me to get out of here so you can get some sleep."

Her hostile expression slowly disappeared. "Actually, I'm not sure I can sleep right now."

"Then I have an idea that might help with that." When he came to his feet, she took a step back. "Relax. I'm not going to throw you over my shoulder, carry you inside and have my way with you." Even if that did sound like a win-win idea.

She tried not to smile but failed. "Okay, then what do you have in mind? A glass of warm milk with a shot of whiskey? Maybe weight lifting? We could jog into town and be back before dawn."

Damn if she wasn't still as sassy—and sexy—as ever. "Let's go for a drive."

SAVANNAH HAD NO IDEA what had motivated her to get in a truck and take off with Sam. She really questioned her sanity when he turned off the main road and onto the familiar road, and she didn't say a word to stop him. She questioned Sam's judgment when she noticed several No Trespassing signs posted on either side of the smooth-wire fence bordering the path to Potter's Pond. That could explain why she hadn't seen one vehicle in what once had been the town's most popular gathering place for young lovers.

"What are we doing here, Sam?" she asked as he turned to the left and headed toward their one-time favorite site beneath the ancient oak that predictably carried their initials. A blatant violation of the rules she'd set out earlier that day.

"Just thought this might be a good place to unwind."

"But we agreed not to—"

"Discuss the pond," he interjected. "We never said we couldn't visit the place."

Leave it to Sam to find a loophole. She afforded him a glance in time to see his killer smile. "Perhaps I should amend the terms of the agreement."

"Maybe you should remember we had some of our best talks here."

"I don't recall much talking taking place." She did recall all those nights when they'd come here on a regular basis to escape everyday life in each other's arms.

"There's always a first time for everything," he said without taking his eyes off the makeshift road.

"Did you not notice all those warning signs?"

"Yeah. Someone's trying to keep kids out of the place."

"Which means we shouldn't be here, either."

"We're not kids."

Very twisted reasoning as far as Savannah was concerned. "I must've missed the one that said Keep Out Unless You're Over Thirty."

Sam barked out a laugh. "I can almost guarantee the new owner is safely in bed in his multimillion dollar mansion and not at all concerned about us or what we do on his land."

She didn't have to inquire over the new owner's identity, but she did anyway. "Let me guess. Wainwright bought the pond."

"You guessed right." Sam stopped beneath the tree, shifted the truck into gear and switched off the ignition. "He plans to build an RV park to draw people traveling north and south between Jackson and Memphis."

"Isn't it kind of off the beaten path?" she asked.

He draped his arm over the steering wheel and stared out the windshield. "Yeah, but if it works, it'll be good for the local economy."

And bad in terms of continuing a tradition. "I suppose you're right, but in a way it's a shame. This old pond holds a lot of history." A lot of their history.

"Do you want to get out and sit a spell to say our official goodbye?" he asked.

"You didn't give me a chance to put on my shoes."

He finally looked at her. "You never minded going barefoot before."

"My feet were much tougher before. Besides, we don't have any lawn chairs and I really don't want to sit on the ground."

He hooked a thumb behind him. "I have a blanket in the backseat."

That conjured up all sorts of images of the last time she'd been on a blanket with him. "How convenient," she said. "Do you routinely have midnight picnics out here with your lady friends, hence the blanket in the backseat?"

"I keep it on hand in case I break down and have to sleep in my truck."

A plausible explanation, if Savannah chose to trust him. More important, did she trust herself on a blanket with Sam? "Maybe we should just stay in the truck."

"And miss getting a better look at that?" He pointed at the panorama stretched out before them.

The full moon hovered high above the horizon, casting the water in a shimmering blue glow that contrasted with the inky sky. Several times Savannah had witnessed this same occurrence over Lake Michigan and although she couldn't deny the beauty in it, the Chicago city lights somehow defused the effect.

Admittedly, she would greatly enjoy soaking up the scenery seated on a blanket, as long as she remained upright. Not willing to borrow that kind of trouble, she unbuckled her seat belt and said, "Let's sit on the hood like we used to do."

"Works for me."

Being shoeless didn't work at all for Savannah. Sam, on the other hand, happened to be wearing a pair of heavy boots designed to thwart burrs and rocks and any living thing that might be lurking in the grass. "You better hope I don't step on a snake when I get out of this truck," she called to him as he slid out of the driver's seat.

Savannah barely had her door open before Sam was right there, scooping her into his arms as if she weighed little more than a cotton ball. She laughed from being caught by surprise, from sheer giddiness when he deposited her onto the hood. "Thanks for being my own personal pack mule and saving my feet," she said as he claimed the spot beside her.

"You're welcome."

Despite her solemn vow not to remember, as she took in the scenery, thoughts of days gone by unfolded in Savannah's mind. Life had been so easy back then, filled with excitement and anticipation and moments of sheer joy.

"We had some good times here, didn't we?" she said without regard to the self-imposed regulations for continuing their relationship.

"Some great times," Sam added. "We could've set the back forty on fire. I barely had the truck stopped before we were all over each other."

He said the last line in a rough, sexy voice, and Savannah felt the impact as if he'd launched a sensory grenade. More scenes invaded her brain, some of which would make a statue blush. Clothes flying, bodies entwined, long, slow kisses, provocative touches.

She chose to defuse the recollections with humor. "Considering the way we used to go at it, you would've thought we'd invented making out. At least hanging out here saved you some money since we rarely went out on official dates."

He frowned. "I bought you plenty of burgers at Stan's."

She tapped her chin and pretended to think. "Oh, and I forgot that you took me to a movie in Jackson twice in four years."

"I sprung for a bottle of cheap wine that one night."

One night she didn't care to remember. "While we're at it, let's not forget the expense of the condom you always carried in your wallet."

"Before I stopped doing that when we both found out what that does to latex."

Savannah was immediately thrust back to the summer before their senior year, when Sam had returned from a two-week baseball camp in Vicksburg. Her parents had been in town with friends that night, and she and Sam had barely made it to her bedroom. It had been a frantic, fiery session of lovemaking resulting in a broken condom—an accident in the making.

"Fortunately the pregnancy scare was only a false alarm," she said.

Sam sat forward, arms resting on his knees as he studied the ground. "Yeah, real fortunate."

His sullen tone completely threw Savannah. "Nothing like learning our lesson the hard way," she added.

He leaned back against the windshield and stacked his hands behind his head. "I don't think we learned a damn thing. I remember another couple of times when we weren't all that careful."

So did Savannah, and she'd always wondered if on some subconscious level she'd wanted to get pregnant. "That still didn't stop your penchant for parking."

"And I don't recall you ever turning me down."

"I guess you're right about that," she conceded.

Sam looked sufficiently smug. "I rest my case."

"Hey, I'm the attorney, so stop stealing my lines."

When she playfully slapped at his arm, he caught her hand and held it firmly in his grasp. "Looks like you're still bent on bruising me even after all this time."

She needed to wrest her hand away. Needed not to react so strongly to his touch, to the memories. "I never bruised you, Sam." Her voice sounded slightly shaky, and oh, how she hated that reaction.

"Oh, yeah, you did bruise me," he added without releasing his grasp. "When you pinched me."

Okay, maybe he wasn't so far off base. "I only pinched you because you used to pin me down on my back and tickle me. You knew I couldn't stand that."

"I recall a few times when I had you on your back and you didn't mind a bit."

The minute Sam loosened his grip, Savannah tugged her hand away and pulled at the hem of her shirt. Yet she still hadn't quite recovered from his touch, and continuing this conversation could very well lead them both into treacherous territory.

With that in mind, Savannah kept a safe distance between them as she lay back and stared at the stars. She closed her eyes as a slight breeze drifted over her face, bringing with it more wonderful summer scents and one less-than-pleasant remembrance. "Do you know what I regret the most about the way we ended things?"

"You didn't punch me."

She could hear a smile in his voice. "No. I regret that we didn't go to the prom together so we could have that last dance."

Without warning, he sat up, scooted off the hood and when his feet hit the ground, he turned to her and said, "Don't move. I'll be right back."

When Savannah heard the door open, she looked back to see Sam leaning into the cab followed by the sounds of country music floating through the open windows.

Sam soon returned but instead of reclaiming his place

beside her, he held out his hand. "Guess we'll just have that last dance now."

Savannah was both taken aback and extremely determined to protect her heart. "That's really not necessary, Sam."

"Yeah, it is. I owe it to you for breaking my promise."

The promise to take her to the prom, a plan three years in the making. Savannah had gone with Gary Alders, another high school hunk, but only as a friend, although she made certain Sam hadn't known that.

After Savannah hesitated, Sam added, "For old times' sake."

She harbored serious misgivings about that. "You're asking me to dance on the grass, subjecting my bare feet to burrs and heaven only knows what else."

"It's fairly soft grass that looks to be clear of critters," he said as he surveyed the area. "And it's not like we haven't done it before."

Yes, and that in itself was a problem. Those former dances had led to other things. For that reason, she grabbed for the only other excuse that came to mind. "I'm not sure I remember how to dance."

"I'll help you remember."

Hadn't he done enough of that already? She could continue to weigh the pros and cons, or she could just can the qualms and humor him. "All right, I'll do it. And you ought to be glad I'm not wearing shoes, otherwise I might crush your toes."

He took her by the waist and set her on the ground, then gave her a gorgeous grin. "That's why I wear boots."

Before she dove into this spontaneous dance, Savannah engaged herself in a mental pep talk. Yes, she would have to touch him. Yes, she would have to revoke the rule to keep him at a distance. Most important, she had to steel herself against any unwanted or unwarranted emotions.

Yet when Sam took her hand into his, the contact, no matter how innocuous, left her feeling as if it were somehow too intimate. And when he put his arms around her, she journeyed back in time when just like tonight, they'd danced to a radio, not a band, on blanket of grass, not a scuffed wooden floor.

The song happened to be a sultry country classic, perfect for a couple that wanted up-close-and-personal proximity. Not so perfect for former lovers who still had miles of acrimony between them. She promised herself to keep everything in perspective, to keep a safe berth between them, even as she inched closer. Amazingly she hadn't forgotten how to dance, but then he was leading her perfectly. No surprise. Sam had always been the kind of man who was very good at a lot of things.

He held their joined hands against his chest, while she kept her eyes lowered to avoid his gaze. She caught the clean scent of soap and felt the warmth of his back beneath her palm, causing her stomach to dip with exhilaration, as if she'd boarded a runaway roller coaster bound for danger.

When the music transitioned into a ballad, Savannah's concerns over getting too close dissolved in the moment. She automatically rested her cheek against his chest where she could hear the steady thud of his heart

while they swayed in sync, as if they could still antici-
pate each other's every move. As if they'd never been
apart.

He'd always made her feel so safe, so secure. He'd
been her touchstone, her teacher in many instances. For
years she'd tried to convince herself that she'd exaggerated the power he'd possessed over her. That she'd fallen
victim to an overblown concept of true love. But right
then she wasn't so sure.

As they continued to sway together, the moments
seemed almost surreal to Savannah, until reality crept
back in. She abruptly wrested out of Sam's arms and
took a few steps back.

"What's wrong?" he asked, looking and sounding
extremely bewildered.

She chafed her arms with her palms. "I'm just too
keyed up for slow dancing." And she'd been much too
caught up in the moment.

"Are you ready to head back home?" he asked.

She should be, but she wasn't. "I'm still too restless to
sleep. I could try, but I'll probably stay awake thinking
about this thing with my mother." And thinking about
him.

"I know of one way you can get rid of some energy,
if you're game."

Savannah was almost afraid to ask. "That depends
on what you're going to suggest."

"I suggest we go for a swim."

As far as she was concerned, Sam had totally lost
his mind. "Now, that sounds like a banner idea, wading
around in the dark with all sorts of unseen creatures."

Sam sighed. "It's a man-made lake, Savannah, not the Amazon River. About all you're going to encounter is a perch, not a piranha."

"Or a catfish." The thought of running into one of those slimy, whiskered bottom-feeders made her cringe.

"Look, Savannah, the fish are a lot more scared of you than you are of them."

That happened to be a fact, but it didn't change Savannah's biggest concern—swimming in the dark with Sam. She hoisted herself back on the hood. "Sorry, but I forgot to bring my suit."

"You don't need one."

Now she was beginning to see where this whole swim idea could be heading. "I'm not going to go skinny-dipping, if that's what you have in mind."

His slow-burn smile told her that was exactly what he had in mind. "You can wear your clothes, or you can wear your underwear. It's not like I haven't seen you in less before."

Before, she hadn't minded if he did see her. But now that didn't seem so prudent. She'd also left her bra at home and that meant she'd either have to wear a wet T-shirt or go topless. Either way, she'd be rather exposed. "I don't know, Sam. Bandying about half-naked in a murky pond with you seems a little scandalous, don't you think?"

He used the truck for support while he toed out of his boots and took off his socks. "First of all, I'm damn sure not going to bandy about. Second, there's not one soul in sight to start a scandal. And last, if you're worried that I might try to compromise your reputation, don't.

It's a big pond, which means we don't have to get near each other. But if you want to stay here and fidget instead of working off some frustration with a swim, be my guest. I'm going for it."

After Sam pulled his shirt up and over his head, the sight of his bare chest made speaking almost out of the question. "You are absolutely crazy, Sam McBriar."

He tossed the T-shirt onto the hood, reached for his fly and grinned. "Maybe so, but you always liked me that way."

Yes, she had. In a way, she still did. She hoisted herself back up on the truck and tried to keep her dangling legs completely motionless, a difficult task considering she had a near-naked, muscled man standing nearby. "I believe I'll just sit here and *fidget* while you fend off the fish."

Sam shrugged. "Your loss. But just so you know, I'm about to take off my jeans, in case you want to cover your delicate eyes."

She wouldn't close her eyes now if her life depended on it. "My *delicate* eyes have seen your boxers before."

"I'm not wearing any."

Savannah couldn't manage even one appropriate comeback for his commando status. She simply stared at him, mouth partially agape and imagination running full steam ahead.

At least he had the decency to turn his back before he stripped out of his jeans, yet that didn't stop Savannah from shamelessly studying his narrow hips and the back of his well-defined thighs and calves as he sauntered toward the bank. He could definitely serve as grand marshal in a butt parade, she mused as he walked into the pond, obscuring her view.

Once he was waist-deep in the water, he turned and said, "Feels great. Are you sure you don't want to try it?"

She started to comment on the possibility of snakes, but she knew exactly where that would lead. "I'm fine."

No, she wasn't. Not when he dove down beneath the surface and came up a few seconds later, skin glistening in the diffused light as he slicked one hand through his hair and ran a palm down his sternum in perfect male-model form. "Come on, Savannah. Back in the day, you wouldn't have let a few fish stop you from having a good time."

At the moment, the wildlife had little to do with her reluctance. The wet, wild man did. "Give me one good reason why I should jump into a catfish-infested body of water with you."

"I'll give you two." He counted them down on his fingers. "You need to relax, and you're itching to take a risk or two even if you won't admit it to me or to yourself."

He could read her like the Sunday paper. As uncertainty crowded her thoughts, she recalled her first summer in Placid when she'd come to this place with Sam. They'd been only buddies at that point, yet poised to move beyond friendship. He'd convinced her to take her turn with the rope tied to a tree that hung over the deepest part of the pond, encouraged her to let go while he waited below to catch her. The feelings had been thrilling when she'd released that rope, dropped into the water, surfaced in his arms—and kissed him for the very first time, changing everything.

She dearly wanted to experience those emotions again. She wanted to toss her structured life to the wind and act on impulse.

In the name of lunacy, she was going to do it. She was going to bare it all and have a watery frolic with the former boyfriend.

"Okay, I'm coming in," she called out, garnering Sam's attention.

"I figured you would eventually."

Savannah couldn't see his face in the dim light, but she could hear the satisfaction in his voice. "First you have to promise not to look until I'm completely covered by water."

He raised his hand as if taking an oath. "I promise to be the gentleman my daddy taught me to be." Then he lowered his hand and added, "But I can't promise I won't grin while you bare it."

"You can grin all you want as long as you keep your eyes closed."

"It's a deal."

In spite of her suspicions that he might not comply, Savannah pulled her shirt over her head, just as he had a few minutes earlier. She shimmied out of her shorts and briefly weighed leaving her panties intact, but that meant she'd have to wear soggy drawers home—or not wear them home at all. Either way, she could be setting herself up for a questionable invitation. As if she wasn't doing that now.

Savannah pitched all her clothes aside along with her

inhibitions and headed toward what could be another experience to deposit in the memory vault. Sam appeared to be obeying her request to keep his eyes shut as she tested the water with a toe. He confirmed that she'd given him too much credit when he said, "Nice tan lines."

She practically flew into the pond, inadvertently falling forward and landing facedown in the water. She swam a little beyond Sam and when she emerged, she tried to appear as if she'd planned the whole thing, only to be met by Sam's laughter.

"I'm so glad I amuse you," she said as she pulled her sopping hair back and twisted it into a knot at her neck.

"I'm not exactly amused, ma'am," he responded in that deadly Southern drawl. "And you're not exactly covered."

She followed his gaze and only then realized that the waterline came right below her bare breasts. Her first instinct—conceal herself. Her second—let him look his fill, consequences be damned.

If wisdom got a word in edgewise, Savannah would head for the hills. Instead, she chose to swim a few laps as far away from Sam as she could get without straying so much that she couldn't see him. Midway through her second round, something nibbled at her ankle, sending her toward the bank with a freestyle stroke befitting an Olympian swimmer. Right when she reached Sam, she felt it again, and this time she shrieked.

"What's wrong?" he said as he grabbed her arm to keep her afloat since she could barely touch the sandy bottom.

"Dammit, I'm being chased by a sea monster!"

When Sam's laughter echoed across the pond, Savannah dug her nails into his biceps. "It's not funny, Samuel."

He winced and then said, "Would you stop clawing me?"

She loosened her grip but didn't let him go. "This is exactly what I was afraid would happen." She'd end up fish food, and too close to Sam for any reasonable comfort.

"Settle down, Savvy. I'll protect you from the minnow."

"My name is *Savannah,* and it wasn't a minnow," she insisted. "It nearly sucked the life out of my thigh."

He cracked a crooked smile. "Lucky fish."

"You are so...so..." Darned sexy, Savannah thought as he clasped her wrists and pulled her closer. And she was so in trouble when he looked at her as if swimming had disappeared from the agenda.

He moved farther into the pond, taking her with him until her feet could no longer find solid ground, forcing her to hold tightly to his shoulders.

He slowly spun them around, making Savannah all the more dizzy, but not necessarily due to the movement. "What are we doing, Sam?"

"Finishing our dance."

"Do you really think that's such a good idea since we're both naked?"

"Probably not."

With their gazes locked together, Savannah felt as if they were suddenly suspended in a defining moment, where the good part of their past had collided with that continual chemistry. Right then, she didn't care about the possible penalty attached to acting on impulse. She only wanted to satisfy her curiosity.

As she slid her palms over Sam's back, she became keenly aware of the changes since she'd done this over a decade ago. His shoulders were much, much broader, his muscles much more defined. He'd definitely evolved into a man. An extremely tempting man.

He stopped moving and surveyed her face with intense blue eyes. "Do you remember when we used to do this?" he asked, his low voice resurrecting more than a few magical moments.

"Yes, but we always wore our swimsuits back then."

He grinned. "Yeah, at least for a little while."

"True." He'd always managed to divest her of her bikini top if nothing else.

"How about this?" He lowered his head and softly brushed her lips with his, once, twice, before he kissed her in earnest.

Sam had always been such a good kisser—the best, in her experience. So many men believed that the way to a woman's heart meant sticking a tongue down her throat. Not Sam. He used tender persuasion and unhurried exploration. She found herself clinging to him for dear life, fearing the control he had over her yet in some strange way needing to be controlled by him. Needing more from him than she should.

As if he'd read her thoughts, he nudged her until she was flush against him where she contacted the confirmation that he wanted her. And he was very close to having her.

Apparently Sam had a brief moment of clarity when he broke the kiss and put some much-needed space between them without taking away his hold on her. "You better stop me now before this goes any further."

The command hovered on Savannah's lips, yet she could not force it out. She couldn't manage even the slightest protest. "What if I told you I don't want you to stop?"

He looked more than a little concerned. "And I don't want to do anything we'll both regret."

She laid a palm on his cheek. "I don't know how to explain this except to say I need to feel alive. I need to forget all the bad, even if it's only for a little while. I just need—"

He halted her words with another brief kiss. "Trust me, I know exactly what you need."

"I do trust you, Sam, otherwise I wouldn't be here." And that was a truth she never planned to admit.

"Then, babe, that's all I need to hear."

Other men had used that *babe* endearment during Savannah's lifetime, and she'd never cared for it at all. Yet Sam wielded the word with familiarity and so much power that she suddenly didn't give a darn about regrets. She only knew she'd been alone for far too long.

As Sam kissed her once more, Savannah immersed herself in the sensations. She became that girl again, the one who reacted to this boy—this first love—as if time had stood still. And when he breezed his lips down the column of her throat, nothing else seemed to matter except this moment and this man. Not all the old accusations. Not the hateful words. Not even the fact that this was only a temporary diversion from the stress of a hectic life that had had her in a choke hold for years. From the sorrowful reminders of loss.

As Sam closed his warm mouth over her breast, Savannah responded to the gentle pull of his lips with the same intensity as she had the first time he'd done this to her, with a surge of heat and an overwhelming longing for more.

He anticipated her needs by skimming his hand along her waist before sliding it to her belly and lower still. It all began to come back to Savannah, the realization that he did know exactly where and how to touch her. How to make her forget everything but him. How to make her tremble, which he did with every gentle stroke.

Too long, she thought as she began to slip into a welcome haze. Too long since she'd felt this way. Maybe never this way since him.

Sam brought his lips to her ear and told her how good she felt, how he'd been imagining this since the moment he'd seen her in the diner, and then softly whispered, "Let go, sweetheart."

As much as she wanted the sensations to continue, Savannah couldn't stop the powerful release, or the physical jolt that accompanied it. She couldn't seem to stop shaking even as Sam held her close and kissed her gently while the climax began to ebb and her breathing returned to normal. Then came the tears, as unexpected as the quickness in which she'd responded to his touch.

She couldn't quite peg why she'd begun to cry—shame

or sentimentality. She couldn't seem to halt the emotions any more than she could stop clinging to Sam.

"I'm sorry," he said as he stroked her hair. "I didn't mean to hurt you."

He had hurt her, but not from his actions a few moments before. The wounds he'd inflicted years ago should have healed by now, but sadly they hadn't, though Savannah had wrongly convinced herself they had. All that bottled-up pain had somehow worked its way to the surface, and she hated that she couldn't temporarily live for the moment and let the past die.

"I'm okay," she said as she tipped her forehead against his chest so she wouldn't have to see his reaction. After she finally composed herself, she looked up at him and smiled. "I've developed a syndrome over the past few years. Orgasmic hysteria. Some people sing during the throes of passion, I bawl like a baby."

That earned Savannah his notable smile. "That good, huh?"

"Don't get cocky," she said. "It's just been a while for me."

"I know what you mean."

Savannah had a difficult time believing that. She also had one heck of a time ignoring the fact that he was still quite in need of attention. "Anything I can do for you?" she found herself asking against sound judgment.

He brushed a damp lock of hair away from her cheek. "Not unless you can manufacture some birth control."

Now might be a good time to tell him she was on the Pill, even though she hadn't needed it for a while. Then again, that would alleviate one major reason for not completely making love with him right then, and she wasn't quite ready for that.

In spite of her continued caution, a boldness Savannah hadn't experienced in a long while overcame her. She reached between them and followed the same path down his abdomen that he'd followed down hers. She wasn't that naive girl he'd once known, and she was determined to establish that fact with a little touching of her own.

Before she reached her intended target, Sam pulled her hand up and clasped it against his chest. Apparently he didn't appreciate her taking the lead. "Sam, I—"

He held his hand over her mouth, whispered, "Be quiet," then nodded toward the bank.

Savannah followed his gaze to discover a beam of light bobbing in the distance. A light that—to her absolute horror—suddenly swung around and landed right on her face.

"Well, I'll be a monkey's uncle, if it ain't little Savannah Greer."

CHAPTER ELEVEN

"THAT WAS ONE OF THE MOST mortifying experiences of my life."

Savannah's declaration broke through the cloud of silence that had hung over them since they'd climbed into the truck for the return trip to the farm.

As far as Sam was concerned, up until the interruption, it had been one of the best experiences he could immediately recall, even if he had momentarily forgotten his plan to prove he was a better man. "Do you mean getting caught or me copping a feel?"

"Both."

He felt the need to defend himself. "Hey, I handed you the chance to stop me, but you didn't take it. In fact, you encouraged me. It's a little late to take it back now."

She nailed him with a glare. "And you encouraged me to go into the pond without my clothes, knowing what might happen if I did."

She had him on that. "Then let's just say we're both to blame and drop it."

"Agreed."

As soon as he pulled into the drive, Sam shifted the truck into Park and cut off the ignition. "We were lucky Frank Allworth caught us and not Chase's dad. Otherwise, we'd probably be sitting in the county jail for trespassing and public lewdness."

Savannah's eyes went as wide as tire rims. "Lucky? Do you not remember who's married to Frank?"

He'd been trying to forget. "Yeah, and Pearl's got a big mouth. But that doesn't mean Frank's going to say anything to her."

"Oh, sure. I'm surprised she wasn't with him. And on that note, what was he doing there?"

Messing up a damn fine time. "Since he lives across the road, seems Wainwright hired him to sit on the porch at night to protect the place from trespassing teenagers."

"And overage idiots." Savannah powered down the window, leaned her head back against the seat and sighed. "I swear, the minute I stepped back into this town, I haven't been acting like myself."

Sam didn't share that opinion. "You're acting just like the girl I used to know."

"Sorry to disappoint, but that girl doesn't exist anymore."

He draped his left arm over the steering wheel and shifted slightly to get a good view of her face. "I think deep down she still does."

She shot him a dirty look. "Just because we used to be high school sweethearts, and just because I had a serious lapse in maturity a while ago and we made out for about ten minutes, that doesn't mean you really know me."

Made out completely naked and he gave her one hell of an orgasm, he started to remind her but thought better of it. Instead, he chose to prove exactly how well he knew her. "I bet you still set your alarm an hour earlier than necessary because you hate to be late, but somehow you manage to make it wherever you're going with only a couple of minutes to spare. I imagine you still eat cereal for breakfast, the fruity kind with the marshmallows. And it's likely you still pretend you don't care for pro football but you can rattle off statistics till the cows come home. Am I right?"

She muttered something under her breath that Sam didn't understand, but he doubted it was flattering. "You don't drink beer but you like your glass of wine on occasion," he continued. "You own about a dozen pair of panties in different shades of pink even though you won't admit it because it makes you seem too girly."

She sent him a glare that could stop a schoolyard bully's reign of terror. "Are you done yet?"

"Not until you admit I'm right."

She shrugged. "Okay, you're right. You know my habits. Again, that doesn't mean you know me."

She was dead wrong on that count, too. "I still know which of your buttons to push."

She rubbed her temples as if she had one heck of a headache. "Let's just leave my buttons out of this, okay?"

He ignored her acid tone and said, "I also know if you're having fun or not. And lady, a little while ago, you were having a damn good time."

"I don't know that I'd qualify what we did as a good time."

A surge of anger hit him full force. "I'd say by the way you were moaning, you enjoyed yourself just fine.

Or maybe you just didn't get enough of what you *needed* from me."

She fumbled with the seat belt for a second before finally releasing it. "I'm too tired to listen to this."

Savannah's sudden exit from the truck told Sam he'd hit a nerve, but that didn't mean he was done with her yet. For some reason, he wanted her to confess that her life wasn't all that great. That maybe she hadn't found what she'd been searching for after all.

Sam slid out of the driver's seat and followed her onto the porch, where he caught her arm, forcing her to look at him. "You can talk until dawn about how much you love going to work every day to your fancy job and coming home to your fancy condo," he said. "But you sure as hell won't convince me that you're all that satisfied with your life. Otherwise, I don't believe you'd be here with me."

She yanked her arm out of his grasp. "You have no idea what my life is like. Yes, I spend a lot of time at work and yes, I go home at night alone. But what about you? You work like a dog from sunup to sundown to save a way of life that—by your own admission—is dying. And for what? To prove you're a sucker for a lost cause?"

Obviously he was a sucker since he was still trying to sell her on small-town living. "Farming isn't a lost cause, Savannah, and neither is Placid. It's all about community. At least people around here have your back when you need them."

"You mean they know your business."

He couldn't exactly argue with that. "Maybe so, but

I know I can count on them, and they can count on me if the need arises. This place also taught me to shoot straight and when I make a promise, my word is as good as gold. Can you say the same for your Chicago buddies?"

Her laugh sounded skeptical. "Your word is as good as gold? That's rich, Sam. I've seen you break a promise without batting an eye."

He sensed they were about to enter some fairly tough emotional terrain. "I'm sorry about the damn prom."

"I'm not referring to the prom. You promised me you were going to apply to Northwestern so we could go to college together."

"I did." The words tumbled out of his mouth before he could take hold of them.

Savannah stared at him blankly before the comprehension light turned on. "When did you do that?"

He had no good reason to continue this conversation, but he'd already backed himself into the confession corner. Might as well lay it all on the line. "I applied about the same time you did, and I got rejected two days before you got accepted."

"Rejected?" She sounded as stunned as she looked.

"Don't act so surprised, Savannah. Unlike you, I only had average grades and I sure as hell didn't have the means to buy my way in. But they were kind enough to invite me to reapply in the spring."

Her face softened with sympathy and Sam hated that more than her anger. "Why didn't you say something?"

He'd considered it before he'd come to his senses. "I didn't see any point in telling you because it wasn't going to make you any less gone. You already had your head set on getting out of town as fast as that old Mustang would let you, with or without me."

"But you could have come later," she said. "You could have been the first in your family with a degree. You said that's what you always wanted."

"And that's exactly what I got—a four-year degree in agribusiness with a minor in marketing right here in the fine state of Mississippi."

Her voice dripped with sarcasm when she said, "Good for you. I'm so glad you had the decency to finally tell me."

He'd failed to tell her a lot of things. "I just figured you didn't care one way or the other, Savannah. You went on with your life and I went on with mine." And that's exactly how it would be when she packed up and left again in a few days.

"You're right, it doesn't matter now," she said. "But it did that day in the diner when you went on your verbal attack as if I'd done something wrong by trying to better myself."

And he'd been forced to live with his sorry actions for years. "I was a kid with too much pride, and you were a girl who thought her dreams were a whole lot more important than mine." Just like it had been between his own mother and father. "You always thought you were too good for Placid and me."

"If that's what you believe, then I don't see any reason to continue this conversation, even if you are wrong." She whipped around and grabbed the door handle while Sam began the countdown.

Three…two…one.

As predicted, she spun around to get in the last word. "And for the record, I firmly believe all your talk about friendship is a ruse. You want more from me than that, but you don't have the guts to follow through because you're afraid it's more than you can handle."

He was on her in a flash, bracing both hands above her head, trapping her against the door with his body. "Lady, I've got twenty bucks in my pocket and some hard proof down south that says you're dead wrong." He pressed against her, driving home his point.

Her brown eyes reflected the heat that had been brewing between them since that day in the workshop. "Then prove it."

Sam had learned a long time ago that anger was one hell of an aphrodisiac. It made a man do crazy things, even knowing he ran a huge risk on several levels. He had more than a few reasons why he should quit while he was ahead, but the way he felt right now, he probably couldn't stop short of the roof caving in.

When they made it into the house, Savannah didn't bother to turn off the light and Sam didn't bother taking her to the bedroom. He did take off his shirt while she took off hers, and then shoved his jeans down while she did the same with her shorts. After that, he backed her up against the paneled wall with no regard for propriety, like the horny teenage kid he used to be.

Without formality, he lifted Savannah up, wrapped her legs around his waist and sealed the deal.

This wasn't a rosy reunion or at all what he'd imagined when he'd fantasized about making love to her again—taking her up against a wall, his pants around his ankles and his boots still on his feet, for a fast round of raw, mind-blowing sex. Normally, this whole scene would be fine with him—hurried and hot. But with Savannah, he'd wanted to take it slow, show her what he'd learned in her absence. Take her places she'd never been before, at least not with him. But their verbal foreplay and her challenge didn't allow for a lot of leisure.

Sam wasn't all that surprised when Savannah climaxed almost immediately since she'd always been fairly quick to fire. He just hoped the same didn't hold true for him. But when she raked her nails down his back and made a noise that sounded a lot like a muffled scream, she didn't afford him the luxury of taking his good, sweet time.

Sam closed his eyes, gritted his teeth and muttered a one-word curse when the force of the climax roared through him like a freight train. He fought for air, fought to recover, fought to remember the last time he'd felt this damn good. Probably back in their youth, when they'd been so wrapped up in each other that every moment they spent together was an adventure. When he'd convinced himself that he would never find another girl like her. That he would never feel that deeply for another girl. He hadn't and most likely never would, something he'd take out and examine later.

After he slowly lowered Savannah to her feet, they just stood there for a few moments, the sound of their ragged breathing bouncing off the walls of the empty house. If he knew what was good for him, he'd put on his pants and head hell-bound for safety before he asked to stay the night. But where she was concerned, he'd forgotten all the lessons he'd learned about the difference between wisdom and wanting. Speaking of a lack of wisdom…

"We forgot the damn condom," he managed to grate out.

"I'm on the Pill," she said.

"You would've saved me a whole lot of grief if you'd mentioned that sooner."

"And you'll save me a whole lot of worry if you assure me safety isn't an issue."

"Trust me, it's not." He hadn't bypassed the condom route since his marriage ended.

When Savannah ducked under his arm, Sam yanked up his jeans and turned around in time to see her pulling her shorts back into place.

"I need to shower," she said as she snatched the T-shirt from the floor and slid it over her head, much to Sam's disappointment.

"I could use one, too." And he wouldn't mind compounding his mistakes tonight by joining her.

She put an end to that wish when she said, "I'll use the bath upstairs and you can use the guest bath down here."

So much for the afterglow of lovemaking. "Fine." He picked his shirt up but didn't bother to put it on. "I'll meet you in your bedroom."

"We both need some sleep, so you may let yourself out." Then she rushed up the stairs like a house afire.

Savannah had gone from willing woman to ice princess in about ten seconds, and that really ticked him off.

Normally he'd welcome an excuse for a quick exit, at least with most women. But she wasn't most women. She never had been.

For that reason, he opted to spend very little time in the shower in order to cut her off at the pass. After he was done, he scaled the stairs and entered her bedroom to await her return, probably at his own peril. He found it ironic that she was the one shutting down, which was usually his trick. But he also knew how to draw her out. At least he used to know.

For the next twenty minutes, Sam walked around the room and surveyed all the trinkets that had been there since the first time she'd allowed him inside. He made his way to the bed and picked up a pink teddy bear positioned on the pillow. The same bear he'd won at a midway booth at the festival—not long before everything had come apart.

When he heard approaching footsteps, Sam tossed the bear back on the bed and turned toward the door.

Savannah strode into the room while towel-drying her hair and stopped short when she spotted him, looking mighty unhappy that he hadn't left. "Do you not remember how to find the front door?"

He didn't like her attitude any more than she liked finding him still hanging around. "I'm not leaving until we discuss what just happened."

She crossed the room, draped the towel on the footboard, stood before the dresser mirror and started brushing her damp hair with a vengeance. "I don't want to have a discussion. I want to go to bed. Alone."

He didn't intend to give up that easily. "Maybe I need to talk about it."

She faced him while sporting a fairly harsh glare and a tight grip on the brush. "Go home, Sam."

"Not until you say what's on your mind, Savannah."

"I don't have anything else to say."

He took a seat on the padded cedar chest. "Maybe not, but I'm bettin' you're having a nice little battle with some hefty guilt."

She continued to clutch the brush so hard he thought it might break. "Okay, maybe I'm feeling a little guilty. I'm also embarrassed over my actions, which have been less than stellar all night. I think it's best if we forget this ever happened."

Like he could really do that. He also couldn't get a solid hold on his resentment. "Okay. If that's the way you want it to be, no problem. But the next time you need a little comfort, find someone else."

Sam made it to the door when she called his name. And like the fool he'd always been, he turned around. "What?"

"It's not only about the sex," she said as she studied the braided rug beneath her bare feet.

He leaned a shoulder against the door frame. "Then explain it to me because I sure as hell don't have a clue."

"It involves what you told me earlier. If you'd been honest with me about the rejection, then I might have…" Her words trailed off along with her gaze.

Sam didn't care to explore what might have been. He only knew that he felt as if someone had just delivered a solid punch to his gut. To actually think she would have stayed had he handled everything differently was like believing his mother would've eventually returned for him. And even if Savannah had entertained that notion, he wouldn't have wanted to shoulder the blame when she realized she'd made a huge mistake. "What's done is done, and speculating won't give you anything but a headache."

Savannah raised her eyes to him and started to smile but it faded fast. "My dad used to say that."

"Your dad was a wise man. And if he were here, he'd tell you to enjoy your time on earth while you still have the chance."

"Yes, he would have said that. He also would've told me to be cautious when it comes to making snap decisions. Obviously I forgot that advice tonight."

As much as he wanted to ask her if he could crawl under that handmade quilt covering her bed and spend the night, he didn't see any reason to do it. Their previous connection had been severed by mistakes he couldn't rectify. "I better go. Jamie's going to want to leave for the festival bright and early in the morning. I'll hold her off until nine so you can get an extra hour of sleep before we pick you up."

She shook her head. "You two go without me."

He figured she'd try to back out if he let her. He wasn't going to let her. "I'll be back in the morning because I promised my kid you'd go with us. And regardless of what you believe, these days I do keep my promises."

Except for a promise he'd made himself the minute

she'd walked back into his life—not to let her get to him. As sure as sunrise, she was getting to him.

After he left Savannah before she could refuse the festival offer again, he pulled out of the drive for home, and became all too aware that the woman was tracking through his veins like hundred-proof whiskey.

He'd learned long ago how to raise an emotional barrier if he needed to protect himself, and that's what he had to do with Savannah. He just hoped that when she left again, he didn't find himself buried beneath another pile of bitter regrets.

SHE COULDN'T BELIEVE she'd agreed to come. Not that Sam had given her much choice. As promised, he'd arrived at the door at 9:00 a.m. sharp with his daughter in tow and a look that said he wouldn't take no for an answer. And though she'd been reluctant to enjoy herself, once she got past the initial uncomfortable moments with Sam, Savannah had honestly had a good time.

Seeing the festival through the eyes of a child—from the carnival rides to corn dogs—made her appreciate the sheer simplicity of country living and community. Having Jamie present also served as a welcome distraction, a means to avoid thinking about Sam and their wild, wicked lovemaking, as well as the fact that he seemed bent on giving her the cold shoulder. But now that she'd claimed a shaded park bench in the town square's center, leaving father and daughter to tackle the midway games, Sam was all she could think about. Images of his powerful body in motion kept rolling through her mind like thunder. Her face and a few unseen places began to heat up when she considered how undeniably sexy the whole encounter had been. How much she wanted a repeat performance, as if she'd completely lost every last bit of pride and wisdom. Then again, he'd all but said he wanted nothing more to do with her, and that was unarguably for the best.

Greatly needing a diversion, Savannah proceeded to people-watch as the festival patrons looking for a bargain swarmed the various merchant booths. During the course of the day, she'd recognized quite a few folks, and many had recognized her. Fortunately, she'd managed to dodge Pearl Allworth. After she'd relaxed enough to realize the remainder of the town didn't seem to know about the pond debacle, she'd exchanged pleasant greetings with former teachers and classmates and family friends, some of whom had extended their sympathies. A few even expressed their wishes she'd return home for good to assume the role of the town's only lawyer.

But this wasn't home anymore, and in a matter of days, she'd be turning over her childhood house to a man she held in low esteem. If she stopped to consider that now, her good mood would be completely ruined.

Savannah scanned the area to find Jamie standing several feet away at a ring-toss booth while her dad valiantly attempted to win her more stuffed animals to add to the pile in her arms. She remembered how he'd done the same for her years before and how she hadn't been able to part with most of the prizes he'd worked so hard to give her. She also recalled what he'd told her last night about the college application, yet the revelation still didn't excuse the cruel way he'd treated her during that final confrontation. And it didn't discount the promise he'd made one night on the bridge—they'd be together forever. A promise he'd noticeably forgotten, and readily broken.

"Lordy, Miss Savannah, you sure are a sight for this old man's eyes."

Somewhat startled, Savannah looked up to find a tall, lanky African-American man dressed in washed-out denim overalls standing above her, straw hat on his head and a wide smile on his careworn face.

She immediately recognized Reggie Wilkins, one of her father's closest friends, and came to her feet to give him a hug. "It's so good to see you, Reggie."

He looked a bit uncomfortable when she let him go. "Same here, Miss Savannah."

She gestured toward the bench behind her. "Have a seat and tell me what you've been up to."

He hesitated for a moment and scanned the area as if seeking approval. At one time someone might have objected if he joined her, before the racial dividing line had somewhat dissolved due to one unifying factor among the citizens of Placid—poverty.

After Reggie removed his hat and claimed the spot beside her, Savannah laid a hand on his arm. "I'm sorry we didn't have more time to talk at the funeral. And I'm so, so sorry about Etta. She was one of my favorite teachers."

His eyes dimmed from recognizable sorrow over the loss of his wife. "You know, Miss Savannah, it was tough to watch her go, but she's in a better place now, waiting for me."

She would do well to rely on that wisdom when it came to her own father. "How are the kids?" she asked. "Aside from all grown up."

Finally, his smile reappeared, as bright as the sun beating down on the sidewalk. "R.J.'s got a fancy business degree and he's in Atlanta workin' in a bank, if you can imagine that. He got his 'rithmetic skills from his mama. And Lila, she's at the university in 'Bama for the third year. She's going to be a physical therapist. They've both done me proud, just like you did your daddy proud."

And like her, Reggie's children had made a life elsewhere. "So it's just you living out at the farm? That must be lonely."

He shook his head. "No, ma'am, I ain't at the farm no more. I'm living in town now. Mr. Wainwright called in my note because I didn't have the money to pay."

The thought of Wainwright ripping a man's home right out from under him made Savannah sick. "You lost the entire farm, even your house?"

"Yes, ma'am, I did. R.J.'s tryin' to get me to come to Georgia, but my kin helped build this town. They're all laid to rest in the old cemetery on the county road, and so is my Etta, and I can't leave my Etta. So I reckon this is where I'll be buried, too. That's only fittin'."

Savannah still couldn't fathom the power Placid had over someone's decision to remain there, even when they had no real reason to stay. "What are you doing to make a living?"

He shrugged. "Some odd jobs here and there, but I work mostly for Mr. Sam. He hires a lot of down-and-out people around these parts when he can. He's a good man, just like his daddy."

Clearly Sam had earned a stellar reputation among the townsfolk. "I'm glad to know you're getting by. But I'm not too thrilled to hear that Edwin Wainwright seems to be putting people out of their homes faster than a bullet."

"He is, and he's not going to be done till he buys up all the property. Folks here are dirt poor and they don't always understand what they're signing when they borrow from him. Before they know it, they ain't got the money and they ain't got a place to live."

"Sounds to me like this town could use some legal help." Someone to take on Wainwright and beat him at his own game. That certainly explained the previous pleas for her to set up shop.

"Yes, ma'am, we sure could use the help. People can't afford to go all the way to Jackson when they're in trouble. Bo Hudson and young Kyle Parker are about to sign on with Wainwright's bank even though I tried to warn them away. If you could look over some of their paperwork, I'm sure they'd be mighty appreciative of that."

If only she had the means and time to help. "Unfortunately, I'm not licensed to practice in the state of Mississippi." Exactly what she'd told Jess during their meeting. "But I'll definitely do some research and see if I can come up with an attorney who'd be willing to meet with you in Placid."

"We'd be much obliged, Miss Savannah." He rose from the bench and smiled down on her. "Now I best be gettin' over to the church's dunkin' booth for my shift."

Savannah returned his smile. "A dunking booth, huh? Too bad we can't put Wainwright in there. You'd raise enough money to put up one fine steeple."

They shared a laugh before Reggie added, "Maybe we'll be seein' each other again soon."

"I'm leaving in a few days." Saying the words gave her an odd and unexpected sinking feeling in the pit of her stomach.

"But you'll see if you can find someone to help us before you go?"

Reggie sounded so hopeful, Savannah couldn't refuse even if she wanted to, which she didn't. "I'll see what I can do, but it could take some time."

This time, his smile held all the sadness in the world. "That's okay. Most people around here got nothin' but time because they sure don't have much else."

And they had no one to turn to when the going got tough, Savannah realized as she told Reggie goodbye.

She had a fleeting thought that she could apply for a Mississippi license and come back every few months to provide legal aid to Placid's less fortunate. Come back to what? The house had been sold and she certainly couldn't stay with Jess considering her marital problems. Rachel and Matt were expecting a baby and the last thing they needed was a guest. She'd be a fool to ask Sam, even though Jim and Gracie would surely welcome her into their home.

The whole concept wasn't the least bit practical. Surely she could find someone willing to take on a David-and-Goliath cause pro bono. She'd work on that later. Right now she needed to find Sam and Jamie.

On that thought, Savannah craned her neck to locate the booth where father and daughter had been only a few minutes ago. They happened to be standing not too far away, conversing with some blonde who had her back turned to the bench.

When Sam touched the lady's shoulder in a gesture that looked way too intimate, Savannah experienced a little nip of jealousy—until a nice-looking guy dressed in golf attire walked up and put his arm around the unknown woman.

She could be polite and join the group, or she could remain seated and wait for her companions to find her. Since she'd spent all day baking in the sun and probably looked like something a rat dragged in because the cat wouldn't touch it, she chose to stay in the same spot.

After she heard Jamie shout her name, Savannah looked up to see the little girl heading her way, holding hands with the mystery woman, who happened to be pregnant…and of all people, Sam's ex-wife.

CHAPTER TWELVE

SAVANNAH MAINTAINED A strong grip on the edge of the bench to keep from bolting, while Darlene looked just as reluctant to come face-to-face with her former competition for Sam's affections.

On the other hand, Jamie beamed like a headlight over the prospect of introducing two presumed strangers. "This is my mom," she said as soon as they arrived at Savannah's erstwhile sanctuary. "Mommy, this is Daddy's old girlfriend, Savannah."

Chagrin threatened to freeze Savannah like an ice cube to the wooden slats, but proper etiquette dictated she stand and mind her manners. Yet "Hi" was all she could muster at the moment.

"It's good to see you again, Savannah," Darlene said with questionable genuineness.

Jamie's delight was etched all over her adorable face. "You two know each other?"

"Yes," Savannah and Darlene answered simultaneously.

"Did you go to school together?" Jamie asked.

"No," Darlene jumped in without giving Savannah a chance to respond. "I went to school in Brewster, where your Nanny and Grandpa Clements live."

"And I went to Placid High with your dad," Savannah added.

"We were rivals." Darlene's cheeks turned slightly red. "In football."

Savannah tried on a smile. "So I guess you could say we've known each other for a good fifteen years." Some of them not so good, particularly the last year of their official acquaintance.

"Jamie," Sam called, drawing the trio's attention. "Let's go ride."

Savannah was somewhat perplexed over Sam's *laissez-faire* attitude. Most men would have run interference between the ex-wife and former girlfriend for fear of eventual retribution. Then again, she was no longer his girlfriend, and Darlene wasn't his wife, so why would it matter?

Jamie gave Savannah's hand a yank to garner her attention. "Are you gonna ride the tilt-a-girl with me and Daddy?"

Darlene laughed. "What ride is that, honey?"

Jamie wrinkled her nose. "You know, Mommy. The one that tilts the girls while it's spinning around."

Savannah couldn't help but grin. "I know that one well, and no thanks. It makes me kind of queasy."

"What about you, Mommy?" Jamie asked.

Darlene patted her belly. "I don't want to make your brother sick, so I guess I'll sit this one out."

Jamie lifted her chin in indignation. "I'll just go ride with my two daddies, who don't get sick." She then sprinted off in the direction of Sam and the stepfather without looking back.

Feeling somewhat generous, Savannah reclaimed her place on the bench and gestured toward the empty space beside her. "Have a seat."

Seeming somewhat self-conscious, Darlene complied, and for a few uncomfortable moments they didn't exchange a word.

Savannah made the first move to break the dialogue impasse. "Kind of awkward, isn't it?"

"Just a tad."

Small talk would probably make a weird situation somewhat better. "I take it that was your husband with Sam."

She nodded. "Brent. He's a family law attorney in Memphis."

Too bad he didn't reside in Mississippi, otherwise Savannah would have approached him about helping out the townsfolk. "Interesting. Where did the two of you meet?"

"He's a partner in the firm that represented me during the divorce." Darlene sent Savannah a sheepish smile. "Oddly enough, when one man walked out of my life, another walked in."

She probably shouldn't ask, yet she couldn't help but wonder if Sam's version of the split had been accurate. "The divorce was Sam's idea?"

"Actually, it was mutual. The marriage died of natural causes. No drama to speak of. Just enough indifference to fill a football stadium."

Exactly how Sam had described it. "I'm sorry to hear that."

Darlene shrugged. "It's hard to keep a marriage afloat

when your husband is still pining away for someone from his past."

Savannah didn't care to travel down that rocky road, yet she felt the need to set the record straight. "If you're referring to me, I highly doubt Sam gave me much thought after I left."

"He gave you a lot of thought. It's obvious he still does." She raised both hands, palms pointed at Savannah, as if in surrender. "Don't get me wrong, I'm not blaming you at all. I'm only stating the facts, although Sam would be hard-pressed to admit it. But a woman has instincts about these things."

Instincts aside, Savannah had a difficult time believing it. "You know how it is. Sometimes people just want what they can't have. Or maybe what they imagined they wanted."

Darlene gave her a meaningful look. "Sometimes people love someone so much that no one else can live up to the ideal, real or imagined."

Savannah frankly didn't think that was the case with Sam. He still wanted her—he'd demonstrated that last night—but on a purely physical level. Maybe that's all it had ever been. "Regardless, I'm really sorry it didn't work out with the two of you. But at least you had a beautiful child together." The child she'd wanted to have with Sam someday, and she hoped she hadn't revealed her envy through her wistful tone.

"Yes, I'll give you that. I don't know what I'd do without Jamie. And sometimes…" Darlene laid a gentle hand on her abdomen. "Sometimes I worry I won't love this little one as much, but then my mom swears I'll have enough to go around. I suppose that's true since she still loves my little brother, who is about as useless as boobs on a boar hog."

Their laughter drew attention from a few passersby but Savannah didn't care. She was pleased she could hold a civil conversation with Darlene and even share a good laugh. "Do you have a name for the baby yet?" she asked.

"We've been back and forth over the choices and we've come up with a few. I did tell Brent that we cannot name this child after his father."

"What's his name?"

"Baldric. It's a family name. A really inconsiderate family's name."

Savannah definitely agreed with that. "You could go with my personal favorite, Beauregard. I dated someone by that name. Luckily, he went by Beau."

Darlene grinned. "I think it has such a nice Southern ring to it."

After they exchanged several more suspect male names, Darlene said, "Now that I think about it, Brent has two children from his previous marriage—fourteen-year-old Brianna and sixteen-year-old Blake. One more 'B' name and the 'B' hive will be too crowded to handle."

Savannah hadn't realized Darlene had such a great sense of humor, nor could she picture her as a stepmother. Before today, maybe an evil stepmother. "I'm sure you'll come up with something nice and trendy."

"I'm certainly going to try."

They continued to casually converse, discussing old

times and playing the "what happened to" game. They covered pranks executed on their respective high schools and how simple life had been back then, especially during the summer.

When Savannah glanced to her left to see Sam, Jamie and Brent approaching, she said, "The daredevils have returned."

Darlene looked over her shoulder and waved toward the group before regarding Savannah again. "Hopefully they're done with the carnival rides. I'm ready to get out of this heat."

"I'm just glad we had this time to talk, Darlene," Savannah said sincerely.

"I enjoyed it, too, Savannah. It's a shame we didn't know each other better in high school. I think we could have been friends."

"I believe we could have been, too, if Sam hadn't been in the mix."

"You're right," Darlene said with a smile. "Leave it to a man to mess it up. But faults and all, Sam's still a very good man."

"I know." Little by little, Savannah had begun to realize that, through Reggie's revelations and Sam's interaction with his daughter. She also couldn't discount that he'd obviously helped her father during his final years.

Darlene stood and stretched, both hands braced on the small of her back. "That being said, good or not, I think we both agree that most men, even Sam and my current dear husband, regress to cave-dwelling tendencies when it comes to their sex drives and keeping a bathroom clean."

They exchanged another laugh before Brent arrived at the bench, frowning. "Are you ladies discussing us?"

Darlene popped a kiss on her husband's cheek. "Aren't we always?" She gestured toward Savannah. "This is Savannah Greer, Brent. She's a high school friend."

A dozen years ago, Savannah would have never accepted that claim. But now, things were different, proving that with adulthood came the realization teenagers could be awfully petty at times. She stood and took Brent's offered hand for a shake. "It's nice to meet you, Brent."

"Same here," he said. "This is probably the first time two legal eagles have graced the Placid festival grounds."

"That could be front-page news tomorrow." Which, as far as Savannah was concerned, was preferable to the Potter's Pond incident showing up in the headlines.

Darlene hooked her arm through Brent's. "We'll see you all back at the farm. I need to get off my feet before they swell up like a toad." She held out her hand to her daughter. "Are you coming with us, honey?"

Jamie shook her head. "I'm gonna go with Daddy and Savannah."

"Okay," Darlene said. "But hurry up. Grandpa Jim is making his famous homemade ice cream and we don't want it to melt before we have some."

Jamie clapped her hands together and jumped up and down, her ponytail bouncing in time with her movement. "I love ice cream!"

"Calm down, Joe," Sam said. "You're going to cause an earthquake."

"Hope to see you, too, Savannah," Darlene said as she and Brent walked away.

Jamie clasped Savannah's hand and gave it a jerk. "Are you gonna have some of Papaw's ice cream, Savannah?"

Temptation came calling, but reality ruled. "I love your granddad's ice cream, sweetie, but I have to get home. My mother's leaving in a couple of days and I need to help her pack her things." As well as corner her for that long-overdue conversation.

"Your mother's going to be there," Sam said, the first words he'd spoken directly to her since they'd arrived at the festival.

That was news to Savannah, and she wondered why he was just now telling her. Better still, why hadn't her mother told her? Oh, yeah. They were all barely speaking. "Since when did this come about?"

"Since she called us this morning to say she wants to tell everyone goodbye before she leaves tomorrow."

"You mean before she leaves on Monday."

"She told Dad that Bill and May are coming early afternoon and they plan to head out tomorrow night."

Which meant Savannah had little time to spare before her mother left town, taking the truth with her.

A THOUSAND MEMORIES RAN through Savannah's mind as they gathered in the McBriars' backyard for evening camaraderie after a long day. She loved these moments the most, when time seemed to suspend in the company of family and good friends.

Gracie and Darlene chatted about the latest small-town gossip while Jamie slept soundly in her grandfather's lap. Amazingly Ruth had been engaged in a conversation with Brent and she'd actually laughed a time or two.

Savannah decided her mother looked more relaxed than she'd seen her in a while. She'd even dressed in casual white slacks and a sleeveless tailored pink blouse instead of her usual button-up shirt and proper below-the-knee skirt. Of course, Ruth had managed to remain hidden in her room while Savannah showered and changed, and then predictably walked to the McBriars' without waiting for her daughter. Managing to avoid a confrontation could be the reason for stoic Ruth's calm demeanor. But as far as Savannah was concerned, that confrontation would happen tonight, come hell or high water.

In the meantime, while Sam tuned his guitar, Savannah put everything out of her mind and simply sat back to enjoy the scene. Only one thing happened to be missing—her dad.

She tried to force the sorrow aside, tried to disregard the pain of loss. Yet as Sam began to sing, her heart broke a little all over again.

She knew every word as if she'd written it herself because he'd sung it to her at least a hundred times before. She knew every I-love-you in the lyrics, every plea to stay. Every reference to making love and making a commitment. She questioned whether his choice had been meant to stir memories, or if he'd made the selection because it had always been one his favorites. She only knew that the strength of her reaction and recollections practically stole her breath, and so did the occasional meaningful look he gave her as he held her hostage with his mesmerizing voice.

By the time Sam was finished, Savannah realized she'd totally tuned everyone and everything out when Gracie's "Bravo" startled her from a daze. She applauded with the rest of the group while resisting the urge to retreat, to escape all the familiar feelings that made her want to replay the past. If last night proved anything at all, her complete abandon verified how precariously close she was coming to reliving the same old mistakes she'd made with Sam, namely handing over her heart to him.

Savannah felt as if she walked an emotional tightrope, poised to fall at any given moment. With an annoying knot in her throat and a voice telling her to get away, she picked up her empty bowl and walked back into the house, an exact replay of the last time she'd had dinner at the McBriars' two days ago.

In the kitchen, she willed herself not to cry, scolded herself for even feeling the need. Tonight had marked a few moments of happiness and she vowed to keep that in mind. The tears fell anyway.

When the screen door opened, Savannah grabbed a napkin from the holder on the counter and turned toward the sink before swiping away the moisture on her cheeks.

"Are you okay?"

Great. Sam's company was the last thing she needed. "Yes," she said as she rinsed the bowl much longer than necessary before placing it in the dishwasher.

When she felt his hand on her shoulder, she flinched

and he immediately removed it. She didn't find his touch at all repulsive, but she did worry she might crumble in front of him. She had to stay grounded, to show him that he couldn't rattle her with a simple song.

After wiping her hands on nearby towel, she finally felt strong enough to face him. Strong enough to ask an important question. "Why did you choose to sing that particular song?"

He hooked his thumbs in his pockets. "Why not?" he asked, as if he had no idea what he'd done to her with his choice.

"You know why, Sam."

He released a frustrated sigh. "It's a song, Savannah, and I've been singing it for years. Don't try to read more into it."

She hated the fact that his attitude hurt her beyond reason. "I'm so pleased we've cleared that up. Now, why are you here?"

"Because Gracie sent me in to see if you're okay. You looked pretty upset when you left."

No real surprise that he hadn't come of his own volition. "Yes, I was a little upset. I thought about my dad and how much he loved Jim's ice cream and that I have over a hundred text messages from work on my cell phone. I also forgot to have someone water my plants." Her lone ivy that so far had survived her neglect.

He looked totally unconvinced. "Are you sure that's all it is?"

"Believe me, that's enough."

He shifted his weight from one leg to the other, a sure

sign of discomfort, and very unlike him. "Are you sure you're not still dwelling on last night?"

"We had sex, Sam," she said, a little louder than necessary. "We answered a few biological urges and it was pretty good, albeit a little over the top. But it wasn't so phenomenal that I need to cry about it."

His expression turned hard, unforgiving. "Yeah, that's all it was. Hot sex. Glad we cleared *that* up."

Savannah tossed the towel on the counter. "If we're done with this pointless conversation, I need to see if my mother's ready to go."

"That's another reason why I'm here," he said. "Right after you left, she announced she was about to go home because she had things to do."

Savannah doubted a heart-to-heart talk with her daughter had made it to Ruth's to-do list. "You should've said something the minute you walked in here. If she gets a head start, she'll probably lock herself in her room to avoid speaking to me."

Since Sam didn't seem to want to move, she had to work her way past him or stay rooted until he left. When she opted to leave without further ado, he clasped her arm, thwarting her departure and forcing her to look at him.

His features had mellowed somewhat, contrasting with the slight shading of evening whiskers that Savannah had always loved. "After you have that little sit-down with your mom, don't forget to call me if you need to talk."

Emotional overload drove her to say, "That's priceless, Sam. Last night you told me to call someone else, remember?"

Without giving him time to respond, Savannah wrested away and returned to the yard to find everyone standing—and Ruth Greer nowhere in sight. "Where's my mother?" she asked, a slightly frantic edge to her voice.

"She headed on home," Jim said. "She told me to tell you that you should stay as long as you like."

Typical. "I'd love to visit a while longer but I need to help her pack. You know how she is, she doesn't want to bother anyone." She didn't want Savannah's help, either.

"We need to go, too," Darlene added as she braced both hands on Jamie's shoulders. "This one is on her last leg."

"I've got two legs, Mommy," Jamie said, eliciting laughter from the group.

While Sam stood conspicuously in the shadows, Savannah doled out hugs to everyone, including Darlene and even Brent.

Saving Jamie for last, Savannah knelt down on her level. "Be good, sweetie, but like my dad used to like to say, if you can't always be good—"

"Be smart," Sam cut in from somewhere behind her, confirming once more how well he'd grown to know her father.

After giving Jamie a squeeze and a kiss on the cheek, Savannah straightened and said goodbye, feeling somewhat down in the dumps over not visiting with them again in the foreseeable future.

Jamie tugged on the hem of Savannah's T-shirt, garnering her attention. "Are you going to live in Ruthie's house now?"

Savannah shook her head. "I'm afraid not. I have to go back to Chicago on Tuesday." Or she could return on Monday now that her mother decided to leave a day earlier.

Jamie looked up at her with pure innocence. With eyes very much like Sam's. "Are you going to come back soon?"

She chose to answer as honestly as possible. "Maybe someday."

"SHE'S NOT COMING BACK." Sam knew it as surely as he knew the sound of his child's voice.

After putting Jamie's suitcase in the trunk, Darlene turned around and scowled at him. "How do you know that, Sam?"

"Because she doesn't have any reason to come back. The house is sold and she didn't have much to do with her friends in the past twelve years." That included him, but then they hadn't parted as friends.

Darlene leaned back against the sedan like she was settling in for a spell. "Maybe you should visit her in Chicago."

"I've been there and I don't care for it."

"When were you ever in Chicago?"

He probably should've told her long ago. He'd had no reason not to aside from some guilt that had prevented him from coming clean. "I spent some time there when I went to that equipment conference a few months after Jamie was born."

She raised an eyebrow. "I thought that conference was in southern Illinois, not Chicago."

Man, the woman had a memory the size of a wheat combine. "A few of us drove up for a baseball game."

"Did you get in touch with Savannah?"

Even now, suspicion rang as loud and clear as a church bell in her voice. "If you're asking if I went to see her, no, I didn't." The thought had crossed his mind, but he'd been trying to make his marriage work at the time. Seeing Savannah wouldn't have aided that cause, and that's if she would've even agreed to meet with him.

"That's neither here nor there," Darlene said. "What matters is right now. I can sense there's still something between the two of you."

"Like always, your imagination's getting the best of you, Darlene." Only this time, she wasn't entirely off base. "And I'm not sure why you're so worried about my personal life when I've never interfered in yours."

"Look, Sam, you hand over jobs you'd prefer to do yourself to people who need money. You're always there for Jim and Gracie and Lord knows you're a great father to Jamie. I'm concerned because I don't see you doing anything for yourself, and by that I mean settling down with someone special."

He'd already found someone special, and she was about to walk out on him a second time. "Like I told you the last time we talked about this very thing, I'm okay with my life the way it is. No complications or heavy commitments."

"And like I said before, you have no one to come

home to at the end of the day, and I don't mean Jim and Gracie."

Time to lighten the mood. "If you're that worried, you could give me Jamie."

She looked stunned. "Are you serious?"

No, he wasn't, but she deserved a little ribbing for being so nosy. "Sure. You're going to have a spare kid, so why not?" He punctuated the comment with a grin.

Darlene didn't look at all like she appreciated his teasing. "For being such a nice guy, sometimes you can be a borderline bastard, Sam McBriar."

He imagined some women saw him that way on occasion. One in particular, but she considered him a jackass. "Lighten up, Darlene. You know I'd never make you hand over the kid to me full-time, although I would like to have her all summer when she gets a little older. She needs to learn to drive the tractor so she can help me out when I'm old and infirm and *alone*."

"That wasn't exactly what I had in mind for her career choice, but I'll think about it," she said with a reluctant smile. "Now back to you and Savannah."

Just when he thought they'd swept that subject under the rug. "There's nothing to discuss."

She sent him the "yeah, sure" look, the one she used to routinely give him during their arguments. "I've seen those little glances between the two of you. I saw them tonight when you were singing to her. The intimacy was palpable. Brent even commented that he felt like a voyeur during your little performance."

"A couple of glances and a song don't translate into intimacy, Darlene." What they'd done last night, did.

And that was information he didn't opt to share with the ex-wife.

"Wouldn't you say having sex with Savannah is fairly intimate, Sam?"

How the hell did she know that? He couldn't imagine Savannah taking his ex into her confidence. Most likely Darlene was trying to bait him into a tell-all moment. "Did I mention you have one hell of an imagination?"

"No imagination involved, Sam. I heard all about it a while ago with my own two ears, and so did everyone else. Luckily Jamie dozed off or she would have heard it, too. You both should learn to lower your voices if you're going to rely on a screen door for privacy."

Damn. If only he'd heeded Gracie's long-standing order that he shut the door behind him; they didn't live in a barn. "We weren't talking that loud."

"Oh, yes, you were. But then you and Savannah have never been known for your discretion."

Sam assumed that was a direct reference to the legendary breakup in the diner until Darlene added, "For instance, take the pond incident last night."

"How in the hell did you find out about that?"

Darlene snorted. "Good grief, Sam. Getting caught by Pearl Allworth's husband was bound to cause a stir. You've given the good people of Placid something to talk about for years to come. Why, they haven't been as excited since Abe Young got caught stealing bloomers from Harriet Hamilton's clothesline back in the fifties."

"What happened between us didn't mean anything."

She rolled her eyes. "You'll never convince me of

that, Sam. And I think it's high time for you to tell Savannah how you feel about her and see where it leads."

He knew exactly where it would lead—nowhere.

Fortunately, Brent picked that moment to come out of the house, providing another "guy" presence to put an end to the unwanted conversation. "I started to wonder if the two of you had run off together," he said as he joined them at the SUV.

"Not a chance," Darlene replied. "We were just having a little talk about Sam's love life."

Brent draped one arm over Darlene's shoulder and pulled her against his side. "Let me just say, Sam, that you have great taste in women."

Darlene slid her arm around his waist. "Thanks, honey."

In that moment, Sam realized he didn't own one iota of jealousy over his ex-wife's and her new husband's public display of affection. That revealed a lot about his relationship with Darlene. He couldn't deny he'd once loved her, but not like he'd loved Savannah, an admission a long time in the making.

Brent kissed Darlene on the cheek. "Are you ready to go, darlin'?"

Darlene smiled up at him. "Sure."

"Where's Jamie?" Sam asked.

"She's conked out on the couch," Brent said.

Sam saw an escape route and planned to navigate it. "I'll go get her while you start the car to cool it off."

"I'll come in with you and tell your parents goodbye." Darlene released her hold on her husband and headed for the house.

After shaking Brent's hand, Sam took a couple of steps toward the porch before he heard, "One more thing, Sam."

He turned back to Brent. "Shoot."

"Just a few words of advice. You've already let one good woman go. Think twice before you let the other one get away again."

As far as Sam was concerned, Savannah was already gone.

AS CLAWLIKE LIMBS BIT at her legs, Savannah realized that had she not been taught to respect her elders, she'd be cursing her mother about now. Even though the three-quarter moon helped guide her, as soon as she'd entered the thicket right before the bridge, she began to stumble in her haste to get home. Of course, Ruth had brought a flashlight for the journey back to the farm. And of course, she didn't wait around to share it with her daughter.

If she could just get past this rough patch without impaling herself on a briar, maybe, just maybe, she could make it to the house before her mother retired for the evening. If not, their little talk would have to wait until tomorrow.

As soon as Savannah reached the break in the trees, she pulled up short at the sight before her. Ruth stood on the bridge, looking out over the fields, her right hand fisted against her heart.

Panic set in, sending Savannah hurrying to her mother's side, where she lightly touched her shoulder. "Are you okay, Mom?"

Ruth continued to stare straight ahead, a faraway look in her eyes. "The last time your father and I took a walk, we ended up here. 'Ruth,' he said, 'there's nothing prettier on God's green earth than a good piece of land.'"

She suspected her mother might be having second thoughts about selling the farm. "It's understandable if you miss the place once you're gone."

"I'm missing your father." Her sigh carried on the breeze. "Sad thing is, you never really know how much you love someone until they're gone."

How very true, Savannah thought. "I miss him, too. But he's at peace."

"He is now," Ruth said. "Those final days at the hospital were terrible. So many times I'd thought I'd lost him, but then he'd squeeze my hand." She opened and closed her fist as if reliving the moments. "When he stopped doing that, I knew he was gone even though he hadn't drawn his last breath."

She inhaled deeply before continuing. "I'm not sure if he always heard me, but I kept telling him how much I loved him. How much he had meant to me through the years. I don't think I told him enough when he was alive."

Savannah's heart began to ache as the tears began to form. "I wish you would have called me, Mom. I would have come."

Ruth sent her a brief glance before turning her attention back to the panorama. "He asked me not to call you. He didn't want you to see him that way."

That was so like her dad—never wanting to be a

bother to anyone. Never wanting anyone to witness his weak moments, though they had been few. Yet Savannah had seen him that way once, and to this day, she'd never known why he'd been on the porch, crying. She'd probably never know. "I still hate that you were all alone when he died, Mom."

"Not always alone."

That gave her a measure of relief. "It's good to know Bill and May were with you."

"Not Bill and May, Savannah. Sam was there."

Savannah couldn't have been more taken aback. "He came to the hospital?"

"Yes. He'd show up and tell me to take a break even if I didn't think I needed one. But some days I was so tired I'd go home and take a nap. He always promised he'd call if it was time, and I trusted he would. Having him there was a godsend, especially at the end."

Savannah swallowed hard around her shock. "He was there when Dad died?"

"Yes, with that old guitar. In your daddy's final moments, Sam sang Floyd's favorite hymn, the one about the sparrow."

When Savannah could again speak, she said, "That was an incredibly kind gesture on his part."

"He's a decent man, Savannah. But I guess you've always known that about him."

More now than ever. "Yes, he is. And I'm glad you finally realize that."

"I never really took the time to know him before you left. Sometimes I'm too quick to judge."

That admission was almost as remarkable as learning

Sam had kept vigil over her dad. "We all have our faults, Mom."

"Your father didn't have many," she said. "He tolerated me for almost sixty years. He also saved my life."

Now would be a good time to work her way into the mystery surrounding her mother's history, but Savannah acknowledged she would have to proceed with caution. "How did he save your life?"

Even in the limited light, she could see her mother's shoulders tense. "It doesn't matter how. He just did."

Now or never had arrived. Savannah chose now. "I saw your sketches, Mother. I found them in the bedroom. I know I shouldn't have pried, but I felt like I needed to—"

"I know. I'm glad you found them."

Finally, a possible breakthrough. "Was that you in the drawings?"

"Yes."

"And the hands belonged to?"

When Ruth fell silent, Savannah worried the revelations could be over, until she said, "My stepfather was a horrible man."

At least part of Savannah's suspicions had been confirmed. "How was he horrible, Mother? Were you his punching bag?"

"Yes." Ruth turned her face toward Savannah and lowered her eyes. "I was also his replacement wife."

CHAPTER THIRTEEN

BY SUGGESTING THEY CONTINUE the conversation back at the house, Savannah ran the very valid risk that her mother could clam up again. Yet she felt that would be best—moving to a well-lit venue where she could weigh Ruth's reactions if she chose to continue the revelations, and stop her if they appeared to be causing her too much pain.

Once they arrived, Savannah guided her mother to the parlor, sat her down on the small sofa and took the space beside her. "Mom, I understand if you don't want to talk about this," she began, "but it might help if you do."

Turning her attention across the room, Ruth focused on the family portrait taken before they'd moved to Placid. A depiction of much happier times. "When Don began to court my mother a month or so after Daddy died, I really didn't mind all that much because Mama had been so sad and she finally seemed happy. But that happiness ended not long after that."

After a lengthy hesitation, Savannah said, "Go on, Mom. I'm listening."

Ruth drew in a deep breath and exhaled slowly. "I remember waking up in the morning to the smell of pancakes. He always cooked pancakes after he'd beat my mother, like that would somehow make up for what he'd done to her. That's why I hate pancakes."

Savannah couldn't fathom what her mother had endured when she cooked those pancakes every Sunday morning for her own family. "When did he start hitting you?"

"When I turned thirteen, the winter before Mama died. He used any excuse he could come up with. The crops were failing, the tractor broke down, the laundry wasn't done to his liking. I used to hide in the attic, but he always found me."

Savannah shuddered at the thought. "And your mother never stopped him."

Anger as harsh as a Chicago winter flashed in Ruth's eyes. "No, she never stopped him. She'd just take to the bed and let him do what he would to me, as long as he wasn't hurting her. They said she died of pneumonia, but I swear she just got tired of getting hit and gave up."

Savannah prepared to enter some potentially precarious territory. "And the other abuse?"

A fleeting look of shame passed over her mother's expression. "A few months after we buried Mama, I had to go to work at the general store to help put food on the table since Don didn't care to do anything but drink. I always took May with me because I didn't trust leaving her alone with him. When I'd come home, I cooked his meals, washed his clothes and did everything Mama did for him. *Everything.*"

When Ruth covered her face with both hands and sobbed, Savannah laid a gentle hand on her shoulder. "It's okay, Mom. You don't have to continue."

"I want to." As if the proverbial floodgates had opened wide, Ruth pulled a tissue from her pocket, dried her eyes and continued. "Mama and I never talked about the ways between a man and a woman. When he started coming into my room at night, I didn't understand what was happening. I only knew it was wrong and it made me sick to my stomach. I tried to fight, but he was so strong."

The abject terror her mother had endured made Savannah internally recoil. "Did you tell anyone?"

Ruth let go a caustic laugh. "Back in those days, no one told. Papa Don was a *respected* citizen. He rescued Widow Calloway and her children from certain poverty. People believed what a man did in his house was nobody's business. And it really wasn't his home at all, but he still defiled all that was good about it."

Savannah began to recognize all too well the reasons behind her mother's strange transformation when they'd moved back to the farm. "When we returned to Placid, the details came back to you, didn't they?"

Ruth sent her a brief glance. "Yes, and your daddy always blamed himself for bringing me back here. But when the mill shut down in Knoxville, we didn't have much choice. He did what he could to help. He took out most of the old furniture and painted the walls. But he couldn't paint away the memories."

Several issues still muddied the comprehension waters. "I'm beginning to understand what you went through, Mom, and I am so, so sorry. But I don't understand why your anxiety caused you to close yourself off to me."

Ruth refused to look directly at Savannah. "You were so headstrong and stubborn that I thought it best if your father dealt with you."

No matter how hard she tried to push it down, that same old spark of resentment began to rear its head. "You mean easier, don't you, Mom?"

Finally, she turned her weary gaze to Savannah. "Do you really think it was easy, watching you build the kind of relationship with your dad that I always wanted to have with you? But I couldn't do that and protect you."

Now Savannah was extremely befuddled. "I'm not following you, Mother."

Ruth folded the hem of her blouse back and forth, her hands noticeably shaking. "Remember that night when you told me how much you hated Placid and you hated me for bringing you here?"

Savannah lowered her head and pinched the bridge of her nose. "I could be one belligerent teenager."

"Do you remember I raised my hand and almost slapped you?"

The long-forgotten image came back to her. "I hadn't really thought much about it because you didn't actually do it."

"But I wanted to. After that day, I feared I had the meanness in me, just like Papa Don."

Suddenly it all began to make sense to Savannah. "The important thing is that you stopped yourself, Mom. And not once did you ever lay a hand on me."

More tears welled in Ruth's eyes. "I couldn't risk hurting you like he hurt me."

Savannah felt her mother's pain as keenly as if it were

her own. "I just wish you would have told me what you'd been through. I would have been much more considerate." Less temperamental. Less hateful.

"I can't take it back now. I can only say I'm sorry and beg your forgiveness."

Savannah was prepared to take that next step—as soon as she had one more answer. "I do forgive you, Mom, but why tell me now?"

Ruth hesitated before saying, "Because your father asked me to make amends. He wanted to know that after he was gone, we'd rely on each other."

She wasn't sure how to take that. "So this wasn't your idea."

"So many times I wanted to tell you, but I didn't know how. We'd built so much bitterness between us, and I'm at fault for that."

Savannah couldn't ignore her role in that bitterness. "In part, so am I."

Ruth shook her head. "You were a child, Savannah. I should have been more patient with you. I should have been stronger."

"Stronger? You went to work when you were barely old enough to take care of yourself. You survived unspeakable acts and you raised your baby sister. If that's not gutsy, I don't know what is."

"I didn't mind working at the store." Her mother's ensuing smile made her appear twenty years younger and lifted Savannah's spirits. "That's where I met your daddy. He was the cutest boy I'd ever set eyes on. He used to come to the house and help me with the chores. As long as Floyd was there, Papa Don didn't come around."

Another burning question that Savannah had to address. "How much did Dad know about Don?"

"I told him everything right after we married. I had to because I didn't know what it was like to have relations with a man without being afraid. It took years before I felt like a real wife. And in all that time, he stayed patient with me."

"I wouldn't expect any less from Dad." Savannah hadn't expected to be made privy to this much information, either. "I still can't imagine being married at seventeen." She couldn't imagine being married at thirty, either.

"It was tough," Ruth said. "We didn't have two nickels to rub together. We did have a lot of love and we had May. We worked hard to make a good home for her."

"Which you did," Savannah said. "May's very grateful to you."

"I know," she said. "But I made mistakes with her, too. I never told her the truth about Papa Don. She never really understood why I had to get her out of that house before she became his target."

Sometimes honesty wasn't the best answer. "I can fully understand why you'd want to protect her from that, Mom. Especially since your mother never protected you the way you tried to protect me. And even if your good intentions got in the way of our relationship, I know why you did it, and I love you for it."

Ruth looked as if Savannah had handed her a basketful of diamonds. "After you were grown, I wanted to be close to you again. I wanted to talk to you like we're talking now. But I was so ashamed."

Savannah took her mother's hand into hers. "You have no reason to be ashamed, Mom. You had no control over what Don did to you. As far as we're concerned, it's never too late to make amends, right?"

"No, it's not."

When Ruth rose from the sofa, Savannah assumed that was the end of their peace accord, not that she believed everything would be smooth sailing from this point forward. Yet instead of leaving the room, Ruth walked to the antique desk in the corner and opened the drawer. She returned to the sofa and offered Savannah a paper. More specifically, a sketch. "This is for you."

The drawing was both heartfelt and heartrending—a sleeping child secure in the arms of her father. Although the sketch had been done in pencil, the care the artist took to depict every intricate detail showed in the wisps of hair curling around the little girl's cheek and the silver snaps on the man's cuffs. Her hair. Her father's cuffs.

Savannah didn't have to search for the signature in the corner of the yellowed page to know this was her mother's handiwork. She couldn't have seen that signature anyway, thanks to the onset of tears. Never had she viewed something so honest and innocent. Never had she admired her mother's talent—and her mother—more.

After brushing away the moisture with her fingertips, Savannah stared up at Ruth with a good deal of wonder. "When did you sketch this?"

"About twenty-four years ago. You'd been sick with the flu for a couple of days, so your daddy took you outside and sat with you on the porch. I couldn't resist capturing the moment because I knew you'd be grown and gone before I knew it. I drew it out of love for you both."

For the first time in many years, her mother had expressed her love for her daughter. Savannah felt as if a huge weight had been lifted from her soul. "Why have I never seen this before?"

"I wanted to wait and give it to you on the day you had your first child."

Ouch. "I suppose you've decided that's not going to happen."

Ruth smiled. "I still hope for that, but no, I thought now would be a better time. Something to remind you that your daddy was the best of men and that he loved you with everything in him."

Savannah needed no tangible reminders because she carried so many in her heart. She appreciated having the drawing anyway. "Mother, you are such an incredible artist. Did you ever dream of pursuing a professional career?"

Ruth reclaimed her place on the sofa. "As old-fashioned as it may seem to you, marrying your father was my dream, and seeing you succeed was, too." She put her arm around Savannah's shoulders in a surprising show of affection. "I'm proud of you, Savannah Leigh. Proud that you went after your dreams. But…"

Oh, boy. Here it came, just when Savannah thought they'd moved mountains this evening. "And?"

"Don't let your work be your only dream. Those dreams are worthless if you can't share them with someone."

As if that were such a simple feat. "I'll try, Mom, but it's slim pickings these days in the dating world."

Ruth sent her a sly smile and gave her a brief and somewhat awkward hug. "You never know when love will land on your front door."

About the only thing Savannah expected to land on her doorstep would be the neighbor's annoying cat. "Speaking of that, will you visit me in Chicago?"

"Maybe in a few months," she said as she slowly rose from the settee. And before she left the room, she looked back and added, "If you're still there."

Still there? Where else would she be?

SAM TOSSED THE LAST BALE into the hay shed and turned when he heard his name. He found Ruth Greer standing nearby, a small rental truck parked in the gravel drive leading to the barn. When May stuck her hand out the window and waved, and Bill honked twice, he raised his palm in acknowledgment.

"You about to head out, Miss Ruth?" he asked as he pulled off his work gloves and shoved them into his back pocket.

"I am, but I wanted to say goodbye to you first."

She'd pretty much done that last night, which made him wonder if there could be more to this unexpected visit. "I appreciate that."

She glanced over her shoulder as if she were looking for support before bringing her attention back to him. "I also wanted to say thank you for everything you've done for me, before and during Floyd's passing. I might not have made it through this without you."

"No thanks necessary. It was my pleasure. And you're one tough lady, Miss Ruth. You would've handled everything fine without me."

"Maybe, but I'm just glad I didn't have to go it alone. At least now I'm feeling more at peace with leaving here."

That led Sam to ask, "Have you and Savannah called a truce?"

She smiled. "Yes, we have. And she's another reason why I'm here. I need to ask another favor."

"No harm in asking."

Ruth wrung her hands. "She's decided to stay on until the end of the week so she can go through a few more things, or so she says. I'm worried she's having trouble dealing with losing the house, although Lord knows why. She hasn't been there for any length of time in years."

"True, but she's got a lot of memories wrapped up in the place." So did he.

"I know, and that's where you come in, helping her let go of the past."

Like he could help Savannah when he hadn't been able to help himself. "How do you propose I do that?"

"Just promise me you'll check on her now and then for the next few days."

She might as well have asked him to pick up the barn with his bare hands. "I don't believe Savannah's going to take too kindly to that idea."

"Don't give her a choice," Ruth said. "Be persistent and she'll come around."

Or she'd kick him to the curb the minute he showed up at the door. "I can only promise I'll try."

"That's all I ask." She started to walk away before turning back to him again. "You know, Sam, I've been blessed to have a second chance to set things straight with my daughter. If it can happen for me, it can happen for you, too."

Sam didn't believe that for a second, but he needed to make an effort to make amends. He needed to put the past to rest while he still had time. What that involved remained to be seen, but not trying could haunt him for the rest of his life.

SHE HAD TOO MUCH STUFF. Savannah realized that after she'd sorted through the remainder of the items she planned to take with her, those silly little things that only she could appreciate. Since her mother's departure, she'd occupied her time in an ongoing debate with her sensible side—to throw or not to throw away. Her pack rat persona had won out. At this rate, she'd have to find the closest shipping service and send a few boxes to Chicago. She had no idea how she'd cram it all into her limited-storage condo, but she'd deal with that later.

Savannah spent the next half hour wandering through the house, committing each and every room to memory. The knotty pine walls in the kitchen, the outdated rose wallpaper in the bathrooms, the scarred hardwood floors in hallways, spoke to a legacy that she would always embrace, even though her mother understandably could not.

She lowered herself to the bare parlor floor, feeling as

though she would lose an important part of herself the minute she left the house behind. Feeling as if she would be closing a chapter of her life that she'd clung to for so many years. She'd promised herself she wouldn't cry, but that vow went by the wayside when she recalled all the times she'd sat in this very spot at her father's feet, telling him about her day and listening to his down-home words of wisdom. She also remembered Sam meeting her in this room so many times, where he'd steal a kiss before her dad would arrive to remind her that she had a curfew. Golden, precious times that she could never get back, or ever forget.

In a house now devoid of occupants other than herself, Savannah had never felt quite so lonely in her life, nor had she ever lost the desire to return to work. Right then, she would happily call the senior partner and tell him to go to hell—and that idea was unequivocally insane. She'd worked too hard to reach her goals to let a burst of nostalgia hijack her career.

Despite her downhearted state, Savannah forced herself to the kitchen for something to eat. Most of the leftovers had been thrown out and only one can of tuna remained in the pantry. She could top the tuna with a slice of overripe tomato and wilting lettuce. Or she could drive into town and grab something to go from Stan's. That certainly seemed the better option.

Savannah snatched her purse from the counter and on the way out the door, rifled through the contents, including the old greeting-card bundle she'd stuffed inside the bag, in search of her keys. Unsuccessful in her efforts, she paused on the front porch, tucked the cards beneath her chin and dug some more.

Impatience suddenly got the best of her. "Dammit, where are you!"

"Right here, ma'am."

Last she checked, keys didn't talk, and if they did, she doubted they'd speak in a sexy, Southern, man's-man voice since her car had been born in Detroit.

Her gaze shot to the driveway, where she spotted Sam standing beside his big black truck, a brown paper bag in one hand, a bottle of white wine in the other and an overtly sensuous smile plastered on his striking face.

Savannah not only dropped the card bundle, she also dropped the blasted purse and its contents at her feet, where the missing key ring landed on her big toe.

She silently cursed the pain and the keys and the man who simply wouldn't stop shaking her up. "What are you doing here, Sam?"

When he held up the bag and said, "Gracie's famous chicken and dumplings," Savannah experienced an overwhelming sense of déjà vu. Different location, but the same scenario during that first reunion on the bridge.

After gathering her mess and her wits, Savannah sprinted down the steps and met Sam halfway on the path. "I was just about to go into town for something to eat. Tell Gracie she saved me from a serious elevation in my cholesterol level."

Sam kept a solid hold on the bag and Savannah's attention. "There's enough for two."

Crazy man, trying to win a dinner invitation. Crazy

girl, about to give it to him, thanks to her sudden inability to be alone. "Have you eaten yet?"

"Nope. Thought I'd join you, if you don't mind letting me in the house."

Not a good idea. "It's a nice evening. We can dine on the front porch."

"Suit yourself." As Sam breezed by, Savannah turned to watch him scale the stairs, completely engrossed in the tight black T-shirt hugging his broad back, the fit of his faded jeans and the swagger in his walk.

While she continued to gawk as if he'd grown a third eye in the middle of his forehead—more accurately, his butt—Sam set the bag and bottle on the table next to her key-swallowing purse. "Gracie didn't pack any plates or utensils," he said as he turned around to reveal her second favorite view. Nothing quite like the added bonus of a belt buckle to enhance a fine, masculine feature.

When she failed to respond, he added, "We also need a corkscrew and glasses, unless you want me to uncork the bottle with my teeth so we can drink out of our shoes."

Snapping to, Savannah strode to the front door and muttered, "I'll get it."

She slapped the screen back a little harder than necessary, angry at herself for once again succumbing to his charms. Last night should have served as their final goodbye, but clearly Sam had other ideas. Apparently so did her hormones, the only logical explanation for her sex-and-Sam thoughts. That, and simple sleep deprivation. Two nights ago, remorse over what they'd done had kept her awake. Last night, learning about her mother's past had robbed her of much-needed rest. And now that she recognized the problem, she could keep a firm grip on her control and in turn, have a glass of wine and sleep like a baby as soon as Sam went home.

She gathered the paper plates and plastic utensils left over from the wake. As far as a corkscrew went, she could only locate a paring knife someone had overlooked in the drawer. They would also have to settle for disposable glasses.

Now if she could just dispose of some extremely sinful images as she made her way to the porch, past the wall where they'd done the deed she'd sworn she would never do again with him. The deed she really wanted to do again.

Only dinner...

Savannah took the chair opposite Sam while he poured the wine. Perplexed, she asked, "Did you use your teeth to open the bottle?"

"Didn't need to," he said as he slid the cup in front of her. "It's a screw cap."

"That purchase must have set you back a couple of bucks."

She expected a frown, but he granted her a grin. "We're in Placid, not Chicago. I'm just glad the town council voted to allow the sale of beer and wine. Otherwise, I'd have to drive two counties over to buy booze."

Not so lucky if her palate couldn't tolerate said booze. "I suppose it will have to do."

After Savannah helped herself to the dumplings, Sam kicked back in the chair and proceeded to stare at her.

"What?" she asked around her first forkful of food.

He laced his fingers together behind his neck. "I'm trying to decide if you look any different now that you've made up with your mom."

Savannah dropped the fork onto the paper plate. "How did you know that?"

"Ruth told me."

"When?"

"When she stopped by and asked me to look in on you."

Didn't anyone ever voluntarily act on her behalf without a request from someone else? "Okay, you've looked, I'm fine, you're obviously not going to eat, now you can go."

"I don't want to go." He leaned forward, took a long drink from the plastic cup and smacked his lips. "I have to help you finish this bottle of fine wine."

The jury was still out on how fine the wine might be. In order to see for herself, she took a sip and scowled. "I believe this comes from the Burns Going Down Winery in No Hope, North Dakota."

Sam let go a hearty laugh. "It's not that bad."

"Yes, it is, unless you like the subtle antifreeze bouquet."

Suddenly serious, Sam leaned forward and spun his fork round and round. "It's none of my business, but I'm curious as to what you found out about your mother's drawing."

Although Savannah was tempted not to answer, she opened the dam and released troubled waters. She told him the gritty details about her stepgrandfather's horrific behavior and about her mother's shame. She also injected her own guilt into the revelation mix. By the time she was finished, she'd consumed two full glasses of the suspect wine.

"It's not all your fault, Savannah," Sam said. "And in some ways, Ruth's not totally to blame, either. I'm just glad you both finally worked it out. Hating is a big burden to bear."

"When it comes to your own mother, you should know all about that." Evidently the stiff drink had loosened her tongue.

"I don't hate her anymore," he said. "I do regret that I didn't clear the air before she died. That's why I'm proud that you did what you did."

Proud? That was a first from him. "Thank you. Now pass me some more of that No Hope, will ya?"

He turned the bottle upside down and shook it. "All gone. Want me to go get some more?"

"If we finished that entire bottle, you shouldn't be driving."

He winked. "You drank most of it, babe, but I don't care to go anywhere at the moment anyway."

"I'm glad," she said. "I kind of like having you here."

So much so she completely discarded all the rationale for why she should want him gone.

With the steel nerves of a stunt pilot, she leaned over and kissed Sam. She blamed her inability to resist him on the liquor, when she knew full well she wasn't drunk. At least not from a few cupfuls of wine. But the way he kissed her back—slowly, provocatively—was more intoxicating than a liter of vodka.

He pulled away and surveyed her face from forehead

to chin before centering on her eyes. "Mind telling me why you just did that?"

"Because I'm lonely."

He didn't appear at all happy over her claim. *False* claim. "And I'm the only man under the age of sixty to keep you company?"

That wasn't even close to the truth. "Okay, I'll admit it. I'm fed up with pretending that I don't want to be with you again. Maybe that's wrong, but that's how I feel."

Savannah halfway expected him to bid her goodbye once and for all. She didn't expect him to ask, "Do you want me to stay?"

"Do you know any reason why I should?"

"Let me spend the night, and I'll give you several good reasons."

Only dinner? "That sounds tempting."

"Just say yes, for old times' sake."

Only tonight... "Yes."

He stroked her arm with his thumb, and Savannah felt it everywhere. "No walls this time."

She could interpret that several ways but she concentrated on the obvious. "No walls, but I still have a bed."

He leaned and kissed her softly. "What are we waiting for?"

A bolt of lightning prodding her to steer clear of him. A celestial message written in the scattered clouds, warning her to be cautious. A moment of lucidity when she recognized the chance she would be taking. If any of those signs did happen to come to pass, she chose to ignore them all.

Without another word or even the slightest hesitation,

Savannah held out her hand and guided Sam up the stairs to her bedroom. The waning sun filtered through the partially open curtains, sending a ribbon of light across the bed. She'd once been in an almost identical situation—standing in her childhood room with Sam, plagued by ambivalence, excited by the prospect of finally giving him everything after two years of making him wait. Yet she wasn't that innocent, impressionable girl now. She knew exactly what was about to happen, including the possible fallout, yet she seemed powerless to halt it any more than she could quiet her racing heart.

As they stood face-to-face, Sam slipped the buttons on her blouse one by one, perhaps to allow her to change her mind. She didn't, not even after he'd removed every last bit of her clothing, from top to bottom, with agonizing slowness. After he seated her on the mattress, he began to undress while Savannah watched with more than a passing interest.

First, he sat on the wingback chair set against the opposite wall and toed out of his boots. Next, he pulled the T-shirt up and over his head and, last, worked his jeans and boxers down his narrow hips, all the while keeping his eyes fixed on hers. Keeping her on edge when he stalked toward her sporting a look and physical evidence that said he meant business. Pleasurable business.

Sam pulled her to her feet, leaned around her and raked the quilt and sheets back, sending several stuffed animals flying. She would have found that comical had she not been in such a needy state.

Savannah expected that same rush of passion, that same uncontrollable combustion that had driven them two nights ago in the foyer. Instead, Sam claimed the place where she had been, moved her between his parted legs and as she stood before him, explored her body with both his eyes and hands as if taking all the details to memory.

She supposed that with age came patience—and experience. He demonstrated that by trailing his warm lips down her torso in a series of light kisses, and he didn't stop there. All those years ago, he'd never been quite so bold. But then, she'd been much more reticent and he'd always respected that. Tonight, he'd clearly decided to pull out all the stops, and she had no desire to stop him.

Savannah felt as if Sam were testing her limits, seeing how much she could take as he used his mouth to bring her to the brink. If he wanted her to beg, he certainly had the method and the means to make that happen. But she didn't have to plead before he brought her to a climax so strong that she shuddered with the force of it. And just when she believed her legs would give way, he brought her back onto the bed in his arms and guided himself inside her.

He kept his gaze locked on her eyes as he moved slowly, surely, keeping her in a state of prolonged bliss. She preferred a frenzied interlude to a slow dance into oblivion, where she didn't have time to weigh the repercussions or consider the consequences. Where she didn't have to feel anything but pleasure.

Yet in that moment, Savannah felt too vulnerable, especially when Sam laced his fingers with hers and raised her arms above her head. She experienced his urgency with every thrust, sensed the tension in his body and saw the struggle in his expression right before he closed his eyes, whispered her name and collapsed against her. He shook with the force of his release and his heart pounded against her breasts as his harsh, uneven breaths broke the silence surrounding them in the place where their lovemaking had begun. A fitting place for it to end, Savannah thought, because after tonight it would inevitably end.

In the meantime, Savannah curled against him, her back to his front, his arms securely around her, and put the fears to rest. She'd wait until tomorrow before she let Sam know that she couldn't let this continue to keep happening. Not if she wanted to leave with her heart still in one piece.

CHAPTER FOURTEEN

APPARENTLY SAVANNAH HAD little regard for her heart. She'd spent three solid, carefree days in Sam's company without giving her fears a second thought. She'd relearned to drive the tractor, shared nightly dinners with Gracie and Jim, accompanied Sam on a day trip to pick up a few head of cattle and gladly invited him every night into her bed—as well as several points in between the front door and the bed.

And the mornings…

Well, the mornings had proven to be her favorite time of day with Sam. This morning was no exception. At some point during the night, he'd flipped onto his belly, his face turned toward the opposite wall. He had one arm bent above his head on the pillow and his hair curled softly at his nape. Savannah knew it would take only a touch to rouse him and he would keep her happily engaged in another memorable round of lovemaking for hours on end. But she needed to leave him be to make certain she was prepared to return tomorrow to a life without him.

She touched him anyway, tracing her fingertip down his spine to where the sheet covered his bare bottom. As predicted, he rolled to his back and greeted her with a winning smile.

"Woman, you're going to land me in the emergency room," he said, his patently sexy voice grainy with sleep.

She lifted the covers for a peek. "You look healthy and raring to go to me."

"Haven't you seen those commercials that claim a four-hour erection is cause to seek medical attention?"

She laughed in spite of the fact his hand landed on her breast. "I believe they mean four *continuous* hours. Besides, I haven't seen you taking any pills."

"I don't need pills," he said as he nuzzled her neck. "I only need you."

And she needed him, much more than she should.

The shrill of her cell phone resting on the nightstand prompted Sam's groan and forced her to check the ID. For the past few days, she'd ignored calls from her immediate superior. Unfortunately, this call couldn't be ignored.

Brushing Sam's wandering hand aside, she sat on the edge of the bed, pulled the sheet up for cover and answered with a professional, "Savannah Greer."

"You need to get back here immediately, Ms. Greer."

Grant Zurkle, senior partner of Zurkle and Zurkle, was nothing if not a straight shooter. And Savannah found herself right in the line of fire. "I'll be returning to work on Monday, Mr. Zurkle."

"Not Monday," he said. "Tomorrow. You have to start preparing briefs for the Smithfield trial."

Trial? "Mr. Smithfield agreed to a settlement two days before I left."

"And we convinced him to withdraw that agreement.

We're going to take this one all the way, and you'll be sitting second chair on the case."

She clinched her teeth against the expletive threatening to spew out of her mouth. Normally, sitting second chair would be a boon, but she could only think about having to cut her vacation short and the unwelcome challenge. "Mr. Zurkle, he's guilty on all counts of sexual harassment. We don't stand a chance of winning."

"We've dug into the plaintiff's past and found enough to bring her credibility into question."

Meaning they would put the victim on trial. Savannah instantly thought about her own mother's abuse and the absolute injustice of it all. "Again, I feel that—"

"It doesn't matter how you feel, Ms. Greer. As long as you work for this firm, you will do as you're told and represent the rights of our clients to the best of your ability."

What about the victim's rights? she wanted to say, but reconsidered when she visualized a bright shade of red traveling from his round cheeks to the top of his bald head. One more verbal misstep and she'd find herself unemployed after putting in four-plus years of blood, sweat and sucking up. "Fine. I'll be in the office first thing in the morning."

"You'll be in *my* office, 7:00 a.m. sharp."

Zurkle hung up without so much as a goodbye, leaving Savannah wishing she'd told him to shove it where the sun don't shine.

She turned to Sam for support only to find he'd left the room. Most likely he was in the shower and that led Savannah to grab her robe hanging on the footboard. If

she hurried, she could join him, a surefire way to forget
the unpleasantness of the conversation. A prime opportunity for another round of lovemaking. A last round.

Savannah refused to succumb to the serious bout of
depression threatening to destroy her final moments
with Sam. On that thought, she hurried into the hall
only to meet him head-on on the landing.

He was fully dressed but still unshaven, a duffel bag
thrown over one shoulder.

"Where are you going?" she asked as he started down
the stairs.

"Home," he said without making any form of eye
contact with her.

Savannah tried to match Sam's steps but since his
stride was too long, she called his name before he managed to escape out the door. "Wait, Sam."

He turned and stared at her, something akin to anger
calling out from his cobalt eyes. "Party's over. I've got
to go work and so do you."

Party? Nice to know how he viewed the past few
days. Just one big party. "That's it? You're not even
going to tell me goodbye?" She wanted more than that.
She wanted a kiss goodbye. She wanted him to say that
what they'd shared had meant more to him than just a
good time. It had certainly meant more to her.

"Bye," he said curtly, then left out the door.

Savannah hugged her robe close as she sprinted down
the remaining stairs and followed him onto the porch.
"I deserve better than this, Sam."

He faced her again, truck keys in hand. "You're right.

You deserve better. You made that real clear twelve years ago."

Nothing like being slapped by a past that obviously wasn't going to go away, at least in Sam's mind. "I thought we'd moved beyond that. I thought this time we'd have a civil parting."

"Okay. Civil it is. Have a nice life in Chicago."

She hated his scorn, hated that she had to explain her motives. "You knew I was eventually going to leave."

"On Friday," he said. "I was ready to let you go tomorrow."

She couldn't imagine what difference a day would make. "I wish I could stay until tomorrow, but you heard the conversation. I don't have a choice."

"We all have choices, Savannah. Sometimes we don't always make the right ones."

"Meaning?"

He leaned a shoulder against the porch's support post. "I should have let you go for good and left it at that. Then I wouldn't be standing here, believing like a fool that things could be different this time. That you might even decide to stay."

"You never asked me to stay, Sam. Then or now." And though she'd never admitted it to herself, that had crushed her beyond belief.

He inclined his head and studied her a long moment. "If I had asked you to stay back then, would you have done it?"

She lowered her eyes in an effort to escape his scrutiny. "Probably not."

"And now?"

When she didn't immediately answer, he said, "That's what I thought. The answer will always be the same. You don't belong here, and I do. You're going to leave and I'm going to stay. That hasn't changed, and it never will."

So many things she wanted to say crowded her mind, including an urge to tell him she still loved him, maybe even more now than before. But to what end? He had been right. They lived two separate lives and no common ground existed between them.

Yet before he slid into the truck and drove out of her life once and for all, she had one final question she needed to ask. "If I had stayed, and by some miracle we'd had a future together, do you honestly believe we would have made it like Rachel and Matt?"

Sam turned his gaze to her again and this time, Savannah witnessed the anger dissolve, replaced by a sadness she'd never before seen in his eyes. "I guess we'll never know."

As Savannah sat on the porch step and watched him drive away, she experienced an intense sense of loss. Loss of her dad, of the house behind her, of a man whom she would never, ever forget. And she had nothing left to do but cry.

SAM SPENT A GOOD FIFTEEN minutes hammering nails into a paddock fence that didn't need repairing. But he couldn't think of a better way to vent his frustration unless he put his fist through the barn wall.

"You got something against that piece of wood, son?"

Sam tossed the hammer into the toolbox, stood and

brushed his palms together as he faced his dad. "What time is it?"

Jim took a toothpick out of his mouth and pointed it at Sam. "It's time for you to tell me what's got you so peeved that you decided to beat a fence to a pulp."

He settled for a partial truth. "I've got to herd about twenty head of cattle into the catch pens in hundred-degree heat so Matt can give them their shots."

"Is Savannah stopping by later?"

"She's gone." The words burned going down like he'd swallowed a shot of lye.

"Not yet," Jim said. "I just stopped by and she was sitting on the porch, having some coffee."

"Take my word for it, she's leaving. Her damn job isn't going to wait another day." He couldn't mask the anger in his tone, something that wouldn't be lost on his dad.

Jim cocked his head and put on the lecture look. "Did you say all you needed to say to her?"

"I told her goodbye." The hardest goodbye he'd ever had to deliver.

"Did you mention that once she's gone, you're going to mope around the house like a whipped pup for years?"

"Let it go, Dad."

Jim sent him a champion scowl. "Your stupid pride's going to land you nothing but alone."

He'd been alone before and survived. "There are worse things."

"Yeah, like letting the love of your life get away again." Jim narrowed his eyes and rubbed his chin. "Unless you don't love her."

When Sam declined to reply, his dad added, "Do you love her, boy?"

He did, and that was the problem. It had always been a problem. "Okay, yeah, I love her. Are you happy now?"

"Then get the corncob out of your keister, Sam, and tell her. And while you're at it, ask her to stay."

He'd thought about confessing his feelings for the past three days and again this morning. In the end, he didn't figure it would make any difference. "She's not going to stick around no matter what I tell her."

"It's worth a try. She might even surprise you."

That would be the shock of the century. "Let's just say I did ask her to stay and she agrees. What if she decides being with me isn't what she wants? Then I'd be no better off than I am now."

Jim patted Sam on the back. "I understand, son, because I've been in your boots before. Why do you think it took me so long to make Gracie my wife? I had to be sure she wasn't going to leave me high and dry like your mother did."

For the very first time, his dad had admitted that he'd been affected by his wife's departure. "What changed your mind?"

"Gracie did. One day, after we'd had some worthless argument, she looked straight at me and said I could stop testing her because she wasn't going anywhere."

Sam had never doubted Gracie's loyalty to them. Not once had he ever feared she'd leave like his mother. "It's different. Gracie lived with us, not in some city hundreds of miles away. She had a reason to stay."

"Then give Savannah a reason to stay. Don't let her

take off without at least tellin' her how you feel, son. Let her know that she'll always have a place to come home to. Otherwise, you're going to spend the rest of your life wondering if being honest might've made a difference."

"It's a pretty damn big risk, Dad."

"One that you need to take, just like all the chances you've taken with this farm. Even if you fail, you'll be a better man for trying."

His dad had made some convincing points. "I'll think about it."

Jim's frown returned. "Don't think, boy. Just do it." He took a couple of steps away from Sam before turning back around. "One more thing. Savannah told me she didn't plan to leave until after sunset so she could beat the heat and avoid traffic. That means you still have a few hours to figure out how you're going to handle this."

When his dad walked away, Sam made the decision to take Jim's advice. He just hoped he had enough time to do what he needed to do. He had something old to find and something new to buy. After that, he'd seek out Savannah—and he knew exactly where he would find her.

THE SKIES HAD FADED FROM blue to orange, indicating the time to leave had come. Yet Savannah felt compelled to witness one last sunset, to reflect on good times and to say farewell to a pivotal part of her life that she would always remember fondly. The bridge seemed the perfect place to do that.

As she stepped onto the aged wooden slats, Savannah experienced an overwhelming sense of regret. If the truth were known, she didn't really want to go, but she knew she couldn't stay. She had no real reason to stay. She no longer had any kin to visit, no home, no one who cared whether she returned aside from a few old friends who had their own lives to lead. That included Sam.

Earlier that day, she'd spent a couple of hours at Stan's, practically jumping out of her skin every time the door had opened in hopes he would walk in and beg her to stay. A ridiculous white-knight fantasy that could only be achieved in fairy tales. Her relationship with Sam had never been a fairy tale. Far from it. And now she needed to put the past to rest, once and for all.

As she geared up to go, a noise caught Savannah's attention. She glanced to her left to see a tan oversized envelope, partially secured by a piece of tape to the railing, flapping in the breeze. Curious, she moved close to find her name scribbled across the front. She could think of only one person who would leave her a note— or a letter, as the case appeared to be.

She detached the envelope, released the metal clasps and pulled out a document. More accurately, a deed transfer—for her mother's house.

Savannah scanned the contents and discovered Sam's name listed as the grantor and a blank space awaiting her signature as the grantee. None of this made sense. Sam didn't own the house; Edwin Wainwright did.

In desperate need of further explanation, Savannah turned over the envelope and a note fluttered out, landing at her feet. She grabbed the piece of paper from the ground before it could fly into the gulley below the bridge.

She recognized the handwriting immediately, and the importance of the missive that read:

In case you ever need a place to call home...
Love, Sam

She was totally floored, both by the gesture and the way in which Sam signed the note. Utterly baffled over what it all meant.

When she heard the heavy sound of footsteps, Savannah turned to see Sam heading her way. And as he stood before her, she realized the cockiness he'd displayed that first day in the diner had disappeared. In fact, he looked humble and maybe a little hopeful.

Savannah held up the document and asked, "What is this all about?"

He hooked both thumbs in his pockets and shrugged. "Exactly what it says it is. All you have to do is sign the form in front of a notary and the place is all yours."

The simple explanation didn't quite suffice. "How did you manage to make a deal with Wainwright?"

"I owned a piece of property he wanted, so I traded him for it. It just so happened he hadn't done anything with the paperwork on your folks' farm, so that made it a lot easier."

Nothing about this situation seemed easy. "I really appreciate this, Sam," she said as she slipped the papers back into the envelope. "But what am I going to do with the house? I can't very well move it to Chicago."

"I was hoping you'd live there."

Savannah's heart executed a little leap in her chest

over the prospect of keeping the farm, a place she could visit from time to time. Maybe she could hire a caretaker. Maybe she could ask Sam to oversee the house. Odd, she'd been so opposed to that in the beginning, before she'd faced leaving for good.

Savannah was on the verge of speaking, only to have Sam add, "Before you nix that idea, I have a few things I need to say to you. Things I should've said a long time ago."

This she had to hear. She was dying to hear it. "I'm listening."

He drew in a deep breath and released it slowly. "After you left the first time, I tried to convince myself that what I felt for you wasn't real. I was just a kid caught up in all the excitement of first-time sex and—"

"Wait a minute," Savannah interrupted. "You told me you'd been with that Jones girl before me." A twenty-one-year-old woman who'd reportedly made it her goal to deflower most of the young men in Placid.

"We never got past third base."

Savannah's shock gave way to sheer delight. "That means I was your first."

Sam looked a little self-conscious before he recovered his tough-guy demeanor. "Yeah, you were my first, the same as I was yours. Can we just move on now?"

She couldn't quite hold back a smile. "Sure. I'm all ears."

"Anyway, Darlene always claimed that I never forgot you and that's a big part of the reason why our marriage didn't work."

"And when she said that to me, I told her I didn't believe it."

"She was right, Savannah. Every woman I've been with I've compared to you."

It dawned on Savannah that she'd done the same. She'd only had two serious relationships since her departure from Placid, and she'd held both men up to standards set by Sam. Neither had achieved those standards, and neither had won her love. Then again, Sam had yet to mention that emotion. "Are we talking only about sex, Sam?"

"I tried to tell myself that's all it ever was. When you came back into town, at first I decided I wanted to remind you of what you'd been missing."

Now it all began to make sense. "That's why you danced with the girl at the bar and then kept throwing out all the innuendo."

"Yeah, and later, I wanted to prove to you that I could be the man you always wanted me to be. As far as the sex goes, I didn't plan on that. In fact, I wanted to avoid it. Getting that close to you again scared the hell out of me. It still does."

Savannah had her own fears, as well. "Okay, so it's not about sex, but you haven't really said what this is all about."

He paused a moment and she finally saw real vulnerability in his dark blue eyes. "I love you, Savannah. I always have and I probably always will. That's what this is all about."

Savannah suddenly realized he'd never actually said the words to her before. Many times in the past she'd expressed her love for him, and he'd always been the typical "Me, too" kind of guy.

She could tell the admission was costing him quite a bit from an emotional standpoint. What would it cost her to reciprocate? She couldn't very well lie, though the truth could lead her into another maze of confusion. "I love you, too, Sam, more than I ever thought possible. But where does that leave us now?"

He took the envelope from her grip. "That's where this comes in. When I said I'd hoped you'd live there, I meant I want you to live there with me full-time."

Savannah found herself caught up in the perfect emotional storm as wave on wave of concerns blew through her mind. If she agreed, she would have to leave her career behind, but then she would build a new one geared toward people who really needed her services, not those who could pay well for sound legal representation. She would have to abandon city life and her condo—a tiny condo with sterile furniture and one wilting ivy—for the constraints of country living. No more shopping at will or dining at four-star restaurants. No more bumper-to-bumper traffic or harsh winter winds. No more waking up alone.

Perhaps she'd reached a point where she craved an easier pace, good friends and a good man to love. A few of her single female colleagues would be appalled to see a career-minded woman presumably sacrificing her dreams. Savannah saw it as exchanging one dream for another—a future with Sam in a town that needed her more than wealthy executives with money to burn.

To that point, Sam had stood there patiently awaiting her answer, but before she could give it, he said, "Dammit, Savannah, it takes Jamie less time to decide what she's wearing every morning, and that involves about an hour."

For that he deserved to be kept on the hook a little longer. "I can't stay, Sam. Not right now."

All the hope drained from his face. "Fine. At least I tried."

When he made a move to leave, Savannah grabbed his arm and forced him to face her. "I can't stay because I have to go back to Chicago and clear out the condo and put it up for sale. Oh, and I have to call my boss and tell him to kiss my ass."

Sam frowned. "Are you sure you want to do that?"

"Don't worry, he's heard the word *ass* before. I'm almost positive he's been called that a time or twelve."

He didn't appear to be in a joking mood. He verified that when he said, "I'm serious, Savannah. I have to know that after you leave, you're going to come back."

Even in adulthood, the sins of his mother haunted him. Savannah thought of one way to reassure him. "I'm going to come back because you're coming with me. I need help moving all my shoes."

Finally, he smiled. He also took her into his arms and kissed her gently, sincerely. "I'm not sure the house will hold all your shoes. Then again, we're going to have to redo the whole thing before we get married, otherwise your mom won't come for a visit."

Savannah hadn't even considered that problem. She hadn't considered much of anything except that Sam had said the word *marry.* "That has to be the worst proposal

I've ever heard, Samuel McBriar." The only proposal she'd ever heard. The only proposal she'd ever wanted to hear.

"You're right. Maybe this will help." He took a step back, shoved the deed into his back pocket and withdrew a ring from his front pocket. But not just any ring, Savannah discovered when he held it up. The promise ring he'd given her on her sixteenth birthday. The same ring she'd thrown at him that long-ago day in the diner.

"This will have to do until I can buy you another one to replace it," he said as he slipped it on her left ring finger.

Savannah stared at the tiny diamond chip through a haze of tears. "I can't believe you held on to it this long."

"I wasn't about to give it up even after I had to give you up. I did give up on believing you'd wear it again."

"This time I promise I won't take it off and throw it at you."

"I promise I won't give you a reason to throw it," he said, and after a slight hesitation added, "And now that we have that settled, will you marry me, Savannah Greer? It doesn't have to be tomorrow or next month or even next year. Just say you'll do it before we're as old as Dad and Gracie."

She couldn't resist teasing him any more than she could resist him. "I don't know, Sam. Tomorrow might be too soon, but next month doesn't sound like such a bad idea. I think we've waited long enough, don't you?"

"Yeah, about twelve years too long."

"Should we return to our house and finalize the deal with a little bed boogie?"

He presented her with a beautiful, heartfelt smile and a somewhat sinful wink. "Sounds like a plan, but I have one more thing to tell you."

For heaven's sake. Once the man started talking, it was darn hard to shut him up. "As long as you hurry. As you know, patience isn't my strongest suit."

"It's about the gulley."

He wanted to discuss a drought-ridden creek bed? "Okay, I'll take the bait. What about the gulley?"

"I'm going to dig a channel so it catches water when it rains."

Far be it for her to question farming technique. "Because you want to irrigate the crops?"

"Because my dad once told me that a bridge isn't any good without water under it. Since you've been back, I've learned he's right."

"So have I."

Savannah slipped her arm around Sam's waist and led him across that old beloved bridge, the place where it had all begun. The place where she'd recently discovered that if a person didn't kill those feelings for an old love, they would remain dormant until one summer day years later, they broke through like spring grass, changing your perspective, disrupting your comfortable life—and granting something you never realized you'd wanted so badly, and thought to never have.

Samuel Jamison McBriar, her first lover—her first love—was now undeniably destined to be Savannah Greer's last.

* * * * *

Harlequin Super Romance®

COMING NEXT MONTH

Available October 11, 2011

#1734 IN THE RANCHER'S FOOTSTEPS
North Star, Montana
Kay Stockham

#1735 THE TEXAN'S BRIDE
The Hardin Boys
Linda Warren

#1736 ALL THAT REMAINS
Count on a Cop
Janice Kay Johnson

#1737 FOR THEIR BABY
9 Months Later
Kathleen O'Brien

#1738 A TOUCH OF SCARLET
Hometown U.S.A.
Liz Talley

#1739 NO GROOM LIKE HIM
More than Friends
Jeanie London

You can find more information on upcoming
Harlequin® titles, free excerpts and more at
www.HarlequinInsideRomance.com.

Harlequin Romantic Suspense presents the latest book in the scorching new **KELLEY LEGACY** *miniseries from best-loved veteran series author Carla Cassidy*

Scandal is the name of the game as the Kelley family fights to preserve their legacy, their hearts...and their lives.

Read on for an excerpt from the fourth title
RANCHER UNDER COVER

Available October 2011
from Harlequin Romantic Suspense

"**W**ould you like a drink?" Caitlin asked as she walked to the minibar in the corner of the room. She felt as if she needed to chug a beer or two for courage.

"No, thanks. I'm not much of a drinking man," he replied.

She raised an eyebrow and looked at him curiously as she poured herself a glass of wine. "A ranch hand who doesn't enjoy a drink? I think maybe that's a first."

He smiled easily. "There was a six-month period in my life when I drank too much. I pulled myself out of the bottom of a bottle a little over seven years ago and I've never looked back."

"That's admirable, to know you have a problem and then fix it."

Those broad shoulders of his moved up and down in an easy shrug. "I don't know how admirable it was, all I knew at the time was that I had a choice to make between living and dying and I decided living was definitely more appealing."

She wanted to ask him what had happened preceding that six-month period that had plunged him into the bottom of the bottle, but she didn't want to know too much about him. Personal information might produce a false sense of intimacy that she didn't need, didn't want in her life.

"Please, sit down," she said, and gestured him to the table. She had never felt so on edge, so awkward in her life.

"After you," he replied.

She was aware of his gaze intensely focused on her as she rounded the table and sat in the chair, and she wanted to tell him to stop looking at her as if she were a delectable dessert he intended to savor later.

Watch Caitlin and Rhett's sensual saga unfold amidst the shocking, ripped-from-the-headlines drama of the Kelley Legacy miniseries in

RANCHER UNDER COVER

Available October 2011
only from Harlequin Romantic Suspense,
wherever books are sold.

SPECIAL EDITION

Life, Love and Family

Look for
NEW YORK TIMES AND *USA TODAY*
BESTSELLING AUTHOR

KATHLEEN EAGLE

in October!

Recently released and wounded war vet
Cal Cougar is determined to start his recovery—
inside and out. There's no better place than the
Double D Ranch to begin the journey.
Cal discovers firsthand how extraordinary the
ranch really is when he meets a struggling single
mom and her very special child.

ONE BRAVE COWBOY,
available September 27 wherever books are sold!